Risking It All

By T. J. Kline

Hidden Falls Novels
Risking It All
Daring to Fall
Making the Play

Healing Harts Novels
Heart's Desire
Taking Heart
Close to Heart
Wild at Heart
Change of Heart

Rodeo Novels
Rodeo Queen
The Cowboy and the Angel
Learning the Ropes
Runaway Cowboy

Risking It All

A Hidden Falls Novel

T. J. KLINE

AVONIMPULSE
An Imprint of HarperCollinsPublishers

This is a work of fiction. Names, characters, places, and incidents are products of the author's imagination or are used fictitiously and are not to be construed as real. Any resemblance to actual events, locales, organizations, or persons, living or dead, is entirely coincidental.

Excerpt from *Daring to Fall* copyright © 2017 by Tina Klinesmith.

Digital Edition MAY 2017 ISBN: 978-0-06-265184-6
Print Edition ISBN: 978-0-06-265186-0

Avon Impulse and the Avon Impulse logo are registered trademarks of HarperCollins Publishers in the United States of America.
Avon and HarperCollins are registered trademarks of HarperCollins Publishers in the United States of America and other countries.

FIRST EDITION

17 18 19 20 21   HDC   10 9 8 7 6 5 4 3 2 1

Therese, without your kind, generous, loving heart
this book would have never been born.
You were my inspiration and, someday,
I hope to grow up to be more like you.
I love you, my friend!

Chapter One

GIA MANCUSO PULLED onto the deserted shoulder of the highway and climbed out of the car quickly, leaving it running and the headlights shining in the darkness, praying the newborn baby wouldn't fully wake up. It was nearly one a.m. and she was almost home, but Bella had been fussy the entire ride across California from San Diego to Hidden Falls, and Gia had no clue what to do to console her. Swinging her arm around in a circle, she tried to work out the kink she'd gotten from driving with her arm twisted in the back seat while holding the pacifier in Bella's perfect little mouth. It was the only thing that kept her from wailing, and Gia had moved her hand only for a few seconds to work the cramp out of her palm before she heard the distinct *plop*. Who'd have thought that a baby a few days old could spit a pacifier so far?

Climbing into the back seat, Gia searched for the silicone item that was the only thing keeping her clinging tenuously to her sanity. Not finding it on the seat or the floorboard, she turned on the dome light, cursing her luck. It wasn't like her car was a passenger van; there were very few hiding places in the Lexus sedan. Bella squinted her eyes and, without even opening them, let out a screech that sounded like a bad driver locking up a set of worn-out brakes.

Squeezing her eyes shut against the sound and giving up on her search, Gia pulled a bottle of water from the case she'd bought for the trip to her parents' house and tugged the can of formula from the diaper bag on the floorboard. She'd been trying to make it the rest of the way before feeding Bella, but desperate times called for desperate measures. She poured the plastic scoop of powder into the bottle, spilling a good portion on her wrinkled camisole, before filling the bottle with lukewarm water. She shook it vigorously as Bella screamed with impatience.

"I'm trying," she muttered to the baby.

Once Gia had made sure all the powder was mixed, she popped the bottle into the baby's mouth, instantly quieting her as she sucked at it greedily.

Gia pulled the door shut and unsnapped the harness over Bella's chest so she could burp her halfway through the feeding. She closed her eyes for just a moment, willing herself to relax, and let her head drop on the headrest of the back seat with a sigh of relief at the first silence in nearly five hours. They weren't far from home, only a few more miles, but after driving all day and stopping several times to feed, burp, change and console the wailing child, Gia was exhausted. Soon she'd be back home, even if she would now be a twenty-six-year-old woman temporarily living with her parents.

Your parents and your niece, she amended. *Daughter*, she mentally corrected herself.

As of right now, no one but her mother and sister knew Bella wasn't hers, and until she could decide what to do, she needed to keep it that way. No one needed to know that her sister, in trouble again, had abandoned her daughter the day after giving birth, leaving Gia to pick up the aftermath Lorena left behind, just like she always did.

Except this time, that "aftermath" was a child.

Gia might be able to manage multimillion-dollar marketing campaigns, but she could barely manage to keep houseplants alive. She didn't know the first thing about babies. She couldn't handle this on her own. At a loss, she'd called her mother, who insisted she keep quiet, request some family leave and return home until they could come up with some sort of plan as to what was best for little Bella.

She had a sneaking suspicion from her mother's constantly lowered voice that she hadn't even told Gia's father that she was coming home or that she'd be bringing his first grandchild with her. Her mother never failed to minimize the trouble her sister got into, and now, with her father finishing his third round of chemotherapy, she doubted her mother had told him the truth, leaving Gia to be the one to break the news and bear the brunt of her father's disappointment. It wasn't fair but, as the baby of the family, Lorena had always been her mother's favorite and the child who seemed to do no wrong in their mother's eyes. When she did, their mother covered for her. That was the way it had always been. Gia had no reason to believe it would change now.

The quiet purr of her car engine and the haunting hoot of an owl in the woods on the side of the highway lulled her. Most people would be afraid—on a long stretch of deserted highway, darkness surrounding her with a cacophony of night sounds—but this was home, where she'd grown up, where she'd once been broken and had left the pieces behind. Gia could feel her body relaxing into the leather seat and braced her arm against the bottom of Bella's car seat, trying desperately not to give in to the urge to sleep.

The soft crunch of gravel jerked her upright as headlights bathed the interior of her car in white light, blinding her. Reports of women being carjacked, kidnapped or murdered filled her mind, and she hurried to snap the buckle of Bella's seat again. Dropping the bottle, she lunged forward, attempting to climb over the console into the driver's seat to get the hell away from whatever killer might be approaching her car.

It took only a few seconds to realize how big a mistake she'd made.

Gia had always been well endowed, but she'd never expected her curves to get her stuck partway between her front and back seats. She wiggled, trying to twist sideways to make it easier to pull herself forward. Gripping the edge of the steering wheel, Gia used it for leverage, tucking one knee under her as she tried to force herself through. It was no use. She was hopelessly stuck, now unable to move forward or back. She was a miserable excuse for a guardian and prayed her stupidity wasn't about to end with her and Bella on tomorrow's news, murdered on the side of the highway, mere minutes from their destination.

She craned her neck to see the flash of red and blue lights washing through the back window of the car as a thin white beam of light flashed through the window, into her eyes. She held up a hand, trying to make out any of the features of who she prayed was really a cop, even if it meant someone would witness her embarrassing predicament. The back door opened and Gia heard a deep rumble of laughter.

"What brings you back to town, Gia?"

Gia closed her eyes, wishing she could crawl under her car. How was it possible that after nearly ten years of avoiding him, she was now caught in this position by the one man she never wanted to see again, the same one who'd broken her stupidly naive heart at nineteen?

"Andrew McQuaid," she muttered to herself. He shone the light on her rear end, and irritation welled. "You think instead of ogling my ass you might actually help me?"

She felt the hands that had carried her to her first heights of ecstasy reach for either side of her hips. The same hands she'd sworn would never touch her again after she found out about the bastard's cheating ways.

"Hey," she squealed, trying to squirm away from his touch, willing herself to ignore the way her heart leapt into her throat. "What the hell are you doing?"

"Exactly what you asked me to do. I'm helping you."

"Not like that!" She swung a hand at him, slapping her own butt in the process, but at least he let go of her.

"How exactly do you propose I help, then?"

"I don't know. You're the cop."

Andrew laughed, still leaning into her car, bent over awkwardly behind her. "Honey, I really don't see any other way."

She glared at him over her shoulder. "Don't call me that."

"Fine." Andrew moved into the car, practically sitting in the back seat, and slid one hand through an opening by her waist, in front of her bent knee. The other slid around her calf and managed to pull it out from under her. "There. I'm going to tip your right hip down, but you're going to have to manage to twist your shoulders to fit . . . um . . ." He searched for a polite term he could use for her boobs. ". . . the girls through," he finished with a chuckle.

Gia felt the rush of heat flood her face. "Let's just get this over with."

Andrew's hands closed on her hips again, practically cupping her right butt cheek in his palm. "Bend your right knee and I'm going to pull on three. One . . . two . . . three."

Gia managed to twist her body as Andrew pulled her backward, and she slid through the space as if she'd never been stuck at all. Andrew dropped into the seat, carrying her with him. Gia landed in his lap with one of his muscular forearms under her breasts, the other hand cupping her inner thigh, sending a blast of heat between her legs. It was the worst reaction she could have ever imagined having.

Until she realized that hard ridge beneath her rear wasn't his gun.

ANDREW PRETENDED HE hadn't thought about Gia Mancuso since she'd thrown his engagement ring back at him that cold January morning. She never would tell him why and had gone back to college early from her Christmas break, leaving him with a broken heart, broken dreams and no answers to his questions. It was the last time she'd spoken to him.

Her visits home since then had been quick, never

long enough for him to get more than a glimpse of her with her parents or helping at their restaurant before she was gone again. He'd heard she eventually took a high-power marketing job in some beach town in Southern California. Almost ten years later and he still had no clue what he'd done to cause the breakup, but he didn't doubt for a second it had been his fault.

He'd always been the black sheep of the McQuaid clan and embraced his rebel-without-a-cause stigma, whether a nineteen-year-old kid or now, as a seven-year veteran of the sheriff's department. In fact, he willingly flaunted his bad-boy reputation, especially since he had two goody-two-shoes older brothers who didn't quite understand the perks that came with it.

But with Gia, he'd been different.

They'd been explosive together, in every bit of their relationship, but especially in the bedroom. The truth was, he'd thought about her often. There had never been another woman who could turn him on faster, or piss him off just as quickly. It didn't seem that much had changed. He was sporting a rock-solid erection already.

He'd be damned if he'd thought it possible for this woman to be even sexier than she'd been at nineteen, but somehow she managed it.

"Think you could let me up?" The annoyance in her voice rang loud and clear. She reached for the back of the driver's seat, trying to pull herself off his lap, but his arm around her ribs held her fast.

Andrew let go as if she were covered in hot coals,

and she maneuvered her way out of the car to stand on the shoulder of the road. He willed his hormones to calm down. Shit, they were responding like he was a nineteen-year-old kid again. It hadn't been that long since he'd been with a woman.

But it feels like forever since I've been with Gia.

Planting her hands at her hips, she shot him an impatient, expectant look. One that warned him it was time to move along. The baby in the car seat beside him hiccupped. Before he realized what was happening, two dark eyes opened and blinked twice, just before the baby vomited over the side of the car seat onto him.

"Ugh!" He slid out quickly, not knowing what to do. He'd been thrown up on plenty of times in the line of duty, but this was different. He wanted to look authoritative, in control, not covered in baby puke.

"Shit!" Gia shoved him out of the way and slid the baby from the car seat. The baby whimpered quietly before letting out a wail of protest, and Gia lifted the child to her shoulder, patting its back. "Oh, Bella. I'm so sorry, sweetheart."

Andrew stared at her, dumbfounded. "Wait."

The child let out a loud belch and hiccupped, settling almost immediately. Gia moved around to the other side of the car, sliding the infant back into the car seat and buckling the safety harness. "Hand me a burp rag out of the bag to clean up this mess on my seat." She held out a hand.

"Um?" He wasn't sure what she expected from him.

He was still standing with vomit on his crotch, staring at her, trying to wrap his head around the fact that she had a kid.

"The bag. On the floor. Hand me a cloth from inside."

He lifted the bag onto the seat and started digging through it. "Which one? You have about twenty in here." He pulled out three different cloth items.

Reaching across the seat, she slid the bag toward her with a sigh and a very annoyed eye roll. "That is a onesie, that is a blanket and that is a bib." She reached inside and pulled out a towel smaller than the one he used to wipe his face at the gym, holding it up for him. "This is a burp rag."

"How would I know? I don't have kids." Andrew took a step backward, shutting the car door. He watched her intently as she stood up and made her way around the back of the car to where he stood at the driver's door. "And since when do you?"

Gia looked away, busying herself with climbing into the back seat and wiping up the mess. "Obviously, recently. Bella's three days old tomorrow. Well—" she corrected herself, realizing the time "—today."

Andrew let his gaze slide over her, taking in every curve as she tucked the rag back into the bag on the back seat and stood, facing him. She arched a brow and planted a hand on her hip, as if daring him to say a word. A slow grin spread over his lips. He'd never been afraid of her temper, even though she intimidated most other men. She'd been a challenge but one he'd always been up for taking on.

Unlike her sister, Lorena.

Andrew didn't want to think about that drunken mistake. Guilt gripped him. That had been almost a year ago now, and he'd been in a bad place that night. Thankfully, afterward Lorena had up and left Hidden Falls. No one had seen her since.

He didn't realize how long he'd been staring at Gia until she crossed her arms over her chest. "You have something you want to say?"

Andrew shrugged, his stance mimicking her defensive one. "You look good, Gia. I would have never guessed you'd just had a baby."

"Thanks, I guess." Something flickered in her hazel eyes, something he didn't think he'd ever seen in them before—deception. She looked away quickly, glancing back at the baby in the car seat. "I should get going. I'm sure Mom is waiting up for us."

She reached for the handle of the door but he held it shut, his hand along the window frame. She was hiding something and he wanted to find out what it was. "How's your dad?"

Giovanni Mancuso had been a staple in Hidden Falls since he'd arrived nearly thirty years ago and opened Rossetti's. It had become the premier restaurant in town, but after his cancer diagnosis nearly a year ago, things had begun to fall apart for him and his wife, Isabella. Rossetti's was closed almost as many nights as it was open now that Gia's sister wasn't here to help them run it and Isabella was too busy caring for Giovanni to be there all night or find someone else who could run the place for her.

"The same." A flash of pain flickered in her eyes, different from what he'd seen there moments ago.

"And your sister?"

Gia narrowed her eyes at him. "What makes you ask?"

Why *had* he asked about Lorena? After what had happened that night, Lorena wasn't a subject he wanted to discuss with anyone, especially Gia. Although it was highly likely that Gia would find out about what happened that weekend, he wasn't enough of an idiot to bring it up, and there weren't really any other reasons for him to ask about Lorena, unless she had an outstanding warrant, which was entirely possible. The woman was trouble.

"She sort of took off and left your mom to run the restaurant alone. With your dad sick, I just wondered if she was coming back anytime soon to help . . ."

"Which is the reason I'm here now." Gia reached for his wrist, sliding his hand from the car door. "So, if you don't mind, I've been driving all day and I'd like to get home sometime tonight."

He wasn't put off by her easy dismissal. She'd avoided him for almost ten years. He didn't expect anything different now. He might have *hoped* for something more, but he didn't expect it. Andrew reached down and opened the door for her. "Just had to stop and do my job, make sure everything was okay."

"Well, we're fine. Thank you." She slid into the driver's seat as the baby slumbered in the back.

"How long are you planning on staying? Maybe we could have dinner before you leave again." It was a long shot, but why not give it a try?

She turned toward him slowly, piercing him with a look that could have cut steel. "Absolutely. I'll pencil that in for two days after hell freezes over."

Chapter Two

GIA RAN A hand over her eyes and reached for the pot of coffee, tipping it forward.

"Hey, *piccola*, you might actually want to grab a mug *before* you pour that and get it all over my sink."

"What?" Gia looked down and saw that she didn't even have a coffee cup on the counter. "Oh, my . . . Sorry, Mama. It was really late by the time we got in last night. Then I had to unload the car and get Bella to sleep again. I think it was after two before I climbed into bed. Then she woke to eat again at four."

Three hours of sleep last night just wasn't enough.

Her mother wandered over and patted a plump hand against Gia's cheek. "*Piccola*, it's going to be a long time before you sleep through the night again."

Gia gave her mother a tight smile at the term of endearment, the Italian word for *little one*, but couldn't help the pang of bitterness that squeezed at her heart. Of course, it was just assumed that she would care for Bella without question or concern for her own future. It had always been expected that Gia would simply watch out for her younger sister, regardless of whether it was warranted or reciprocated. As a result, she was here figuring out what to do next with her sister's newborn baby while her sister had run off with some guy.

Her mother passed her a mug. "Thanks, Mama. Are you heading into Rossetti's for the breakfast crowd?"

Her mother shuffled away without answering, reaching for the cream she kept in the refrigerator. None of that fake nondairy stuff for her parents. It was all-natural, a throwback to the way they'd grown up in the old country, even though they'd immigrated to the States nearly fifty years ago. Both of her parents still believed in traditional methods, which was part of why Rossetti's, their family's Italian restaurant, had done so well.

It was also part of the reason Gia was in this predicament now. Family loyalty was just another of her parents' old-school values they'd ingrained into their daughters. Well, into Gia, at least.

"Not this morning." She slid the cream onto the counter beside Gia.

"But don't you need to go in and prep for lunch and dinner services?" It had been a few years since she'd helped her parents in the restaurant, but most of her teen years were spent and fondest memories were made in the kitchen. She still knew exactly what needed to be done.

So many times she'd wanted to come home, but she'd found herself using her job in San Diego as an excuse to keep her too busy to return except for holidays. In truth, it was just too hard to be in Hidden Falls. Being here made it hard to keep up the pretense. It was too easy for people to peer through the facade she barely kept in place—fantastic job, success, and a family that was the picture of perfection. It was nothing more than fancy wrapping paper on trash. It couldn't mask the stink of mistakes, regrets and lies.

They didn't see the struggle she had to be taken seriously in her job because she was a woman. They didn't see how she spent most weekends binge-watching entire seasons of television shows on Netflix because she refused to go barhopping with women just wanting a one-night stand. And she certainly didn't want anyone to see how much it hurt to face both Andrew, after what he'd done, and her sister. Her homesickness was a small price to pay to keep her hurt hidden.

"Sit down, *mia dolce*," her mother's voice broke into her thoughts. "We need to talk before your father wakes. You need to know what's really going on."

Dread slithered into the pit of her stomach, writhing and coiling. Gia pressed a hand against her belly, willing the attack of nausea back. She couldn't handle anything more, but with her father's cancer not responding to the last round of chemotherapy, she couldn't help but worry about him, and her mother.

Reaching for her hand, her mother curled her fingers

around Gia's. The same way she had when Gia had been a little girl. But it didn't bring her comfort now; it only made her more afraid.

"Mama? What's going on?"

"I know I told you to come home because of Bella, *piccola*, but there's more that we need to discuss and make plans for."

"Daddy." Gia's voice warbled slightly, and she cleared her throat.

"In a manner of speaking. You know how sick your father is, and I've been trying to take care of him, but it's nearly impossible for me to do that and run the restaurant. Your sister was helping but, well . . ." Her mother sighed and gave a small shrug. "Your sister has to live her own life, I suppose."

Gia wanted to roll her eyes. Her sister's version of "living her own life" meant leaving the rest of the family in limbo while she had a good time. This wasn't like "finding herself" after high school. She'd walked away from her child. Not because she couldn't be a good parent but because she didn't want to be bothered to try.

Gia knew her mother was working up to a point, and she'd rather have all the bad news at once, not this beating around the bush. "What's going on, Mama?"

"A lot of bills have been piling up. Medical expenses, mostly, things he told me the insurance company would handle, but they didn't." Angry tears filled her mother's hazel eyes, so like Gia's own, far too expressive of her inner thoughts. Gia easily read the shame, and concern.

"There's a company, Fortune Industries, that wants to put up a big-box store where the restaurant is. They're trying to buy up the entire area. If we sell, it would give us the money to pay all the bills plus have some left over. We could give your sister the money to open her own restaurant like we promised years ago."

Gia felt her eyes widen at her mother's words. Were her parents nuts? Her sister had just walked away from her child *and* the family restaurant without giving anyone a reason or a second thought. Now her mother wanted to give her money too? She opened her mouth to question her mother's sanity but thought better of it.

Her mother covered her face with her hands, sobs wracking her body. "But your father refuses to sell."

Because he knows Lorena.

Gia rolled her lips inward, trying to fight the bitterness choking her, and slid from the chair to squat down in front of her mother, reaching for her hands. Her mother leaned forward, embracing Gia in a tight hug, her entire body trembling as she cried and Gia rubbed her back.

"Oh, Mama."

"I was hoping to convince your father, but—"

"Why didn't you tell me sooner?"

Her mother hiccupped, wiping at the tears on her cheeks. "You know your father. He's a proud man and didn't want me to burden you with this, especially when Lorena was helping at Rossetti's. But now that she's gone, and with Bella . . ." Her words trailed away, as if the answer was obvious.

It wasn't. Instead, everything had just become more cloudy, more convoluted. More confusing.

Rossetti's was her father's pride and joy. He loved it as much as he did his children. He'd saved up every nickel and dime to open it, first as a tiny hole-in-the-wall serving typical Italian food, and eventually turning Rossetti's into *the* Italian dining establishment. Not just for people in Hidden Falls but for the entire area. People traveled for hours to enjoy her father's authentic Italian cuisine, waited weeks—months, sometimes—for a reservation. They'd been talking about opening a second location, something that Lorena had been pushing them to do, and had even begun talking to the bank about it until her father's diagnosis came in. Her parents realized they wouldn't have the time or financial resources, and then Lorena bailed, leaving her parents to figure out how to recoup what they could of their initial investment.

"What does Daddy say?"

"*Dolce mia*, you know your father. He just wants to go back to cooking. But the treatments aren't working, and his oncologist suggests your father take it easy and try an experimental drug. But the insurance won't cover the cost, and we don't have the money unless we sell. But he refuses to give up the restaurant. Said he'd rather—" Her mother's voice cracked, choking up, making her unable to speak.

Die. He'd rather die than give up the restaurant.

Gia didn't need to hear her mother say the words.

She loved her father dearly, loved his passion and knew Rossetti's was his dream, but she wouldn't let him risk his life for it.

"It's okay. We'll figure this out." Gia knew she was simply saying words, nothing more than platitudes. She had no idea how she could make this work or whether anything short of selling the restaurant could help them. Not that selling would make her father well, or bring Lorena back for Bella.

When it rains, it pours.

"You have to help me tell him and convince him to sell. Maybe now that Bella's here, when he finds out he has a granddaughter to live for, we can change his mind."

"You haven't told him?" Her mother shook her head, looking down at her hands sheepishly. "Mama, you tell everyone *everything*."

Her mother pinched her lips together but didn't deny it. Gia knew it was just the way her family was. They shared. Histories, stories, rumors. It was just how her mother—and all Italian families, for that matter—were. They were a tight culture within a small town. Everyone knew everyone's business. But they were also loyal to a fault, which was exactly what her sister took advantage of so often.

"We have to tell him, this morning," Gia insisted.

"I know. But we can't tell him about what Lorena did. He was devastated when she left town. I can't imagine what it will do to him to know . . ."

"What? The truth? That she abandoned her baby?" Her tone was soft but adamant.

"Gianna Maricella Mancuso!" her mother scolded. "You don't know what she's going through. You have no right to judge."

Gia tipped her head and closed her eyes, feeling defeated. Why did she always have to be the voice of reason, the one to point out the obvious that her mother wanted to ignore, especially where her sister was concerned? And seeing as how she was the one caring for her sister's baby, she had every right to judge.

"Mama, I don't like it either, but that's what Lorena did. It's a fact. Lies aren't going to help Daddy accept anything."

"And the brutal truth could make him even sicker." Her mother's eyes held a stubborn determination Gia knew well. She was convinced that her way was best, and there was no changing her mind. "It's more important to convince him to sell the restaurant. We can tell him the rest of it later, after. He can only handle one disappointment at a time."

"How is the restaurant more important that Bella?"

Her mother scowled at her. "It's not, but I want him to be happy about her. We should tell him that she's your child."

"Mine? Mama—"

Her mother held up her hand, refusing to hear any argument, and rose, taking a deep breath and squaring her shoulders. "*Piccola*, your father knows you are strong and smart and independent. He knows that you don't need a man in your life. You've already proved that. He'll be happy for you, and about Bella."

"He knows Lorena is a screwup. It would come as less of a shock just to admit Bella is hers."

Her mother shot her a glare that withered any further argument. "Do not talk that way about your sister. She's a *farfallina*, a little butterfly flitting from flower to flower. Someday she will find a place to land. Until then, she needs to know her family loves and supports her."

And in the meantime, while she "flitted," Gia was forced to put her life on hold. Biting back the things she wanted to say, Gia clenched her teeth.

"Then what does that make me?" she finally muttered into her coffee cup as she sat down at the table again.

Her mother's hands landed on her shoulders as she pressed a kiss to the top of Gia's head. "You are *forte*."

Strong? That was her mother's idea of a compliment?

"You are the rock that your father and I rely on." She poured another cup of coffee and carried it out of the room, leaving Gia to her worries.

Her parents were in debt, enough that her mother wanted to sell the restaurant they'd owned for nearly thirty years. Her father's cancer wasn't responding and needed an experimental treatment. And her sister had not only abandoned her parents, but her child, and no one knew where to find her or if she was ever planning on returning.

Gia dropped her forehead into her palm, closing her eyes and wishing she had the energy to drive eight hours back to San Diego. This was turning out to be a fan-*freaking*-tastic morning.

SOMETHING WASN'T RIGHT at Rossetti's. As he drove past, heading home after his shift, Andrew noticed the lights were on and there was a solitary Lexus in the parking lot. It was only six thirty in the morning. Why was Gia here already?

Andrew had immediately recognized the car from the fiasco on the side of the highway last night—mostly because there weren't many luxury sedans in Hidden Falls—and pulled off, sliding his Challenger neatly in beside Gia's car. He was beat, and unsure why he'd stopped, especially after how Gia had given him the cold shoulder last night, but it was as if his body was operating independently from his brain.

Andrew tugged at the front door but found it locked. It wasn't unusual. Most people in Hidden Falls just accepted that Rossetti's being open before dinner was a hit-or-miss thing now thanks to Giovanni's cancer.

Getting no response to his knock, Andrew pressed his ear to the door. He could hear the faint sound of music coming from somewhere inside the restaurant. Obviously someone was here. Andrew walked around the building to the back entrance, found the door slightly ajar and slipped into the building. From back here, he realized that what he'd first thought was music sounded more like a wounded cat wailing in time to the country music on the radio. Andrew nearly choked on the laughter that wanted to burst from his gut.

Gia was good at a lot of things—organization, math, photography—but being a good singer had never come close to making her list of attributes. However, she loved music and didn't care that she couldn't manage to carry a tune with a trough-sized bucket. Following the sound, he paused as he reached the doorway of the back office, watching her sway her hips in front of the filing cabinet, dipping low, her hand stroking the cabinet in time with the music.

His body grew hard in an instant, every muscle tensing. She might not be able to sing, but the woman knew how to dance. Andrew quickly adjusted himself and began mentally reciting traffic codes in order to calm his now throbbing body.

Gia had always been beautiful, but having a baby agreed with her. She'd filled out in every place that mattered. She was extremely well endowed, looking like a Victoria's Secret model now with her petite frame and voluptuous curves. Women probably hated her but he doubted she cared. Other than her sister, she'd had never had many relationships with other women growing up. And what she and Lorena had could hardly be called a friendship.

Lorena had always been competitive with Gia, although he'd never quite understood why. While they might look similar, they were as different as night and day and, in his mind, there was no comparison. Lorena would never measure up to her sister. Lorena thought only of herself; Gia thought of everyone but. He lifted his hand and rapped his knuckles on the open door.

Gia jumped as she turned and saw him standing there, holding a hand against her heart. "What the hell?"

Slapping the file she held onto the top of the desk, Gia shot him a look that would have made Medusa cringe as she slid into the chair. "Do you find some sort of pleasure in taking years off my life and nearly giving me a heart attack? Shit!"

The corner of his mouth lifted. "Sorry. I would have announced that I was here, but I figured you wouldn't hear me over that . . . I guess we could call it singing," he teased.

"Ha." She cocked her head to one side. "What are you even doing here, Andrew? We're closed."

He crossed his arms, leaning against the door frame. "Which is why it was odd to see the lights on and a car in the parking lot. I just wanted to make sure nothing was wrong."

"Ah, so you're trying to convince me that you're a Good Samaritan?" She rolled her eyes at him and looked down at the computer screen, opening the file next to her. "Since when?"

He shrugged. "Always?"

She blew air through her lips in disgust. "Sure. You keep telling yourself that."

"I'm a cop, Gia. It's literally my *job* to be a Good Samaritan."

Disappointment rolled through him, making him ache for what should have been. Things hadn't always been this antagonistic between them. There'd been a time when they'd been inseparable, when they couldn't keep their hands off one another. He'd graduated high school two years before she had, but he'd had his eye on Gia Mancuso for years before he finally got up the nerve to ask her out. She'd been a "good girl." A straight-A student, president of her class, heading for big things and reaching for even bigger dreams, despite the lies that were spread about her.

He, on the other hand, had been nothing more than the class clown and local playboy. The McQuaids' troublemaking brother, who cared more about having a good time than he did going anywhere or becoming anything more than what he was. He had no hopes of leaving town, in spite of the fact that his older brother Grant had, eventually finding his place in a professional football career. But Andrew hadn't gotten that lucky and wasn't nearly that disciplined, which was why he'd been shocked when she'd agreed to his invitation to pizza and a movie. Even more surprised to find out she'd been into him for a while but had doubted his interest in a girl like her. He'd been interested, all right. He hadn't been able to get enough of her.

She'd changed him, making him want more, want to *be* more. He finally saw a future for himself and it included Gia at his side. And then, without warning, she'd broken off their engagement.

He pushed himself off the door frame and into the office, slumping into the chair across from the desk. "One of these days, you'll have to tell me what I did to piss you off."

"I don't recall inviting you in." Gia arched a perfect brow and looked down her nose at him. "And please, tell me you aren't serious."

"One day we were like those chick flicks you used to drag me to on the weekends. The next thing I know, you're throwing your engagement ring in my face and refusing to speak to me."

"You *are* serious?" Gia leaned back in the chair, crossing her arms under her ample chest. "You cheated on me."

"What?" The question tumbled from his mouth. The accusation was so ludicrous that he couldn't help laughing out loud, which only earned him another of her death glares.

"I mean, I knew you were a player, but I guess I stupidly thought you loved me the way you claimed to."

"If you really believe that I cheated on you, then you didn't know me at all."

Gia had been the one and only woman who had ever curbed his playboy ways. When they were together, he'd never wanted another woman. Gia's beauty intimidated some people into underestimating her, but she was tough as nails and liked it when she surprised people. She'd sure surprised him. Being with her made him want to be the man she believed he was, the one he pretended to be for her. She was more than enough for any one man to handle, and he really thought he'd found "the One." He knew he'd never find anyone better suited to him, no matter how long he looked. After she walked away, he'd had no interest in trying for forever again.

"I thought I did, which is why it came as such a surprise when I heard about it. From several people, I might add." She shrugged and waved her hand at him. "Don't worry about it, Andrew. You ripped those rose-colored glasses off and taught me a lesson. Maybe I should thank you."

He'd have never hurt Gia that way, and it pissed him off more that people had lied and told her he had. He was even more furious that she'd actually believed it.

He clenched his jaw, the words barely coming out. "That so?"

"Let's just say bad boys just aren't my type anymore. They aren't worth the trouble, or the heartache, because people don't change."

Andrew could hear the hard, pessimistic note to her voice that hadn't been there ten years before. "You have."

"Only because I had to in order to survive."

Andrew rose, moving closer to the desk. She didn't rise. As a matter of fact, she didn't give any indication that he made her uncomfortable in the slightest. Anyone else might have believed her act, but he'd always been able to read those eyes of hers like they were a diary, exposing the very depths of her soul to him.

"I'm not so sure it's survival, Gia. Seems more like hiding to me." He braced his hands on the desk and leaned over her, forcing her to either scoot backward or remain with his face mere inches from hers. "And the girl I knew and loved never ran scared. It'd be a shame if you started to now."

Her eyes flashed with the fire he'd known was inside her, the gold flecks in them lighting up, but she refused to meet his gaze. "I'm not scared."

Andrew leaned in even closer, his lips a fraction of an inch from hers. "No?"

She held her tense position, even when his mouth brushed against hers, sending electric jolts of pleasure rocketing through his body. He wasn't sure why he was torturing himself, other than to prove to her that she still felt something for him, that he wasn't the only one wanted what they'd once had.

"No."

Sliding her hand around the back of his neck, she leaned up, opening her mouth and kissing him full on the lips. The explosion of need rocketed through him as she massaged his scalp with her fingers, drawing him closer. He might have been toying with her, but he wasn't stupid, and there was no way he was going to waste this opportunity. Andrew swept his tongue against hers, dancing in a rhythm he remembered from so long ago. His entire body felt charged, humming with desire too long buried. A groan began in his chest, trying to escape, but she leaned back and took a deep breath.

"Nope. See?" She smiled up at him innocently, as if she hadn't just shaken his entire being to the core. "Nothing at all."

Damn, she sure knows how to crush a man's ego.

"Then I guess I'll head home, since you don't need me."

Chapter Three

GIA WAS UP early the next morning, feeding Bella, when she heard the newspaper hit the front door. It surprised her that anyone still read the newspaper, let alone paid to have it delivered, considering how much easier it was to get current news and updates online. But Hidden Falls was a small town. A lot of things seemed to linger here simply out of tradition rather than necessity.

She lifted Bella into her arms and carried her to the front door to retrieve the paper for her father while she burped the baby. It had been a rough couple of days. Bella was colicky, crying almost nonstop since they'd left San Diego, but she attributed it to the fact that they'd barely been still for five minutes since her birth. The poor baby had been jostled nonstop over the past four days.

Lorena still wasn't returning any calls or text messages. Gia's father had been unusually quiet since her mother had informed him that Gia had become a mother, carefully leaving out any details, while Gia had remained quiet, uncomfortable with all of the lies that just seemed to keep breeding.

As much as she wanted to tell her father the truth, she had to trust her mother's assessment of his condition and didn't go against her wishes. She might not agree about which was more important, but her mother was right about one thing. Bella was safe and stable, while her parents' finances and her father's health situation were falling apart.

After going over her parents' current finances, both at the restaurant and with their accountant by phone, Gia knew her mother's dire prognosis wasn't far off. If they didn't sell and kept going the way they were now, there was a good chance they'd be forced to shut down anyway, which would leave them with no possible way to pay for her father's treatment. As it was, they were going to be hard-pressed to even pay the past-due medical bills he had accumulated, let alone pay any new ones that might accrue.

No matter which way she turned, Gia was caught in this web her family had woven around her. Their mistakes and troubles were now hers. Even if she considered leaving the way her sister had, a deep-seated sense of loyalty refused to let her turn her back on them the way Lorena had. She would grit her teeth and figure a way out of this mess for them. One step at a time.

Walking back into the kitchen, she dropped the paper on the table and sat down, reaching for Bella's bottle to finish feeding her. The baby looked up at her with her intense deep blue eyes with an innocence that made Gia's heart ache.

During a routine doctor's visit in college, she'd discovered it would be difficult for her to conceive due to polycystic ovary syndrome. It had only made her desire for a houseful of children grow stronger. Lorena, on the other hand, seemed to see this child as a nuisance. As often as Gia prayed that her sister would come to her senses, that she would come back for her daughter, she couldn't help the twinge of pain and jealousy that pinched her heart at the thought of returning Bella to Lorena. She just couldn't comprehend her sister's attitude about abandoning her child.

Lorena didn't want to be a mother. She didn't even want to help their parents. How would she ever manage to deal with dirty diapers and early morning feedings? From the first moments after Lorena had showed up on Gia's doorstep, it had been Gia to dry Bella's tears, to hold and comfort her. It was Gia's finger the little girl gripped as she ate, her neck that Bella nuzzled into as she fell asleep. It might have only been a few days, but Bella had touched Gia's heart and bonded with her, regardless of the fact that she hadn't been the one to give birth.

During the day, Gia hoped her sister would come to her senses, but in these early morning hours when no one else was around, she prayed Lorena would stay away. And then the guilt ate at her for her harsh judgment. The reality was that Bella was not her child, even if she might want her to be.

But life wasn't about her right now. Gia couldn't make decisions about her own future any more than she could make them about the restaurant. Her priority was family now, and being there for others. And until some more permanent arrangements were made, she was here only to make sure everyone else got what they needed, yet again, even when it meant letting go of what she wanted, whatever that might look like. Gia wasn't even sure anymore.

Images of Andrew came to mind, haunting her even as she tried to brush them away. She did *not* want Andrew, and that kiss she'd stupidly given him yesterday should have proved that, regardless of whatever fantasies her sleep-addled brain might conjure.

But if she let them come, the memories were comforting, even if they were those of a naive girl. She'd once thought he was a bad boy with a heart of gold. She was convinced he was just misunderstood. Until her sister had come to her right after New Year's, after Gia had shown her the engagement ring he'd given her, and told her he and Lorena had made out. She hadn't wanted to believe Lorena, but when several other girls confirmed seeing them together, she'd realized her white knight existed only in her imagination. There were no fairy tales, no happily-ever-afters, in real life, especially hers.

She'd questioned her feelings, her decisions and her dreams. Brokenhearted, confused, angry and feeling more than justified, Gia had told him he could shove his ring and his lies where the sun didn't shine. Just before she walked away—*ran* away was a more appropriate description—and hid from both Andrew and her insecurities. Trying to bandage her wounded pride with school, and later work, and healing her heart with a string of first dates that never turned serious and shallow relationships. Not because there was ever anything wrong with them. There was something wrong with her, something that wouldn't trust again, something that had never quite healed. Returning to Hidden Falls had opened the floodgates of her memories, reopened the wound she hadn't realized had been festering for so many years. Yet something about her return felt right. Almost as if she were coming full circle to close the door on the pain of her past once and for all.

She looked down at her niece, finally sound asleep in her arms with the bottle still in her mouth. Ten years ago, she'd been imagining that she and Andrew would be raising a family together. She'd never have suspected she would hate him and be raising her sister's child alone.

"Guess who's back in town?"

Andrew's brother Ben stood at his shoulder while Andrew poured the hops into the barley malt mixture that had come to a boil. His home brewing hobby had turned into a stress reliever that all his brothers benefited from, but it was something he'd have preferred doing without this conversation.

"Do I care?"

"I'm thinking the answer to that question is yes."

Ben seemed far too excited at the prospect of revealing the news for Andrew to let him have the satisfaction. "Gia."

"How'd you know?" Ben looked disappointed and Andrew congratulated himself on the fact.

He and Ben were close, especially since they spent most days working with one another on various emergency calls around the town—Ben with the fire department and Andrew as a sheriff's deputy—but it also led to plenty of spirited competition between them. That and the fact that there was barely a year's age difference between them.

Setting the timer for thirty minutes, Andrew turned to face his brother. "Because, like you, I can read that rag we call a town newspaper and saw it in there this morning."

"Well?"

"Well, what?" He walked to the sink to wash his brewing equipment, setting it aside to dry.

"Well, what are you going to do about it?" Ben sat down in the chair Andrew had vacated, crossing his arms over the back of it. "I mean, it's Gia."

"And?"

"Look, I know you like having this reputation of being an asshole cop and all, but we both know you had it bad for her. Real bad."

"I was a kid and stupid."

"You were twenty-one and proposed," Ben corrected him.

Andrew rolled his eyes. "Going through with it would have been a huge mistake."

Ben stood up, clearly irritated with Andrew's lack of enthusiasm. "You want everyone to think you're this player who couldn't care less, that you don't *do* relationships. But you did with Gia. I know it and, damn it, so do you."

Andrew dried his hands on a towel, ignoring his brother. He didn't want to talk about his past with Gia. It was just that—the past. Rehashing it wouldn't change anything. She'd been pretty clear yesterday with that kiss that she'd been over him a long time. He would probably never know why she thought he cheated on her, nor did it likely matter at this point, but the fact that she'd so readily believed it was probably a blessing in disguise. It had saved them both the heartache of realizing how little they really trusted one another.

"Just because you and Emma are engaged now doesn't mean you need to start matchmaking."

"Fine," Ben said, throwing his hands into the air and letting them slap his thighs. "Pretend you don't care. Pretend none of it happened."

Andrew spun on him. "What the hell do you want me to do? She doesn't want to see me. She's made that much clear."

Ben's eyes widened for a moment, his brow lifting high on his forehead in surprise, and Andrew realized he'd said far too much. His brother had picked up on it like a bloodhound following a scent. Ben shot Andrew a smug grin.

"And how would you know that?"

"She's made sure not to see me whenever she visited in the past."

Ben narrowed his eyes suspiciously. "There is more to it than that."

Andrew sighed. Ben wouldn't let this go until he found out.

"Okay, I saw her the other night. She was almost to her parents' place. On the side of the highway. I thought she had car trouble." His palms itched with the memory of holding her curves as he tried to help her get unstuck, letting his fingers move over her . . . He dragged his mind back to the present. "Did you know she has a kid now?"

"Gia? Are you sure? She got married?"

Andrew couldn't help but think about the way she'd kissed him, driving home her point. He doubted she would have done that if she were married, especially in the middle of her accusation. If he knew one thing about Gia, it was how much she despised liars.

"I don't think so, but I saw the baby myself, in the

back seat of the car. Cute little thing too, when she wasn't screaming or throwing up on me."

"Yeah, um, gonna need those details," Ben promised, then shook his head. "Gia was pretty straight-laced, contrary to the rumors."

"People change." Andrew shrugged. It was the same thing he and Gia had discussed yesterday morning, and he wondered if he was wrong. Maybe she was right. Maybe people *didn't* change; maybe they just revealed their true colors.

"I just find it hard to believe that someone like Gia, Miss Responsibility herself, would end up a single mom. I mean, there's nothing wrong with it and it happens all the time, but she always planned out every scenario, researched everything, worrying about the minutiae. She's too careful. I doubt she'd change *that* much."

"I did," he pointed out.

"No, you didn't," Ben scoffed. "You just want people to believe you have. Gia saw the real you from the start and brought it out for everyone else to enjoy. She was good for you."

Ben chuckled, moving from the chair when the timer went off so Andrew could pull the home-brew mixture off to cool.

"And for the record, no one believes it. Everyone knows what a nice guy you are. You only think you're hiding it. But by all means, keep wasting time trying if you want."

GIA'S PULSE RACED as she stared at the e-mail on her laptop.

> Any idea when you might be returning? This
> project is time-sensitive and, unless you're
> returning soon, we need to assign it to Angelo
> Martinez to cover.

She'd been working toward heading up this marketing campaign for months, fought hard to prove her capabilities against more experienced men at the company, including Angelo. She'd even offered to present the campaign remotely, but the firm had declined. She couldn't fault them for needing a body, a face for the client to relate to. That didn't stop her from feeling like her career was slipping through her fingertips. The tighter she gripped, the faster it seemed to dissipate.

However, in light of her father's illness and the situation with Bella, it seemed far less significant than it had once been. In fact, being here with her family, even as dysfunctional as it currently was, she knew it wasn't only loyalty keeping her rooted. Gia was home, for the first time in a very long time.

She would be as up-front and honest with her boss as she could be, without making any commitments either way. It wasn't that he was denying her the time off, but he did have a business to run and he deserved some of the details, like when she planned to return. She cringed as she typed the response.

I've returned home to help my ailing father. I'm not
sure how long it will be but I'm formally requesting
four weeks of leave. I have no doubt that Angelo
will do a great job taking over this project. I
apologize again for this inconvenience.

She sent the e-mail and closed the laptop before she
could second-guess her decision. She hadn't promised to
come back, any more than she'd said she wouldn't. This
would buy her some time to decide where she wanted to
be. But for now, she was needed here and family came
first. She would figure out her job situation when the
current crises were averted.

Gia's cell phone *ping*ed with a text notification and
she glanced at the screen, expecting it to be her boss's response. Her heart skipped a beat before thudding painfully in her chest.

Call me.

She quickly dialed her sister's phone number.
"Lorena, where are you?"

"Some truck stop outside Denver. Bobby has a show
here tonight and then we're heading to Cheyenne. A
performance at some county fair or something." The
roar of a diesel engine nearly drowned out her sister's
words. "What's so urgent that you had to text me, like,
twenty-five times?"

Gia couldn't believe how blasé her sister sounded.

"Your daughter, for one thing. She needs you. Come home, Lorena."

Her sister sighed impatiently into the phone. "No, she doesn't. She has you."

Gia didn't miss the bitterness in her sister's voice. "What am I supposed to do? I'm not her mother. I'm not even her guardian. I don't have a birth certificate for her. She hasn't seen a doctor since you left the hospital." Gia could hear the panic rising in her voice and glanced over at Bella, sleeping soundly in her bassinet, one tiny hand curled at her chin while her mouth twitched as if she was sucking on a bottle.

"I already told you what to do. The birth certificate form already says she's yours. I told you, I gave them your name at the hospital. Just finish filling it out and sign it. Then you can take it to the courthouse."

"But she's *not* mine." *Not really, even if I do love her like my own.* "Have you even told the father?"

"Yes." Lorena's voice was stilted and Gia knew she was lying. Lorena must have sensed distrust in Gia's silence. "Fine, I told Bobby she was stillborn. I knew he didn't want kids but I thought he'd change his mind and propose when he found out I was pregnant. I was wrong."

"He has a right to know he has a daughter."

"If he didn't care when I was pregnant, why would he care now?" Lorena sniffed slightly.

"Give him a chance to see her. He might change his

mind." Gia knew she was projecting her own desires on her sister.

"She might not even be his, Gia."

Gia's stomach dropped to her toes. "Please, tell me you're joking." Lorena didn't sound like she was.

"Stop acting so high and mighty, Gia. Trust me, I know you would never end up in this sort of predicament. Perfect Gia never screws up. She always makes the right choices."

Gia wondered at the hatefulness in her sister's tone. This wasn't the girl she'd grown up with. She'd been spoiled, but Gia didn't know when Lorena had become so selfish, jealous and competitive. But she had to know right from wrong. And this was so very wrong.

Gia ignored the anger welling up inside her and took a deep breath, trying one more time. "Bella needs you, Lorena. I need you. Mom and Dad need you."

"Are you *home*?" Lorena's bitter laughter cut through Gia. "Did you run back to Mom and Dad?"

"Dad's getting worse. He needs a new treatment, and they need our help or they are going to lose the restaurant."

"Good. I hate that place. I hate everything about it."

"You loved the restaurant."

"No, I loved the idea of running my own, some place far from Hidden Falls, but that didn't happen. They made me a promise, then jerked it away."

"What were they supposed to do, Lorena? They

didn't have the money after Daddy got sick." Gia rubbed her free hand at her temple, trying to massage away the pain building behind her eyes, but it did nothing for the pain in her heart.

"You always were a Goody Two-Shoes."

It was hardly the worst thing her sister had ever called her. "Lorena, please, come home." She was begging, but what other option did she have?

"Sorry, sis. I've finally gotten the chance to have my freedom and I'm taking it, with Bobby."

"What about Bella?"

"She's yours now, or give her up for adoption." Her voice caught on the last word and she paused a beat, her voice softening slightly. "I can't take her. She's better off with you anyway, Gia."

Before Gia could argue, the phone disconnected. She tried calling Lorena again but it immediately went to voice mail, and Gia knew her sister would continue ignoring her calls until she was ready to talk again. Typical Lorena, stubborn, childish and only thinking of herself.

Gia rose and walked over to the bassinet, staring down at the sleeping baby, running a hand over her downy head. How could her sister have carried Bella for nine months, felt her move, looked into her face and then walked away? What if she changed her mind later?

"What are we going to do now, Bella?" she whispered. As if in response to her voice and touch, Bella's mouth opened, curving into an involuntary smile that broke Gia's heart. "I won't leave you, *mio dono*, my little gift."

Chapter Four

GIA COULDN'T STAND being cooped up in the house for one more minute. Her parents were arguing, loudly, about what should be done with the restaurant. If that weren't bad enough, especially since they didn't realize or seem to care how loud they were and whether they woke Bella, then her father cornered her in the living room and started asking questions about the baby.

Why hadn't she told them she was pregnant? Why hadn't they noticed when she came home for the Fourth of July? Who was the father, and were they still together? He was suspicious and far too intelligent for her to believe they could keep this ruse up for long. She had to get out of the house or risk telling him the truth.

Lying to him, for even this short amount of time, was eating away at her, making her feel like a fraud. She'd begged her mother to let her tell him the truth, but she'd pleaded with Gia for patience, to wait until after they'd changed his mind about the restaurant and he started on the new medicine, giving him strength to handle the truth. Seeing the fearful anguish in her mother's eyes had forced her to agree. However, it had also helped her make another decision—to file for guardianship and adopt Bella rather than forge the birth certificate. If she was having this much difficulty lying to her father for a few days, she could never lie to the world for eighteen years.

Especially since she trusted Lorena would come to her senses in a few weeks. Once she did, her sister could be a real mother to Bella. Gia's heart lurched painfully at the thought, but she forced herself to swallow the pain. She had to remain logical about this decision, to set her emotions aside to do what was best for Bella. If her sister didn't change her mind and return within a few months, then she would proceed with adopting Bella.

Unclipping the car seat and hooking it into the crook of her arm, Gia carried it into the restaurant with her purse and the diaper bag swinging from her other shoulder.

"Gia!" Heather had been working as a waitress at Rossetti's since Gia had convinced her father to hire her friend in high school. "I wondered when you were coming in to say hello." She slid a ticket onto the counter for their chef and turned back toward Gia. "And who is this little bundle?"

"This is Bella," she answered, deliberately avoiding

stating any familial relationship. It would come out eventually, but her father deserved to know first. "I'll be right back."

Gia carried Bella to the office and pulled out the cloth baby-carrying wrap she'd purchased, winding it around her body the way the instructions stated. After several attempts, she was finally able to get it fitting correctly on her body, and she lifted Bella from inside the car seat, slipping her into it and snuggling her close. Having Bella at the restaurant while she was here wasn't an ideal situation, but it was the best she could do for the time being. Once she had Bella settled with her pacifier, Gia headed back out to the main dining area.

"Oh, my God! Is that you, Gia?"

"It's so good to see you!"

"How are your parents? We haven't seen them here forever."

Voices called to her from all around the room at once and she tried to welcome each person, thanking them for coming, the way she'd seen her mother do for so many years. She felt comfortable, basking in the warmth from people she'd grown up with. Beneath the glow of electric candlelight, Tuscan decor and classic Italian music playing quietly through the speakers, Gia felt at home. Avoiding as many questions about herself and Bella as possible, she inquired about local families, who had come, who had gone, and what each person was up to now, surprised at how well the tactic worked.

As the lunch crowd thinned, Bella began to fuss, and

Gia headed to the kitchen to prepare her bottle. She'd no more than entered when Rusty cornered her.

"You know what's going on, right?" Rusty had learned everything he knew about cooking from her father and was the closest thing Gia had ever had to a brother. In the twelve years she'd known him, he'd never been one to beat around the bush.

"Gia, I know what your mom thinks, but this place, it's not wearing your dad down. It's what's keeping him alive. He didn't start going downhill until she refused to let him come in anymore." Gia frowned, and her shock must have registered on her face. "She didn't tell you?"

She shook her head. "No, she just said Fortune Industries was looking to buy Rossetti's and that they needed the money."

"Something like that. They're a Fortune 500 company. Their stock is worth almost as much as Apple's and Microsoft's. They only want it just to tear it down and put up some big warehouse store. I know about your parents' money troubles. Your mom wanted me to help convince your dad to sell, but I won't do it. Losing Rossetti's would kill him."

"Rusty, he can't keep working here. He's too sick."

"Gia, I love your dad, you know that. He was there for me when my own dad took off after he divorced my mom, and I get that your mom is the one making all the decisions now, but this isn't a good one. I understand what she's trying to do, but she's missing the forest for the trees." He shook his head sadly. "She's desperate,

Gia. I've never known her to lie to your dad before, but she's telling him the restaurant is losing money. It was doing fine until she started closing it for breakfast and lunch four days a week."

Gia couldn't help but think of how it had been her mother's idea to lie about Bella as well, despite Gia's protests. She'd also been the one to keep their money troubles hidden from Gia and hadn't told either her or Lorena just how sick their father really was. Rusty was right. It wasn't like her mother, and Gia needed to figure out why she was doing it.

She finished preparing Bella's bottle and tested the formula on her wrist before adjusting her in the carrier. "I have to feed her. Let me think. I'll be back in a minute."

She hurried toward the swinging doors leading back into the dining room. "And Rusty?" He turned, and she couldn't help but feel grateful that, in the face of her sister's betrayal and her mother's odd behavior, Rusty was watching out for her father. "Thanks for telling me. I really appreciate it."

How HAD SHE managed to miss this?

Gia stared at the headline of the paper:

Can Rossetti's Hold Out?

The article went on to detail the offer Fortune Industries had made her father. It also went on to speculate why he was holding out and was bold enough to suggest what sort of negotiations her family could make. Her mother wasn't wrong about the sum being enough to solve their money troubles. The amount nearly made her blush. However, knowing her father, it wasn't even close to the value he would put on his livelihood.

Letting it go would devastate him. This restaurant had been the heart of Hidden Falls since before she was born. It had once been the heart of their family, keeping them bound together. She'd left school in the afternoons to spend her evenings at Rossetti's doing her homework. She'd learned to cook cacciatore before most of her friends could tie their shoes. Math lessons had been taught with debits and credits or cooking measurements, and she'd been helping her mother with the accounts payable and receivable before most kids had gotten their driver's permits. Rossetti's was as much a part of her heritage as her Italian genes.

She looked down at the paper again.

Hidden Falls isn't giving up on Rossetti's and will do whatever it takes to keep this staple in the black, even if Fortune Industries and Giovanni Mancuso's illness aren't making it easy for the Mancuso family to turn down that kind of money.

Hackles rising, Gia crumpled the paper and threw it into the trash. *Figlio di troia*, she cursed.

What did this reporter know about her family, or what it would take to keep the restaurant afloat? They had only a few people left on a bare-bones staff, which made them incredibly shorthanded. With her mother the only transportation for her father to and from doctors' appointments, there was no one left to run the early shift, and from what she'd seen, dinner service had fallen far from its heights of music and dancing in the back room with exotic Italian dishes designed to tease the senses. Now it was nothing more than basic fare again. None of her father's specialties were on the menu any longer, and the live band on weekends had been replaced by CDs on a loop.

Bella squirmed against the front of Gia, and she rubbed her hand over her back until she quieted. In an effort to get Bella back to sleep, Gia stood and rocked her body from side to side, finding it calmed her as well. Her own nerves were stressed to the point of snapping like an overstretched rubber band.

"Which is the better option, *bella*?" she asked aloud, directing the rhetorical question at the child.

There was a quiet knock at the door, just before it opened a crack and a familiar face peeked around the edge. "You drive all night and don't even call an old friend?"

Instantly recognizing his deep voice, Gia hurried to the door and opened it the rest of the way. "Ben!"

"In the flesh." He leaned in to one side and gave her a hug, careful of the baby braced in front of her. "I'm guessing this is the baby I've heard people talking about. She is pretty, Gia. Congratulations."

She heard the question in his tone but chose to ignore it. Gia pulled the cover back from her face so he could get a better look at Bella. "Thanks. I'm sort of partial."

She'd always gotten along well with Andrew's brother. Handsome, kind and smart, he'd empathized with her about dealing with their younger siblings, although he'd had five of them compared to her one. Ben might have been a few years older than she was, but he'd never failed to say hello to her during her short visits home over the past years, in spite of how everything had ended with her and Andrew.

"She looks like you." Gia smiled tightly, trying to figure out a way to change the subject. He shot her a curious glance. "No ring though?"

She held up her hand, dismissing his observation with a shrug. "Didn't work out."

"For you, or Lorena?"

Gia's heart plummeted to her toes, and she couldn't help the fear that closed her throat, prohibiting her from swallowing, let alone answering his point-blank question.

"So, she *is* Lorena's."

"Ben, please, you can't tell anyone."

He held both palms out to her as he sat down on the edge of the desk. "It's not my story to tell." His gaze slid over her empathetically. "I hear you ran into Andrew when you got back."

"Couple times. Did he tell you what happened?"

"Nope," he said matter-of-factly. "You know Andrew. He just stuffs it all inside." He pretended to shove his fist into his stomach.

She rolled her eyes. "Yeah, he's a deep well of emotion, that one."

"Come on, Gia. Cut him some slack. It's been almost ten years since you two split. You can't still be holding a grudge."

"He cheated on me with my sister."

"Allegedly," he added, crossing his ankles in front of him. "Did you ever ask him about it?"

"I didn't have to. People saw them together. I assumed that one of you guys said something, which is why he never even apologized. He was caught. What could he say?"

"He never talked about it or what happened, so I didn't push." His brows lifted high on his forehead. "Don't you think he should have at least had the opportunity to defend himself?"

She looked up at him pointedly. He had at least a foot on her but she wasn't about to back down. "He had plenty of opportunity. And since when do firemen interrogate people?"

He pushed himself from the desk and chuckled. "No interrogation, just pointing out the obvious. I gotta get back to the station, but I stopped in to pick up my lunch, and was hoping you might be here so I could say hello." Ben headed through the door before stopping and leaning back inside the office. "You guys were good together, Gia. You always brought out the best in each other. He was happy with you. I haven't seen him that way since."

She watched Ben leave, her hand finding Bella's back again, absently rubbing in circles. She and Andrew *had* been good together—at least, she'd thought so—until he'd given it all up for a quick romp with her sister.

ANDREW HEADED IN for his evening shift at the station early. As much as he might want to try convincing himself it wasn't because he was hoping to catch a glimpse of Gia again, he'd have been lying and he knew it. He hadn't stopped thinking about her since he'd left the restaurant the day before. Nor had he been able to stop thinking about what Ben said. Gia *had* brought out the best in him. She made him want to be a man who deserved the trust she had in him.

The parking lot of Rossetti's was more packed than it had been in weeks as he drove in, looking for an empty spot. It likely had everything to do with the article in the paper this morning calling for people to help save the place that had become an institution to the small town, one of the few things that made it more than just a dot on the map. Either way, he doubted he'd be able to get his dinner in time for his upcoming shift, even if he ordered it to go.

But that's not why you're here, is it?

Andrew cast the thought aside and parked his car in

front of two trucks. It wasn't really a parking spot, just an empty lot, and he would have ticketed anyone else who tried it, but what the hell? There were some perks to being a cop in a small town. He pocketed his keys and headed for the front door.

"Look at what the cat dragged in. What are you doing here?"

Andrew turned around slowly and cringed when he saw Grant leaning on the back of Ben's truck, with their twin brothers, Jackson and Jefferson, climbing out of the back seat. Andrew let his chin drop forward to his chest. What were the odds of running into his oldest brother, Grant, in the parking lot? He should have been with his fiancée and stepson.

Their sister was the only sibling not present, other than their brother Lincoln, who was currently on a national music tour. *Damn!* Maddie would have kept their harassment to a minimum, provided she wasn't leading the pack torturing him herself.

"Where's Maddie? She's gonna be pissed to find out you four went out to dinner without her."

He started to walk past the group, only to have Grant reach for his shoulder. "You didn't answer the question."

Andrew shrugged him off. "Since when do you care about my eating habits?"

"Since when do you get all defensive over a simple question?" Jefferson asked.

"Since Gia came back and he's rethinking his mistake, letting her get away," Ben pointed out to the other four.

"Oh, no you don't." Jackson wagged a finger at Andrew. "You had your shot with her. You need to give one of us a chance."

Jealousy filled him. Andrew crossed his arms over his chest, deliberately puffing himself up, letting his gaze slide over his youngest brother. "We have a rule, remember?"

Years ago, the six brothers had agreed to never date a girl any of the others might have an interest in. It had been Grant's idea, always the one to head off any trouble between the brothers before it could start, and the rule had seen them through high school, when the pool of dating-age girls was much smaller. As they grew up, and began to find themselves attracted to different types of women, it seemed to matter far less.

There was no way Andrew was going to let Jackson date Gia. Not if he had any say in the matter.

Jackson laughed. "Where was that loyalty when it came to sleeping with Lorena."

Lightning fast, Andrew grasped the front of Jackson's shirt and slammed him against the back of Ben's truck. "Don't ever breathe a word about that again, you got it?"

Jackson, taken by surprise, raised his fists, ready to fight Andrew off, but Ben and Grant jumped between them before either could take a swing, pulling them apart.

"What's the matter, Andrew?" Jackson taunted.

"Afraid Gia might start comparing the two of us and find out you were lacking?"

"Shut up, you idiot." Ben dragged Jackson toward the front of the restaurant as Jefferson followed, shoving his twin through the door.

"Get inside and get us a table."

Andrew pulled his arms free from Grant's grasp and ran a hand through his short hair. "What the fuck? Next time, let me at him. That kid needs to get popped in his big mouth."

"Sure, because you didn't do anything, right?"

"He started it," Andrew said, realizing exactly how much he sounded like a five-year-old tattling to a parent. "He better not ask her out."

"Why? Because she's yours?" Grant leaned against the edge of the truck. "She's not property, man. You can't just claim dibs." Andrew glared at his brother. "You let her go, Andrew."

As if he needed a reminder.

"She dumped me," he clarified, unable to hide the bitterness in his voice.

Grant tucked his hands into his pockets. "Either way, it's over. You didn't go after her, and you didn't fix things when you had the chance. You think she hasn't dated anyone over the last ten years? Shit," he said with a chuckle. "She's got a kid. Obviously she's moved on. She grew up. Why didn't you?"

Andrew shot his brother a warning look, and Grant

laughed again. "My point is that you can't hold Jackson to that rule with a woman you dated ten years ago. I asked Bethany out after Ben did."

"She wasn't interested in Ben."

"Lucky for me, but the fact remains, bro." Grant draped an arm over Andrew's shoulder. "Maybe tonight isn't the night for you to get dinner here. Go grab a burger across the street."

Andrew shrugged off Grant's arm. The thought of Gia and Jackson together was enough to make him want to put his fist through a wall. Maybe he should skip dinner altogether and do some DTAC training before he went on duty tonight instead. Beating the crap out of some snot-nosed rookies as "the red man" might be just the perfect way to blow off some steam. Or maybe he should get to the bottom of this with Gia, once and for all.

Chapter Five

GIA WAS FRAZZLED. She'd already been forced to call her mother to come and pick up Bella for the evening while she filled in for a missing waitress and a no-longer-existent hostess. She was thrilled with the unexpected turnout, or would have been if she'd had the staff to handle it. It looked like the entire town seemed to be at Rossetti's tonight due, she was certain, to the article in the paper. More people than she'd imagined must read the damn thing. She'd never seen this kind of a crowd here, but if her parents had this much support from the town, she might be able to figure out some way to turn the tide in her father's favor.

Running to the front of the restaurant, she cringed at the line of people stretching out the doors, mentally trying to fit everyone. She already had four parties to seat with more in the waiting area, and the phone rang nonstop with no one to answer it. Reaching for a stack of menus, not even bothering to count them at this point, she stood in front of the crowd.

"June, party of three; Parker, party of two; and Baylor, party of six. Please follow me."

She led the way as the largest group was settled at their table on her left before directing the other two to theirs on her right and passing each menus. Gia promised their waitresses would be with them shortly but deliberately failed to explain how long "shortly" might really be. Not that they seemed to care. At least she'd managed to hurry their busboy along and get water delivered quickly.

Speed-walking to the front, she spotted Ben and the McQuaid twins. All three cast bright smiles in her direction and she wondered, like most of the people in town, how one family could have so many good-looking men in it. She couldn't help but smile back at the three of them as she headed their way.

"Please tell me you guys are ordering to go. We are swamped." She looked up at Ben, bumping him with her elbow. "And what are you doing back already? You were just here at lunch."

"I'm a growing boy. I need my carbs," he said, patting his flat stomach.

Jefferson looked around. "That was a smart move, to have the paper run that article. Looks like it's paying off."

"What do you mean?" Gia cocked her head to one side, confused.

He looked surprised. "The big front-page spread about Rossetti's. I just assumed you set it up."

"I saw it, but I didn't run it."

He shrugged. "It was a brilliant marketing move, and since you're some high-power marketing executive, I figured it was your idea. Either way, it looks like it helped."

Jackson shook his head. "And you call me an idiot," he muttered. "Hey, Gia."

He closed the distance between them, enveloping her in a bear hug. She'd gone to school with the pair and had watched girls throwing themselves at the two rodeo stars for years. Jefferson was the more serious of the two while Jackson was the clown, but both were great guys.

She smiled at the trio. "It's a good thing Jefferson wears his hair short enough to still see that scar or I'd never be able to tell the two of you apart."

Jefferson winked at her. "Chicks dig scars."

"Sure they do. Until they find out that you got it when your drunk ass fell out of the truck." Jackson rolled his eyes at his brother and shot her a cocky grin. "It's easy to tell us apart. I'm the smart, good-looking one. He's the one with only a few brain cells left after his stupid bull-riding stint." She tried to bite back her smile at their banter.

"There are four of us tonight, Gia," Ben said, curbing their flirting. "Grant's just . . ." He paused and looked back over his shoulder. ". . . parking the car."

"Okay. Well, you guys can either hang out at the bar

or stay here, but it's going to be about a thirty-minute wait for a table."

Ben and Jefferson met one another's gaze. "Bar," they replied in unison.

She laughed. "I'm sure you three know the way." She waved a hand in the direction of the bar at the end of the walkway. "Tell Nick I said your tab is on me until your table's ready."

"Big mistake, Gia," Ben said with a chuckle as the three men headed to the bar.

Gia turned in time to see Grant come inside with Andrew. Either Ben had miscalculated their party or Andrew was crashing. Butterflies immediately took up residence in her stomach and heat settled even lower, even as irritation filled her chest.

"Hey, Gia! You look fantastic." Grant greeted her warmly, like the old friend he was, bending to wrap her in a hug, lifting her off the ground.

She'd always liked Grant. He was charming and sweet and had never failed to be anything less than a gentleman, unlike his brother, scowling beside him. Andrew bobbed his head in greeting, as if she wasn't worth wasting his breath.

"Thanks. I saw that hit you took, and your retirement. You're okay now?"

"Yep, healed up and looking forward to the next chapter in life, which includes getting married."

"Congratulations! Anyone I know?" Like the rest of the McQuaids, there was a long line of women wanting to get a ring from Grant; however, his celebrity status had doubled his prospects.

"Bethany and her son moved here last summer, so you might have seen them around. You'd like her."

"I'd love to meet her."

Andrew sighed from beside him. "Now that you two are all caught up, mind if I place an order to go? I have to get on duty."

Gia arched a brow at Andrew's snide tone. She slid a glance over him, trying not to notice the broad expanse of chest stretching his T-shirt or the way his biceps bulged, pulling the cotton.

"If you're really in that much of a hurry, I'm sure you could get a burger across the street," she pointed out before turning her attention back to Grant. "The rest of the guys are waiting in the bar if you want to head back."

Grant laughed out loud and looped an arm around her neck. "I've missed you, Gia. And I've really missed watching you give this guy shit."

She couldn't help the smile that tugged at her lips, especially when Andrew stalked past, clearly annoyed.

"I'll be right there to take your order, Officer Sunshine," she called after him. Grant's laughed echoed in her ears as she reached for a handful of menus. "Miller, party of six, follow me."

ANDREW SAT, FUMING, at the bar while ice slid down the beer bottles in front of Ben and the twins. Grant nursed his club soda while Andrew glared at his iced tap water weeping condensation onto the marble counter.

Jefferson peered at him from around Ben's side. "What is your problem, man? You look like someone just crapped on your car."

"He's just pissed because Gia snubbed him." Jackson took a long swig from his beer. Andrew clenched his fists at his sides, using every ounce of self-control not to knock his brother from the bar stool.

"Cool it, Jackson," Grant muttered under his breath.

"Okay, boys, I finagled a table for you. Give me five minutes to get it cleaned off." Gia scooted past Nick pouring drinks behind the bar and pulled a notepad out from underneath. "So, what'll it be, Sunshine?"

"Sunshine?" Jackson laughed. "Him?"

"Yep," Gia said, shooting Jackson a smile with perfect straight white teeth.

Her dazzling smile hadn't changed one bit. It still made her eyes glitter like diamonds. That smile had made him forget everyone else around him more than once.

"On account of his sparkling personality and the way he just lights up a room."

All four of his traitorous brothers burst into laughter. He simply clenched the muscle in his jaw so tightly he thought it might snap.

"Oh, damn! You've got his number." Jackson held a hand to his gut as he laughed harder. "Do me a favor? Marry me and let's spend the next fifty years tormenting Andrew together."

Red-hot rage burst behind his eyes, and Andrew gripped the water glass hard enough that he expected it to shatter in his fingers. Instead of looking outraged, Gia just smiled brighter at Jackson and leaned over the bar toward him.

"Do you really think he could handle the two of us?" she asked in a conspiratorial whisper.

He leaned even closer to her, lowering his voice to match hers, and cut a glance in Andrew's direction. "What do you say we test it out and go to a movie tomorrow?"

That son of a bitch!

Andrew's gut churned with jealous rage as Gia appeared to be contemplating her answer. The idea of her going out with his brother—his younger, wilder and far less responsible brother—was ludicrous. Grant closed his eyes and shook his head slightly. Jefferson, Grant and Ben all fell silent. They knew Jackson was crossing a line, deliberately, and he could see the hesitation in their faces. They were waiting to find out what Gia would do and how Andrew would respond.

"As nice as that might be, I don't have a sitter. If I'm not here at the restaurant, my mom has to be, and she can't do that if she's watching Bella for me. So, unless you know of a sitter I can trust . . ."

Jackson looked crestfallen. "What if I find you a sitter?"

She narrowed her eyes at him, as if she was trying to judge how serious his question might be. "I doubt you could find someone I'd trust with a newborn on such short notice."

"Well, there's always my mom. Or Maddie," he offered.

Gia shot him a dubious look at the mention of their sister. She'd have no way of knowing how capable Maddie had become with kids, or the fact that she was now a speech therapist at the elementary school. Like her brothers, Maddie had raised plenty of hell growing up, and some reputations were hard to shake. He should know.

"Andrew, you're off tomorrow, right?" Jackson's voice grated on Andrew's last nerve. He knew exactly where his brother was heading with this. "You'd be willing to help Gia out, wouldn't you? I mean, who could you trust more than a cop?" he asked, turning back to Gia.

Andrew wanted to lunge past his other three brothers to strangle Jackson. He was deliberately trying to egg on this situation, knowing full well Andrew wouldn't willingly offer to do anything to make it easier for Jackson to date Gia. Now he was stuck. If he didn't agree, he'd look like the jealous asshat, and he didn't want Gia to think that he hadn't gotten over her. He absolutely had.

Liar, a quiet voice whispered in his head.

"Sure, why not?" He slammed back the rest of the water. "And I'll take an order of spinach ravioli."

Emotion flickered in her eyes, shadowing them, and her smile faltered. He turned away from her quickly, pretending to watch the people around them. The reality was that he couldn't look at her. He had no doubt that if he did, she'd easily see the truth in his eyes and realize he'd never stopped loving her.

GIA SHUFFLED INTO her parents' house well after midnight, exhausted and bleary-eyed but surprised to see both seated at the kitchen table. Her mother was feeding Bella but her father was watching for her, waiting for her like she was a teenager sneaking in from a date.

"Gia, I need to talk to you." He might have been sick, and weak, but he was still imposing.

"Can I take a quick shower, Daddy? It was a busy night."

His eyes brightened and his tone instantly changed. She recognized the excited energy snapping in them both. "Really? How busy?"

"Giovanni, that isn't what we need to discuss right now." Her mother looked pointedly at the baby sleeping in her arms and arched a brow.

"Talk first, shower after."

Gia had planned on waking early to talk to her parents about the restaurant, but right now, she was grungy and exhausted and smelled like spices and tomato sauce. She just wanted to crawl into bed and sleep for the next week straight, but thanks to her sister, that was no longer an option for her.

"Okay," she said, sliding into a hard-backed kitchen chair. "What's up?"

"Your mother told me."

Gia shot a quick look at her mother, but she refused to meet Gia's gaze. "What did she tell you?"

"About Bella, and I must say I'm very disappointed in both of you for not telling me the truth from the start."

"Daddy . . ." Gia shot her mother an incredulous look. "I wanted to, but we thought—"

He held up a shaky hand. "I know what you thought. You both assumed that I am too weak to handle the truth. But I am still your father, and lying to me, either of you, is unacceptable."

Gia had seen the disappointment in her father's eyes when she told him she'd had a baby, even though he'd pretended to be happy for her. But what she saw in them now was far worse. Disillusionment clouded his gaze. He was hurt more by the fact that she'd shown a lack of faith in his capabilities. She could also read the worry that he'd lost her respect. Tears welled in her eyes at the pain she'd caused her father.

"Daddy, I'm sorry."

He reached for her hand and squeezed it gently. "I know, *bella*, and I understand that you thought you were doing the right thing." He glanced at her mother, his eyes dark with anger. "But we don't lie to one another."

She bristled, pulling her hand from his. "Then why didn't you didn't tell me how sick you really were?"

Her father closed his eyes, sighing softly. "You're right. Like you, I thought I was protecting you. It was wrong."

Gia's mother raised her brows before turning back

toward the baby. "We need to decide on a more permanent solution about Bella." She brushed a fingertip over the child's plump cheek. "Have you talked to Lorena?"

"I've tried. She refused to come home, and now she's not responding to my messages at all." Gia shook her head.

Sadness filled her at the thought of the choices Lorena was making, the regret Gia was sure she would one day face.

"With me being sick and your mother trying to help, we can only do so much."

"It's okay, Daddy. I need to get her birth certificate straightened out with Lorena, but then I'm filing for temporary guardianship. That way, we can still buy some time in case she changes her mind."

"And if she doesn't?" her father asked.

"Then I'll move forward with adopting her."

Her father closed his eyes and shook his head slowly. Gia knew he was trying to hide his own disapproval of her sister's choices. But Gia wasn't going to let Bella suffer for her sister's decisions. She would make sure Bella grew up knowing how loved she was. She just had to figure out how she was going to manage as a single mother now.

"Okay." His voice was softer now. He pushed himself to standing and cupped his hand on his granddaughter's head. "This is going to be hard for you and we'll try to help as much as we can, but . . ." His voice simply trailed off.

He didn't have to say it. They didn't know what to do either. Neither of them even had the energy to help her with the baby. She could see the exhaustion written all over them after just one night. Raising a child would be expensive and they didn't have the money to help her financially. But they needed to come to a few decisions tonight.

Gia hated to be the one to wear her father down any further, but since they were getting everything out in the open, she also needed some answers from them. "Daddy, why did you call the newspaper?"

"What?" Her mother's head snapped up, and she stared at Gia for a moment before turning to her husband. "What is she talking about?"

"The article about Rossetti's," Gia explained. "In the paper this morning." She looked back at her father. "You called them, didn't you? There was no way to know the details of your deal with Fortune Industries unless someone involved told them."

Her father took a deep breath and walked out of the kitchen. Within moments, he returned with the paper and laid it on the table in front of her mother.

"*Figlio di mignotta*," her mother cursed. "I can't believe you did this, Giovanni. We talked, we decided. How could you do this behind my back?"

"No, you decided." Her father leaned on the kitchen table, his palms flat, his voice steady despite his frail appearance. "I let you make the decision, to buffalo me into agreeing to something I didn't want, and I shouldn't have. I don't want to sell. I want to go back to the restaurant. This is *my* restaurant and I want to run it. This sitting around the house, waiting to die, is going to be what kills me."

Her mother was a superstitious woman, and Gia could tell it was making her frantic that her arms were too full for her to properly make the sign of the cross. Gia rose, lifted Bella from her mother's arms and barely contained a smile when her mother's hands instantly flew over her body, warding off any bad omens from her father's mention of death.

"*Il cielo non voglia*, heaven forbid! Take it back."

"No." Her father's voice was more firm than Gia had heard it since coming home. "I am going back to work, starting later this morning."

Gia could see the determination in her father's eyes and knew that once his mind was set on something, he'd give it every ounce of strength he had to make it a reality. That wasn't going to help them either.

"Daddy, why don't we compromise?" she suggested. "Maybe you can go in a few hours a day, for the breakfast service, when it's quieter."

"I shut down breakfast service," her mother pointed out. "We couldn't afford the staff to cover it."

"What? We had plenty of staff," her father's voice boomed, reminding Gia of the man who had raised her rather than the frail man he'd become since he'd gotten sick. "What other changes have you made without telling me, Isabella?"

"I did what I had to. You were sick. Your treatments were taking a toll on you. We couldn't afford to hire people to cover for the both of us while we were at your treatments, and I didn't want to tell you. You couldn't handle the stress of the restaurant too." Tears filled her mother's eyes as she looked up at her husband. "I did what I had to do," she repeated quietly, as if trying to convince herself. She reached across the table for her husband's arm. "If we sell now, you can retire and we'd still have plenty of money to take care of the medical bills. We could even help Gia raise Bella."

"I won't sell. I don't care how much money they offer. And you had no right making decisions about the restaurant without discussing them with me."

Her father's voice was determined. Her mother's mouth was set in a thin line. They were at an impasse, and Gia knew this wasn't going to end well if it continued. She had to take control of this conversation before it turned into a blame game. Running a hand over the top of her head, she brushed back the stray hairs from her ponytail.

"Here's what I propose." She paused to make sure they were both listening. "We reopen the restaurant for breakfast and lunch. Daddy, you return to run the crew and the service in the morning. Mama, you take lunch, and I'll head up dinner, at least until we get the restaurant back up and in the black. The article today actually helped a lot and was a great idea, Daddy. It brought in a massive crowd tonight, but we need that kind of crowd consistently, and that's going to take some time. And more staff." She tapped her fingers on the table. "Until then, we need something bigger to bring a lot of people in. Some kind of event that draws people." She looked up at her mother. "How long do we have to decide about selling?"

Her mother glanced at her father, waiting for him to answer. When he didn't, she gave him an exasperated sigh. "Six weeks. That's it. Only six weeks. It's just not possible to turn it around in that short of a time. Not with the medical bills too. We need to sell."

Bella began to whimper quietly and Gia rose, rocking her and patting her back until she settled again. "I took four weeks of family leave. That gives us some time to try." She frowned as she tried to organize her thoughts in her sleep-deprived brain. "How much are the medical bills? I have some money saved up that I can give you and get those creditors off your back."

"Almost one hundred thousand dollars." Her mother crossed her arms over her chest. "I doubt you have *that* saved."

"A hundred *thousand*?" Gia asked, nearly choking on the number.

"Chemo is expensive, not to mention his other medications." Her mother glared at her father. "Especially when you let the health insurance policy lapse."

"We already went through this, Isabella," her father said, cutting his wife off with a growl of impatience.

Gia looked back and forth at her parents. Their situation was beginning to make more sense now. Her mother's overbearing decision-making. The way she was demanding her father sell the restaurant she knew meant so much to him. Not to mention the defeat she saw in her father's eyes and his determination to keep the restaurant running, in spite of his illness. He'd made the first mistake and, not wanting him to risk another, her mother opted to take the path of least resistance while her father was trying to prove himself.

Guilt. So much guilt being tossed back and forth. Like children in a water balloon fight, they just continued filling up more when they ran low, trying to be the one to get the last strike.

Closing her eyes, she sighed. The pair in front of her had always been loving, caring parents. They were supportive and attentive, doing so much right as parents. However, guilt had been a skill they'd honed to perfection and used to their greatest advantage. Whether it was to get their daughters to help in the restaurant or to come home for a holiday. It had become such an ingrained part of Gia's life that she hadn't stopped to consider there was far more depth to this issue than either of them just wanting their own way. Her father had made a mistake that could cost her parents everything they'd worked their entire lives for. Now, the aftermath of that mistake was destroying their future.

The sweet sigh that slipped from Bella's lips dragged Gia from her worries about her family's future to her present. She could help them only with the issues they faced today, right now.

"Mama, Daddy made a mistake. A big one, but it was a mistake, and he isn't the only one. Lorena is making one too, but look at how beautiful Bella is. We will get through this together, all of this, one step at a time. Let's at least give my idea a shot."

Gia prayed she was right, because there was so much at stake and so much more that could go wrong. Both for her parents and for her.

Chapter Six

_____

AT ELEVEN THE next morning, Gia answered the knock at the front door of her parents' house to find a very surly, sexy-as-sin man leaning against the frame of the door, his head bowed slightly. Andrew slid his sunglasses off and hooked them into the front of his T-shirt just as a slight breeze slapped her in the face with his scent. Not cologne, just Andrew. The smell she'd dreamed about and wondered why other men didn't have. Like sunshine and laundry soap, mixed with a spicy male scent that was all his own. She felt warmth flood through her, washing over her heart and settling between her thighs.

Nope! Never going there again, she reminded herself.

"Are you really going through with this?" His tone was doubtful, and his eyes registered humor at the thought.

In truth, she'd been having second thoughts all morning about going to a movie with Jackson, but if there was anything that would convince her to go, Andrew's dickish attitude did the trick.

She smiled sweetly. "Any reason I shouldn't?"

Please, give me a reason I shouldn't.

His gaze swept over her, slowly, intimately, and her heart stopped beating for a moment. Gia couldn't quite turn off the pessimistic voice that kept reminding her this was a bad idea. Especially when her body was already trying to shut down her brain's responses to Andrew. In her defense, she *hadn't* been around any men lately. It had been almost two years since she'd had more than a goodnight kiss, not that he needed to know that.

Then again, she'd never been around anyone like Andrew. He'd ruined other men for her before she was nineteen. His deep, slightly raspy voice could turn her bone marrow into molten lava and her limbs to gelatin with only a few words. He only had to look at her with those dark, sultry eyes and she knew exactly what he was thinking, or what he wanted to do. But the younger version of him was child's play compared to the man who stood in front of her now with his T-shirt clinging to every taut muscle, his jeans encasing his hips and thighs tightly, leaving little to the imagination, and that damn cocksure grin on his face she was sure had caused plenty of panties to drop in Hidden Falls, before and after her departure.

Don't forget the ones while you were still here.

The snide voice reminding her of the past, of her inability to hold his interest and his betrayal, made her heart beat painfully against her ribs. It was *almost* enough to kill the desire she felt for him, which made her feel even more pathetic for going through with this.

"I don't know what you're hoping to accomplish, Gia, but it almost seems like you're trying to replace one McQuaid brother with another."

The son of a bitch thought *he* had any right to accuse *her* of any wrongdoing. He was the one who had cheated on her with Lorena, the same night he'd asked her to marry him.

"*I coglioni,*" Gia muttered, turning to head back inside the house. She stopped when his fingers curled around her wrist.

"English, sweetheart. You always did have a way of reverting to Italian when I got you worked up." The smooth huskiness she heard in his voice made it clear he wasn't talking about her anger.

She arched a brow and took a step toward him, tipping her head up and not caring one bit that he had a good eight inches on her. She stabbed her finger into the immovable wall of his chest, trying to ignore the sizzle that shot up her arm at just the touch.

"I said, you've got some balls." The smile fell from his face and he looked suddenly unsure. "Coming here and insinuating anything about me when you're the one who messed around with my sister."

Color drained from his face, confirming beyond a shadow of doubt that what she'd been told all those years ago was true. Pain wrenched at her heart. While she'd acted on the accusation, there had been a small part of her that hoped he had some sort of explanation, a reason, an excuse . . . something. But Andrew didn't even try to defend himself.

"You know what they say about those in glass houses, Andrew." She turned her back on him, heading for the living room. He reached for her hand again, and she paused, looking at their connected hands. He dropped it like she'd scalded him.

Oh, she burned all right, but not in a bad way, and she hated her own weakness. How could she still feel anything but resentment for this man after what he'd done?

Andrew scrubbed a hand over his mouth and jaw, looking apologetic. "Gia, I—"

"I don't want to know the details." She threw up her hands. "And I certainly don't want to talk about it. It's in the past. *We* are in the past. And for the record, me going out today with Jackson has absolutely nothing to do with you. Got it?"

He licked his lips and rolled them inward before nodding, his dark eyes chagrined. "Got it."

"Good. Now, come inside so I can give you instructions and Bella's schedule."

She could feel the weight of his gaze on her back as he followed her. She'd agreed with her parents that they needed to stop lying to protect one another, yet everything she'd just said to Andrew was a whopping load of bullshit. Her date with Jackson *was* about him. She *did* want to talk about what happened and she had never, ever been able to leave her feelings for him in the past.

GIA SAT IN Jackson's old pickup truck, feeling slightly nauseated as it swayed on the turns and bobbed down the highway.

"Sorry," he murmured, as if reading her mind. "I forget how different riding in this ol' Chevy is than being in a new car. They may not make them like this anymore, but that's because they aren't for everyone."

She held one hand to her stomach. "I feel like I'm on a boat."

"You are looking a little green. I thought maybe it was just the thought of going out with me." Jackson laughed, but he slowed down as he took the next curve on the highway.

"No. Why would you think that?" She cracked the window, letting the warm scent of pine slip in and soothe her tumultuous stomach.

He simply arched a brow and turned back to the highway as he took their exit. "Gia, I think we both know that this is sort of a one-time thing. You have a history with Andrew and, let's face it, while I'm not opposed to pissing him off once to make a point, I wouldn't want a woman, even one as great as you, to come between him and me. He's a pain in my ass, but he *is* my brother, and I love him."

Gia sighed with relief. She liked Jackson, she really did, but even she had realized, as soon as he picked her up, that there was no sexual chemistry between them. They could tease one another, joke around and talk incessantly, but there was no electric current like the one she felt with Andrew.

Damn it. Same story, different guy. But she knew Jackson was right, and relief flooded through her.

"So, what do you propose we do?"

Wicked mischief glinted in his green eyes. "We tell him what a great time we had. Convince him we're in love in order to make him suffer."

She rolled her eyes. "What makes you think he'll even care?" She thought of Andrew's earlier comment about replacing him with his brother and felt herself growing irritated all over again.

Jackson laughed. "Trust me, he cares. A lot." He shook his head as he pulled into the parking lot of the movie theater and turned off the truck. "And regardless of what you'd like everyone else to believe, I think you do too."

"That was a long time ago, Jackson."

He gave her a half-shrug. "Maybe. And maybe neither of you was ready back then. But time can fix a lot of things, Gia."

"It can also fester a lot of wounds that never healed," she pointed out. "I'm not here to rekindle things with Andrew. I'm here to help my parents."

He nodded, seeming to accept the change of topic. "So, how long are you planning on staying?"

"A few weeks."

His lower lip jutted out as he rubbed the slight cleft in his chin. "That should be enough time."

"For what?"

Jackson faced her, his eyes glinting with mischief. "For all of the pieces to come together."

"What?" She watched as he jumped out of the driver's seat and hurried to her door. "What is that supposed to mean?"

"Nothing," he said with a laugh, reaching for her hand and dragging her toward the ticket window. "I hope you like scary movies."

Gia got the distinct impression Jackson had more up his sleeve than just tormenting his brother, and she was about to look guilty by association.

AFTER AT LEAST seventeen texts from Jackson updating him on their date, Andrew turned off his notifications and tossed his cell phone onto the coffee table. If he saw one more message about how pretty Gia looked or how good she smelled, he'd throw the damn thing out the window. There had been at least seven pictures of them. Taking a walk near the fountain as they waited for the movie to start, another selfie in the theater. #FirstDate. His response was concise and to the point—#FuckOff.

The last one must have been taken without her realizing it. She'd been laughing, with her head thrown back, hair tousled around her shoulders and eyes lit with glee. Gia was so beautiful it made his chest ache.

And she'd been his until he'd royally screwed up.

Andrew exhaled slowly, trying to control the jealous rage threatening to overtake him. He didn't deserve Gia, never had. Although he'd never admit it to Jackson, his brother and Gia were perfect for one another. Jackson was a good man, people adored him and he had a great sense of humor. Not to mention how highly he valued loyalty, honor and family, the same way Gia did.

Well, except for asking Gia out, but Andrew could hardly fault him for that. Who wouldn't want to date Gia? Who wouldn't want her in their life?

A raspy cry came from the playpen Gia had moved into the living room for him, and he jumped up to retrieve Bella. He'd never spent much time with babies. In fact, he'd never spent *any* time around them unless it was on a call. Gia had given him an infant crash course before she'd left on how to diaper, feed and burp her, under the mistaken assumption that he already knew how to care for an infant, reminding him that those three things would encompass all of Bella's basic needs while Gia was gone. She'd texted once they'd arrived at the movies that she'd be back within a few hours. She was already thirty minutes late, and Andrew wasn't sure what he was supposed to do now, having already done each. Andrew slid an arm into the playpen, scooping up the infant and holding her in the crook of his arm the way Gia had instructed.

"Hey, Bella, what's the matter?" he murmured. The infant grunted in response, rubbing her mouth at the neck of Andrew's T-shirt. "I don't know what to do for you until your mom gets back."

"Here."

Gia's father shuffled into the room and held out a bottle. Andrew hadn't even realized he was in the house. When Gia said she didn't have a sitter, he'd assumed she'd left him home with Bella alone. But one look at the man was enough for Andrew to realize he simply didn't have the energy to handle a newborn, even for a few hours.

Giovanni looked older than Andrew remembered. He'd heard people talk about how sick he was, heard about the cancer that wasn't responding to even the most aggressive treatments, but this was the first time he'd seen the ravages close up. Giovanni had once been a barrel-chested brute of a man, looking like a mafia hit man stereotype with his slicked-back salt-and-pepper hair and his chiseled jawline. He could stand toe-to-toe with any of the McQuaid men and almost be eye level, and Andrew was sure that, in his younger days, he could have probably taken any one of them in a fight.

But the man in front of him barely bore a resemblance. Giovanni looked tired. Not just physically, although his body seemed frail enough to break if he moved too fast. He looked emotionally exhausted, wrung out, like he was finished fighting. Even his dark eyes that had once danced with mirth, the way Gia's did, now seemed dulled and almost glassy, sunken deep into his skull. He'd always been intimidating, larger than life with his thick Italian accent and hands the size of hams, but he'd never been unfriendly, even after Andrew and Gia had split up.

"Haven't seen you around this house in a long time, son."

He instantly felt like the young man he'd once been, dating Giovanni's older daughter, and the nervousness that had curled in his belly the night he'd asked for his permission to propose to Gia returned now. He'd seen Giovanni over the years, but always from a distance. He'd never again returned to face him.

"That's true, sir." He took the bottle from the older man, nodding his thanks, and slid onto the couch, hoping Giovanni would follow his lead and do the same. He looked ready to fall over.

"You hurt my girl, you know. If I was younger man . . ."

Giovanni had every right to take him to task for the pain he'd caused Gia, and Andrew wouldn't begrudge the man the opportunity. Slipping the bottle into Bella's pouting mouth, he prayed the old man wouldn't hit him while he held her.

"I did, but I never meant to," he admitted.

Giovanni crossed his thin arms over his chest, puffing it up. "Does she know about you and Lorena, or what really happened before she ran off?"

Damn small towns and the gossip that made the rounds faster than shit through a goose. If he ever found out who had spread the rumor, he'd make sure they spent an uncomfortable few hours in cuffs in the back of his patrol car.

"I'm not sure how she found out, but it sounds like she does."

Giovanni narrowed his eyes. "You sure? Because if I know my daughter, she wouldn't have let you in this house, let alone anywhere near Bella, if she did." A smile tugged at his mouth. "If she'd knew the truth, you'd be lucky if you weren't walking with a limp."

"I wouldn't have thought so either, sir, but from what she's said, I'm pretty sure she knows."

Giovanni nodded slowly, edging closer as Andrew lifted the baby to burp her, patting her back gently. He ran a hand gently over the baby's head. "My granddaughter is lovely."

"Like her mother," Andrew murmured.

Giovanni shot him a knowing look, and Andrew worried he'd said too much. This man had every reason to hate him.

"You do realize Gia isn't her mother, don't you?"

"What?" The shock must have registered in Andrew's eyes.

"Lorena," Giovanni clarified. "She left Bella with Gia right after she was born."

Andrew suddenly understood the old man's questioning.

He mentally did the math. When he'd seen Gia on the side of the highway, she'd mentioned that Bella was only a few days old, which meant she was conceived about ten months ago. Around the same time he'd gotten hammered and woke up with Lorena.

Giovanni's bushy brows pinched between his eyes. "Yeah, I heard the stories. Hidden Falls is a small town and word spreads quickly. You need to have a talk with Gia, especially since she's planning on adopting Bella if Lorena doesn't return. Her paternity is bound to come up."

"How did you—"

"I like you, son. I always have." Giovanni shook his head as a slow grin slipped over his thin lips, forcing wrinkles into the corners of his weathered eyes. "You remind me of myself, and you tend to get in your own way."

He eyed the recliner for a moment before finally sliding into it with a sigh and folding his hands over his stomach. "My wife thinks I don't see things, but I do. I think sometimes I see things more clearly than she does. Lorena has always tried to be like Gia, wanted everything Gia had, regardless of the cost to get it, and you got caught up in Lorena's games."

"What Gia and I had was a long time ago." Andrew looked down at Bella, trying to comprehend the fact that this could be his daughter. "I loved her. You know that, right?"

"Mmm-hmm, even after she left. Everyone could see it, even if you didn't think so. Which only gave Lorena another reason to go after you."

Andrew felt the dread curl in his chest. He thought he'd hidden his feelings for Gia. Hell, he'd moved on, grown up and given up on ideas like true love, but apparently everyone who knew him at all saw something he didn't even realize he was revealing.

"You never went to LA like you said you were going to."

"After Gia left, I decided to stay in Hidden Falls."

"Look, I don't actually know what happened between you and Lorena." He held up a hand when Andrew started to speak. "As her father, I don't think I want to, but believe me when I tell you, she took great pleasure in telling anyone who would listen about how she was the sister who won. About how she managed to have something that Gia never would. She said the two of you were leaving together."

"But—" Andrew felt his mind spinning. He'd been with Lorena only the one night. He had planned on moving to LA when he and Gia were engaged, but never since.

Giovanni held up his hand again, cutting Andrew off. "I told you, I don't want to know, but you need to talk to Gia and explain what happened before she finds out on her own."

"She's never going to forgive me for this."

Giovanni pushed himself to standing. "Sure she will, if you give her what she needs."

Andrew's gaze met the old man's, the intensity in Giovanni's eyes surprising him. "What's that?"

Slapping his shoulder as he walked out of the room, Giovanni let out a soft chuckle. "Well, now, I guess that's up to you to figure out, son."

Chapter Seven

THE HOUSE WAS nearly silent when Gia finally entered. Only the quiet tick of the grandfather clock in the hallway broke the serene calm. She felt bad being almost an hour later than she'd told Andrew she would be, but she and Jackson had begun talking business, and she'd lost track of time while helping him figure out a marketing strategy to promote his new horse-breeding venture. It had struck up a brainstorming session with the issue the restaurant was facing, and he'd come up with the idea for an easy event that she was sure would earn a hefty sum quickly for her father with minimal investment, if she could convince the other McQuaid men to go along with it.

And that would only be possible if she could release the grip she held on how Andrew had hurt her.

"Hello?" she called quietly, not wanting to wake her father in his room upstairs. "Andrew?"

When she didn't receive a response, she headed into the living room where she'd set up everything Andrew would need to watch Bella for the evening. Her heart stopped beating when she saw the pair sleeping on the couch. Braced in a corner of the cushions with his stocking feet on the coffee table, Andrew had Bella curled against his massive chest, both sound asleep. Bella's head was tucked safely under his chin, which was tipped down toward her protectively. The baby looked so tiny in his arms with his palm covering her back, but the picture was the epitome of tenderness.

Gia's heart shattered.

This was exactly what she'd dreamed of having, what they'd talked about for their future, before she'd gotten the doctors' prognosis, before their future together had fallen apart.

Had been torn apart, she mentally corrected herself.

Andrew had planned on joining a police department in LA while she finished college. Then, a few years down the road, they would start a family. They'd discussed how they'd raise them here in Hidden Falls, close to family. First marriage, then at least four kids.

Until he'd turned his back on it and thrown it all away to sleep with her sister.

He'd been her dream, but she'd never been his.

Tears filled her eyes, blurring the pair on the couch,

and she tried to blink them back, unable to understand how something that happened so long ago could still cut so deeply. Maybe it was because once she'd broken off their engagement, she'd never allowed herself the time to grieve. Or maybe it was because she'd never stopped loving Andrew, in spite of his betrayal.

She couldn't believe that. Because if that were true, it would make her hopelessly pathetic.

Gia dabbed at her eyes, willing the tears back, as she bent over Andrew, laying her hand over his on Bella's back. "Andrew," she whispered, trying to wake him gently. "I'm back. Why don't you let me take her?"

His eyes flicked open, completely alert, but he didn't move otherwise. His gaze was dark, intense, and Gia's mouth went dry at the desire he didn't even bother to try to hide. She was suddenly unable speak.

"Gia," he whispered, lifting his hand to her cheek, brushing his thumb over her cheekbone.

She knew it would happen. Didn't even want to stop it. When Andrew curled his fingers into her hair and guided her down toward him, she welcomed it. As his breath moved over her lips, she parted them, seeking his kiss. From the moment his mouth brushed against hers, at the first tentative taste of him, she knew she was lost.

Being kissed by Andrew was like coming home.

It was familiar and easy in so many ways, his touch taking her back in time, but it was also new and exciting. She sighed into him, loosening her grip on their past for a moment, allowing herself to experience the difference between the teen she'd once loved and the man he was today. When he swept his tongue against hers, her pulse throbbed, heating her body in slow, languid waves of yearning, spreading gradually and destroying every defense in its path. She was the first to deepen the kiss, her hand moving over his jaw, leaning into him, seeking more from him.

Bella wiggled, giving a little grunt as she lifted her head slightly and bumped against Gia's jaw. It was enough to jolt her back to the reality of the situation instead of the fantasy she was letting herself get swept away in.

What she and Andrew had was in the past. She had too many troubles on her plate already without adding her better-off-forgotten feelings for Andrew to the mix. Between her sister, Bella and her parents' restaurant, she had no room in her life for any more complications.

And Andrew was the most dangerous complication she could imagine.

WHEN HE'D OPENED his eyes to see Gia standing over him Andrew had thought, for a moment, it was a dream. He hadn't intended to kiss her but now that he had, he wasn't about to apologize for it. He'd been fantasizing about kissing her this way since the day she'd told him to leave. But never once had it been like this. As arousing as each fantasy had been, not once had he felt ready to explode with longing. Not once did his heart practically pound out of his chest, racing like a wild stallion over the open plain. Never had his hands shaken with the need to touch her. This was what those dreams should have been. This was right.

Then when Bella bumped against their chins and Gia withdrew, he knew it had been a mistake. He could see the distrust flickering in her eyes, like candlelight. If he ever hoped to gain her forgiveness, he needed to regain her trust first.

"Sorry," she muttered, scampering backward quickly even as she tried to slide an arm under Bella. "I'll take her."

"Why?"

"To put her back in her bed."

Andrew let her take the baby. "No, I mean why are you sorry?"

"Because . . ." Gia glanced back over her shoulder at him and twisted her full lips to one side, nibbling at the corner. He cocked his head and arched a brow, waiting. "Because."

He chuckled. "Contrary to how it might feel at times, Gia, we *are* adults. We can kiss and it doesn't have to mean the end of the world. It can be just a kiss."

She opened her mouth, about to say something, then bit her lower lip again, looking stung. He immediately regretted his words, wondering what she'd been about to say.

"So, how was your *date*?" he asked, changing the subject.

He wasn't even sure why he asked the question. Jealousy flared up again, hot and bright as the sun. He had no desire to hear the details of how she and Jackson hit it off, or anything else that might have happened while they were out.

"It was nice. A good movie, and we stopped by the drive-in after for milkshakes." She headed down the hallway for her room. He followed her but stopped short in the doorway, not willing to enter her room, watching as she laid Bella down on her bed, tucking rolled blankets on either side of her.

"And?"

She turned and touched a finger to her lips, indicating he should remain quiet, then pressed her hand against his chest, urging him out of the doorway, shutting it behind her. He took only a single step back. With the door shut, it left little room for her between him and the door. Andrew looked down at her, trying to ignore the fact that he was getting an eyeful of her ample cleavage. His mouth practically watered at the sight of her and he felt his body jerk to attention.

"And nothing. We talked about business, and Jackson came up with a great idea to help my parents."

Andrew could hear the admiration in her voice and it singed him. Clenching his fists at his sides, he had only one thought—how quickly he could get home to beat his brother to a pulp. His next inclination was to push her up against the door and kiss her until she couldn't even remember his brother's name. Somehow he managed to rein the desire in, barely.

"Did he?"

She laid a hand against his ribs and looked up at him, her eyes soft and pleading. "Yes, and I need your help."

Dear God, help me.

If she continued looking at him that way, he'd give her his right arm. Maybe his left too.

Andrew felt any inclination he might find to deny her disappear like some magician's trick. One touch from her, one look, and his willpower crumbled. He had no ability to deny her, never had, but she didn't realize that, and he wasn't going to let her figure out that she was his Achilles' heel.

His hands found her waist and he took a step toward her, pressing her back against the bedroom door. "My help?"

He needed her, had never stopped wanting her, and since her return, Andrew felt like his entire world had been upended. But regardless of the chaos she brought into his life, she made him feel like he was alive again. Like he'd been holding his breath since her departure ten years ago, and he was finally able to inhale deeply.

"Andrew," she began, her hands landing on his forearms. He could hear the rebuff in her voice and leaned forward with a heavy sigh, balancing his forehead on the door above her. "Why don't we go back to the other room, where we can talk?"

The talk he'd had with Giovanni was in the forefront of his mind. Talk. Yes, that's exactly what they *needed* to do and the last thing he actually wanted to do. Because if Giovanni was right and she didn't know what had transpired between him and Lorena that night, it would be the last thing he discussed with anyone—just before she buried him.

"Sure. Let's do that," he agreed unenthusiastically.

Andrew took a few steps back and let her lead the way, trying not to enjoy the view and failing miserably. She was beautiful, had grown even more so with time and maturity. Physically she was what every woman aspired to be—curvy but thin. However, emotionally, she was what every person *should* have aspired to be— tough, fair, loyal and kind. She was perfection, wrapped up in a feminine package that drove him wild.

"Okay, so here's the plan," she said, leading him back to the couch and sitting down, tucking one leg under her. "Jackson said Grant and Ben have ladies in their lives now, so we don't want to make this a bachelor auction, but your entire family holds a sort of local celebrity status. What if we had a McQuaid Trade?"

"Come again?" He couldn't possibly have heard her correctly. "Trade . . . for what?"

"Anything."

Andrew leaned back against the couch. She couldn't possibly have thought this through completely, and he wondered if Jackson had really come up with this idea or if he'd been too afraid to tell her no. Hell, poor Linc had enough women trying to trap him into their beds while he was on tour. There wasn't a woman alive who didn't fantasize about nailing Linc McQuaid, country music superstar. And a fiancée probably wouldn't stop women from trying to do the same with Grant, even as a retired NFL player. He frowned, and she must have seen the concern in his expression.

"Well, not *anything*," she clarified. "But you could each offer something up to be auctioned. It *could* be a date or, say, in Linc's case, maybe guitar lessons or a private concert."

"Let me get this right. You're suggesting that I should, as a sheriff's deputy, pimp myself out?"

Her cheeks turned bright pink as the ridiculousness of the suggestion she was making dawned on her. Gia's shoulders sagged. "Well . . . no. I guess not. It sounded better when Jackson mentioned it." He tipped his head to one side, waiting for her to fully comprehend how it would appear. "But people do bachelor auctions all the time."

He nodded. "Yes, for charities." She pinched her lips together. He'd struck a nerve. "Gia, what's going on? Talk to me."

"I just really need something that will help get people coming back to the restaurant. A lot of people. Fast."

"What's the big rush? Because of that article?"

She glanced back over her shoulder at the hallway. "No. Well, sort of." She braced an elbow on the back of the couch and leaned forward, lowering her voice. "Dad was behind that article. He's lost his insurance and has a huge medical debt right now. Dad's not responding to chemo anymore and was approved for a clinical trial, but they won't let him start it until his bills are paid off. If I can't help them get Rossetti's earning the way it used to, they're going to have to sell it, and you can imagine what that would do to him. It's a mess and I have to fix it."

"Aw, man." Andrew rubbed a hand over his eyes.

That certainly explained why the restaurant had been shut down more, the changes that had been made over the last year, and the fact that people had been seeing less of Giovanni. "Is he going to be okay?"

Her eyes shimmered. "I don't know. But I have to do *something* to help." A tear streaked down her cheek, breaking his heart.

"Baby, come here."

He reached for her and she fell against his chest, soaking in the strength he offered. It didn't matter what happened in the past. She couldn't possibly doubt that he would always care about her, and her family. Andrew stroked her back, feeling her tears soaking through his shirt, her arms around his ribs. He knew it should feel strange, holding his ex-girlfriend—ex-*fiancée*—almost ten years after their breakup, while she cried on his shoulder. Instead, it felt right. Like he was the only one who could understand exactly what she was going through and be there to support her. Having her in his arms again felt like he'd been reunited with a part of him he hadn't even realized was missing.

She sniffed and looked up at him, drawing herself back slightly. "I'm sorry."

Andrew brushed her dark hair back from her face, tipping up her chin with his finger. "Don't be."

He stared down at her, wanting to kiss her again, needing to kiss her. It felt like the next logical move. It was what he would have done before, but things had changed between them. They weren't together and he had no right to even hold her this way. He was trespassing on territory that was no longer his. Pushing aside his own desires, he grasped for the conversation they'd been having—ideas to help her family out of their financial situation.

"I have an idea that might be even more profitable than an auction."

Gia sat up, dabbing under her eyes and smearing her makeup, making her look adorably mussed, although he knew she wouldn't think so.

"I'll call Linc and convince him do a concert at Rossetti's. We can fill the ballroom, do a couple of shows over the weekend. He'll bring in far more money than any of the rest of us could."

"Would he do that? *Could* he?"

Andrew shrugged one shoulder half-heartedly. "He owes me. I'll call in a favor," he assured her. His brother didn't owe him jack-crap, but Andrew would make his brother whatever deal he had to in order to make sure

Linc came through for him. Not that he was going to admit that to Gia.

"Oh, thank you, Andrew!"

She threw her arms around his neck, hugging him tight enough to cut off his airway for one glorious second. Not that he was going to complain, not for one solitary beat.

She let go, narrowing her eyes at him. "Is this so you don't have to go out on a date with some random woman?"

He laughed. "Gia, there's only one woman in this town I want to date." The honest words tumbled from his lips before he could stop them. Her cheeks grew pink again and he wanted to kick himself. He cleared his throat. "I should go."

What was he thinking? Up until today, she'd acted like she wanted to gouge his eyes out. She was never going to forgive him. Andrew rose awkwardly and headed for the door.

He still hadn't gotten to the bottom of why she thought he'd cheated on her. Not to mention that this matter of what happened between him and Lorena was still hanging over his head. He had to tell her before someone else spilled the beans. What he really needed was to find Lorena and get some answers from her, because if there was any chance that Bella was his daughter, he needed to know. Just because she was willing to walk away from her child didn't mean he was.

Chapter Eight

GIA STARED DOWN at the documentation for Bella's birth certificate. It bore her name as Bella's mother and a forged signature. Thanks to Lorena, she was caught up in yet another lie she had no control over.

If she were to file the document, no one might ever be the wiser, but she would know. While it was a simple solution for the moment, it would mean living a lie for the rest of her life, lying to Bella as she grew up, and Gia wasn't certain she could do it. What if Lorena changed her mind and decided she wanted her daughter back? Gia would be the one to face charges of fraud. And because Lorena had listed the father as unknown, if Bobby ever did want to file for paternity, Gia would also be forced to fight him for custody. She was caught in a no-win scenario. Especially since the birth certificate form had to be filed with the health department within the next five days. She would have to fly her sister in and convince her to correct it.

Gia dialed Lorena's cell phone again, praying she'd pick up. As usual, it went straight to voice mail. She hoped her frustrated sigh wasn't picked up on the message. "Lorena, I really need you here. I can't turn in this birth certificate. I just can't. Let's correct it and I'll file for guardianship, I swear. Please, just come home."

There was no way for her sister to miss the desperation in Gia's voice. She couldn't live with this lie and only Lorena could fix it. Her phone *ping*ed with a text message and she closed her eyes, hoping that it was from Lorena.

> Linc said he'd be happy to do the concerts. Just needs to know when.

Gia's stomach immediately did somersaults as she read the message from Andrew, trying to convince herself it was only because it was the first thing that had gone right. Surely it had nothing to do with the fact that the man made every cell in her body quiver with anticipation whenever she thought about him. It was like being caught in the middle of an electrical storm.

Not because it's Andrew, she repeated to herself, willing her body to comply with her brain assertion.

She tried to convince herself it had more to do with the fact that Linc McQuaid concert tickets had been selling online for absurd amounts of money within minutes of going on sale. On one hand, it was insane, but Gia couldn't help but celebrate the fact.

Her mind began to spin with ideas. Three concerts would bring huge amounts of revenue for Rossetti's, especially if one was a VIP concert—smaller, more intimate—and included a full three-course meal. Optimism began to take root for the first time since her arrival. She owed Andrew and Linc more gratitude than they would ever understand.

Before she could respond to Andrew, another message came through:

He says he has a break in the tour schedule in just under two weeks.

She'd have to get plans underway fast. That would barely be enough time to print posters and get advertising set up. While she'd worked under tighter deadlines before, she'd had plenty of assistance from the advertising firm and their resources. This time she would be on her own with no resources at all. Gia took a deep breath, squaring her shoulders.

Failure wasn't an option. It couldn't be.

She pressed the button to call Andrew directly. A text seemed too impersonal a way to thank him, and while she would have liked to thank him in person, she didn't trust herself around him. Not after that kiss on the couch. She still wasn't sure how that had even happened. One minute she'd been waking him to leave, and the next she was ready to rip her clothes off for him. Her attraction to him wasn't normal. It was frantic and heady, unexplainable. Until she knew she wouldn't give in to the weakness, she'd was better off keeping her distance from him as much as possible.

If she'd been smart, she would have stayed away from Hidden Falls completely. She'd managed to avoid him for ten years' worth of visits, but now she couldn't seem to go more than a day without seeing him. And being this close to him again was destroying any confidence she had in her ability to keep the hurt she'd felt when she found out he'd cheated on her—with her sister, no less—in the forefront of her mind.

Niggling doubts crept inside, stretching out their dark tentacles, reminding her that Lorena wasn't the most trustworthy or known for her honesty. But there had been others who'd seen them kissing. Others who'd informed her that Lorena's shirt was unbuttoned.

"Gia?" Andrew's voice was husky, as if she'd awakened him, and she glanced at the clock on her nightstand. It was only ten thirty, but he'd probably gone right to bed after texting her. She should have just messaged him back.

"Sorry, were you sleeping?"

"No." He inhaled quickly and she could hear him moving. "I just woke up a few minutes ago. I have the night shift this week."

"Lucky you," she teased, her lips curving into a smile she couldn't quite help. "I'll let you go. I just wanted to thank you for talking to Linc for me, and a text just didn't seem like it was enough."

"You think a phone call is?"

She could hear the playful note in his voice and felt the flutter of butterfly wings in her stomach. She wanted to join his banter, but it would only make it harder for her to keep the protective walls up.

"You don't?"

"I could think of much better ways for you to thank me, Gia. And for most of them, I'd need to see you in person."

"Andrew." It was supposed to be a warning, a reminder that they needed to stop treading this fine line, but what came out instead was a breathless sigh.

"Meet me, Gia." There was a pleading note in his voice. One she hadn't expected from him. "At our spot."

"Their spot" was the patio along the side of the restaurant. Under a covered canopy outside the doors, where small, twinkling lights hung like fairy stars and the water fountain gurgled quietly among the scent of honeysuckle and jasmine that covered the stone barrier wall. They used to wait for the restaurant to close so that Gia could sneak her father's car keys and meet him there. It was where he'd first kissed her, where he'd proposed. Late at night while the rest of the world slumbered, he'd promised to never hurt her, to spend eternity making her happy. It was also where people had seen him leaving his tryst with Lorena. The memory steeled her resolve to remain distant.

"I can't leave. Bella's sleeping."

She wanted to move past her hurt, to become friends again, to find the ease they'd once had with one another. But all of that came at the expense of her heart, and that was a vulnerability she couldn't bare to him again.

"We need to talk." The playful flirtation in his voice was gone, leaving behind a man who sounded far too serious, and it worried her.

Gia ran a hand through the messy waves cascading over her shoulder and brushed them back. "Tomorrow."

"I work the late shift," he reminded her.

"Are you still living on your parents' ranch? I can come by in the morning."

"In the bunkhouse," he elaborated. "You sure you want to come here? With everyone else around?"

Her laugh was quiet. "Who are you kidding? We both know your dad will have everyone out working at the crack of dawn." His groan rumbled through the receiver as if even the reminder was painful. "I'll come over around nine. Everyone should be on their way out by then."

Gia laid a hand over her stomach, trying to convince herself she must have eaten something that didn't agree with her. Her body practically hummed with desire, and she didn't want to admit it was the idea of being alone with him that caused it. Or the possibility that while they were alone, another kiss might happen. Because she wasn't a teenager and her hormones weren't calling the shots. She was a grown woman, in full control of her reactions.

Unfortunately, just thinking it didn't make it a reality. Her body's responses were not coinciding with her logical reasoning as quickly as she wanted.

"I'll see you in the morning, then, Gia." Andrew's voice was a warm caress, making her entire body tingle with anticipation.

ANDREW STOOD ON the porch of the bunkhouse, watching as Gia's Lexus made its way down the dirt driveway, slowing as she approached the bunkhouse. Sliding out of the driver's side, Gia revealed one shapely denim-encased thigh at a time before moving around the car to get Bella's car seat. The pink-and-blue Western shirt she wore over a white camisole made her look young and sweet. And incredibly hot. He couldn't help but appreciate the beauty that had once been his.

Yep, until you went and fucked it up.

He was going to do his best to fix that today. The first thing he needed was get to the bottom of why they'd broken up. Gia wasn't one to believe rumors, or she never would have looked past his reputation in the first place. He'd never cheated on her, so somehow he was going to get to the bottom of why she was so adamant he had. Hopefully, in the process, he could convince her that he was worth a second chance, that *they* were; however, that would mean coming clean about his major lapse in judgment last New Year's Eve.

"Morning," she greeted him, hooking the baby carrier into the crook of her arm before adjusting the diaper bag that immediately slipped from her shoulder and down to the grocery bag she'd looped over her wrist.

Andrew jogged down the steps, reaching for the car seat to free up her other arm. "Good morning. How are my two favorite ladies?"

Gia skidded to a quick halt, the gravel of the driveway crunching under her shoes. "Andrew," she warned, "this is a social call to say thank you for your help. I'm making you breakfast. That's all."

Strike one.

He held up his free hand and shot her a half-smile. "I didn't say anything. If you don't want to be one of my favorite ladies, I know Bella will, won't you?" Gia shook her head as he cooed to the sleeping baby.

"You don't even realize how ridiculous you sound, do you?"

"Bella likes it, don't you?" he said, ignoring Gia's criticism. Leading Gia into the bunkhouse, he settled the car seat on the floor by the couch.

She dropped the diaper bag in the corner of the couch. "I left the playpen in my trunk. I'll be right back."

He deftly slipped the keys from her hand. "I'll get it. You two make yourselves comfortable."

After retrieving it from her trunk, he hurried back inside to see her circling the main room, looking around her. She'd kicked her flats off beside one of the bar stools. He didn't see the grocery bag but assumed she'd already taken it to the kitchen. Without waiting for her to ask, he tugged the playpen from the case and set it up in the dining area, the most central location between the kitchen and living room. Gia carefully laid Bella inside. Before she could do it herself, Andrew plucked the blanket from the car seat and handed it to her. She eyed him curiously, but remained silent.

Once the baby was settled, she crossed her arms, looking unsure of what to do now. "Looks like you guys have grown up quite a bit. It's not that same nasty bachelor pad. I have to admit, I was a little worried about bringing her here."

"Yeah, we actually do laundry now. No more smelly socks and jeans strewn around the room like we used to. Dishes might be another argument." He smiled at her, attempting to get her to relax.

She laughed at the memory and wrinkled her nose. "So, no more chasing each other with sweaty T-shirts. You guys were pretty gross."

"Yet you not only tolerated it, but sought it out." He started to laugh but realized that even their memories were strained, colored by regret and sorrow. Neither of them spoke for a moment, as if she realized the same thing.

"So," she drew the word out. "Are you all living here now?" Their conversation felt awkward and forced, as if she was searching for topics that were safe. Not at all like last night, when it had been comfortably easy.

Andrew walked into the kitchen and plucked two mugs from the cupboard. "Coffee?"

Gia nodded and leaned over the bar, folding her hands as she watched him prepare it from their single-serving maker. He spotted the grocery bag on the counter and emptied the contents into the refrigerator for the time being.

"And, to answer your question, no. It's only the three of us here now—me and the twins. Unless Linc is home," he clarified. "But it's been almost a year since he was home for more than a short visit. Grant, Bethany and James have a place up the road, where he bought some property, and Ben moved into his fiancée's place a few months ago, the animal sanctuary down the road from the ranch."

"Sierra Tracks?"

"Yeah." He rolled his eyes. "They're in that honeymoon phase, so when he isn't at the station, he's usually there."

"You sound jealous," she teased.

He shrugged. "Not really."

He wasn't about to admit that he was. He missed their Guys' Nights, but Bethany and Emma had become a welcome part of the family now. He was happy for Ben, happy for both of his brothers, but he was at a place in his life where bachelorhood seemed more like a trap he'd accidentally fallen into instead of a choice he'd made. In reality, it had been a choice made *for* him, when Gia walked away.

Contrary to what he allowed people to believe, he wanted to settle down. He just hadn't wanted to settle down with anyone but Gia. They'd been connected, on every level, and if he couldn't make it work with her, if she couldn't trust or believe in him, then it was because he just wasn't trustworthy.

It had been far easier to close his emotions off and play the field. It was easy not to disappoint someone when they didn't expect more than a night or two from him. No expectations meant that no one got attached, and no one got hurt.

But from the moment he'd run her plates on the side of the highway the other night and realized it was Gia, it was like a switch had been flipped in him. He wanted everything his brothers had, but he wanted those things only with Gia.

"Aw," she cooed, dropping her chin into her palm. "Are you feeling lonely, Andrew? Guess you're just going to have to find a lucky lady to be your ball and chain."

She'd relaxed enough to be teasing him, and common sense warned him to let the comment pass. Instead he slid the mug of coffee onto the bar in front of her and leaned his hip against the counter, shooting her a cocky smirk as he lifted his cup to his lips.

"Interested in applying for the position?"

If he'd thought he could throw her for a moment, he

was sadly mistaken. "You wish," she countered saucily, not even missing a beat, drinking from her own mug.

"Yeah, I do."

He watched as her jaw fell slightly slack before she caught herself, closing her mouth, slowly sipping the coffee to stall.

Okay, so his blatant honesty had managed to shock her. Might as well take advantage of knocking her off balance and go for the gold.

"I've got to ask, Gia, what makes you so certain I cheated on you?"

Gia's cheeks flushed. Andrew realized he'd never seen her blush so often, and he liked keeping her guessing.

"Wow, um, okay . . . that was straight to the point."

Andrew wasn't going to apologize for being blunt. The honesty between them had always been one of the things he loved most about their relationship. He'd been able to open up with her, to be completely vulnerable with her in a way he never had been with anyone, even his siblings, not before or since. He waited silently for her response.

"I was told that you did." She met his unwavering gaze. "By the girl you cheated on me with."

He took a deep breath, trying to let the tiny bit of vague information sink in. "Mind if I ask who it was?"

"Yes."

So, that narrowed down the pool of women to only a few it could be. First, there weren't many women Gia was close with or who would have been "girls" ten years ago, and of those, only one Gia would still protect for this long after the fact. Lorena. Giovanni's comments suddenly made sense.

"And you trusted this *girl* more than you did me?"

Her chin dipped forward as if he'd just asked the world's stupidest question. "Your reputation sort of preceded you."

It wasn't exactly true. Yes, he'd had a reputation as a bad boy with girls, and he'd dated plenty, but they knew he wasn't out for a relationship, and he'd never cheated on a girl. He'd never even had a serious girlfriend before Gia. Or since.

Where no relationship existed, there couldn't be cheating.

He folded his hands in front of him and leaned over the other side of the bar, meeting her gaze with open honesty. "I never cheated on you, Gia."

"I was told different, by a few people." Her voice was a strained whisper, as if saying the words hurt. "People saw you together."

"While you and I were together, I never even looked at another woman, let alone touched one." His throat choked up with everything he'd felt for her and he swallowed hard, staring at her and willing her to see the truth. "You were everything to me."

Her gaze locked with his and he could see the indecision there. It was a start, for her to question what she'd believed and now he needed to give her some space to think about it. Pushing her would only backfire on him.

He was the first to look away, walking to the refrigerator to retrieve the items she'd brought to make breakfast. "What are you making?"

He moved aside as she came up beside him, taking the produce from his hands and heading to the sink to wash the tomatoes and green onions. He leaned his hip against the counter beside her, watching her work.

"Since you're just going to stand there, you could help. Grab the ham steak and dice it into small cubes."

Andrew shot her a cocky grin and moved behind her, his hands landing against the counter on either side of her hips, pressing his chest against her back. His pulse picked up its pace and heat began the slow descent through his body, curling low in his gut.

"What are you doing?"

Her voice was soft, barely a whisper of breath, and he could feel her chest catch as she tried to control her breathing. She turned her head slightly to look at him over her shoulder, and Andrew caught a floral scent mixed with vanilla from her hair. It took every bit of willpower he had not to wrap his arms around her.

He pulled open the drawer beside her, slipping a cutting board from inside, and leaned down to her ear. "Just trying to help, like you asked."

She closed her eyes, her lashes fanning over her cheeks, her hands stilling under the water. This was how he remembered her—desire evident and fighting for her own self-control—and it encouraged him. He brushed his lips against the spot just behind her ear, the one that used to give her chills and break her arms out in goose bumps.

"I didn't ask for this kind of help," she whispered, her voice husky.

Andrew set the cutting board on the sink and his right arm circled her waist, his hand splaying over the flat of her belly. "No?"

She took a deep breath and stepped to one side, turning to face him, the gold flecks in her hazel eyes shining brightly. "No," she replied, sounding more certain of herself.

"Okay."

Andrew took a step back, taking her at her word. There was a lot of water under their bridge that he needed to dam up before she would trust him again. She might want him, but she was a strong woman, and she might decide that she didn't want to go back to where they'd once been. But he wasn't giving up easily. Gia was worth every bit of the effort it would take to win her back.

She frowned as she looked at him, her expression revealing as much disappointment as he felt, which gave him hope, but she didn't comment on his acquiescence. With a sigh, Gia turned back toward the sink. "You said you wanted to talk."

"I said we *needed* to talk."

He dug in the refrigerator for the ham steak before dropping it on the cutting board and pulling a knife from the wooden block on the counter. He wasn't ready to confess what happened with Lorena yet. Soon, but not quite yet.

"When were you thinking of holding the concert?" he asked.

"Well, you said he could do it in just under two weeks. That's really cutting it close as far as advertising, but it's Linc McQuaid, so I'm not sure I really need to do much advertising. All it will take is a mention on social media and once the word gets out . . ." She shrugged. "I figured I might as well take advantage of him being available that soon." She turned off the faucet. "You'll help me plan it, right? And spread the word?"

"Hang some posters?"

She moved closer and slipped the knife from his hand, bumping her hip against his thigh so he would move over. Gia laughed, the sound surrounding him, warming the lump of ice he'd carried in his chest since she'd left town, and he felt the exterior of his heart begin to melt.

"That's not exactly what I meant."

He leaned back against the counter now that she'd rendered him useless and crossed his arms over his chest. "So, what did you mean?"

Her hand paused over the meat for a moment before she continued to dice it. "I'm going to need printed materials right away, not to mention that I'm going to have to be in touch with Linc to figure out the logistics for when he gets into town."

"Like?"

Her hair fell forward over her shoulder, blocking her face from his view, so he brushed it back. She jumped and nearly dropped the knife.

"Watch yourself."

He liked knowing that his nearness affected her as much as it did him. His entire body was tense, wanting to touch her, to be touched, to feel her against him, but his desire for their future outweighed his impatience.

She glanced his way, looking confused. "What was I saying?"

Andrew bit back his grin.

Yeah, she might try to pretend she wasn't feeling the same way he was, but he could see the truth. "Logistics with Linc?"

"Oh, I was thinking that maybe we should do something 'unplugged.' A session that's low-key and intimate."

"Intimate," he repeated, watching her.

"Yeah, what do you think?"

She looked over at him and must have realized that he wasn't thinking about the concert. The only thing on his mind right now was how intimate this was, her in his kitchen, doing something as trivial as fixing them breakfast, and how much he wanted this every morning for the rest of his life.

Damn it!

Andrew knew he was putting the cart before the horse again and needed to slow down. Logically he knew he couldn't just slip back in time to when they were young and in love, but at moments like this, when she looked at him that way, it was so easy to believe it could happen.

Gia bit down on her lip and dropped the knife on the cutting board. Her eyes flashed with golden fire, hot and hungry, and not for the omelets she was prepping. Her first steps were tentative as she closed the distance between them, pushing him back against the counter and sliding her hands up around his neck, dragging his mouth down to hers.

This wasn't the slow, sweet kiss they'd had in her house. This kiss was filled with fire, explosive desire uncontrolled. Andrew's arms wound around her back, lifting her to her toes, pressing her ample breasts against his chest, burning him through their clothing. Her tongue met his, twisting in a dance he'd spent years fantasizing about. He moved his hand over her jaw before burying it in her hair, trying to memorize every second, every touch, in case it was his last. Her hands slid over his chest, down to the hem of his shirt, and under. Every muscle tensed when her fingertips touched his skin, his entire body jerking to full attention and begging for release.

He needed to stop this before he couldn't, and he was closing in on that very fine line quickly. "Gia?"

"Just shut up and kiss me, Andrew," she muttered against his jaw, her lips pressing kisses over his neck.

He slid his hands over her butt and lifted her, turning to set her on the counter, putting her mouth at the same level as his. Cupping her face between his palms, forcing her to meet his gaze. His pulse raced as he inhaled the sweet scent of her. "Gia, there's a lot we need to talk about."

"We will," she agreed, just before she jerked his T-shirt over his head. "Later."

Chapter Nine

THIS WAS A MISTAKE.

Gia knew it. Andrew knew it, which was probably why he was trying to warn her. But she didn't care. She was tired of being careful, of always doing the right thing. It never worked out in her favor anyway.

She'd been the perfect student, the perfect daughter, the perfect girlfriend, a great sister, and none of that seemed to matter. She was still sacrificing her future for everyone else. She had given up the account that would have promoted her to VP in order to come back to help her parents. She was giving up her savings to help pay for the financial crises looming over them. She was even giving up her future to become the kind of mother her niece deserved because her sister couldn't be bothered to take responsibility.

Gia wanted to make a mistake. She wanted to do

something so completely out of character and throw caution and reason to the wind for a change. And Andrew was here, every woman's living, breathing bad-boy "mistake," looking better than ever and kissing her in a way that had her toes curling.

He was hot—like, *hot*.

There was no other way to describe him. With a body that practically made her fingers ache to explore. Muscles rippled with every movement, taut abs flexing as that V guided her gaze lower to where his jeans dipped on his hips. But as much as he turned her on physically—and holy crap, did he turn her on—that wasn't the entirety of her attraction to Andrew.

He was tough, but incredibly sensitive. Even now, he thought of her needs before his own. His dark eyes searched hers, seeking further explanation for her actions, but she didn't want to stop and think about what she was doing. She'd done enough thinking. Now she wanted only to feel.

"I know what I'm doing, Andrew, so don't ask questions."

"Are you sure?" His voice was strained and low, as if he didn't really want to hear the truth.

"You don't listen very well," she pointed out. "And no, I'm not sure," she admitted as she reached for the bottom of her shirt and yanked it up.

She hadn't planned on pulling this shirt off this way when she'd chosen the fitted pearl-buttoned Western number with the camisole underneath. The two shirts somehow managed to twist together, tangling around her neck with both shirts covering her face and her arms locked straight up above her head. Her position revealed her bra, and her breasts, for the entire world to see. Gia tried tugging her arms back down but the shirts weren't budging.

So much for being seductive.

She heard a low laugh just before she felt Andrew's hands travel up from her shoulders, trying to untangle the shirts. "You do realize that a lesser man would take full advantage of this situation, right? I mean, this is better than using handcuffs."

"Just help me." She twisted helplessly, her arms swinging above her head as she wiggled, the shirts beginning to cut off her circulation.

"Oh, darlin'," he drawled, his voice thick with hungry desire. "Unless you want me to carry you into my room now, you better not do that again."

She jerked one arm down, tangling herself even further but trying to see his face, to read his expression, because his voice was enough to cause warmth to pool between her thighs, making her squirm. His hands landed gently on her knees, spreading her legs apart as he moved between them. With painstaking slowness, his fingers slid up her thigh to caress her waist before gliding up her ribs. Taking his time, he grazed his thumb against the side of her breast and moved it over her heated skin, up her shoulders. With her vision impaired, her other senses kicked into overdrive, and she found it hard to remain still under his touch.

"Okay, stop moving," he warned. "Let me see."

Gia's chest heaved, feeling his ragged breath blow over her neck, hot and moist, as he leaned in to take a better look. His chest rubbed against hers, and her nipples beaded beneath the lace of her bra at the contact. Andrew slid his fingers under the shirts, flipping both inside out. Lifting them over her head, he could slide them up her arms but stopped so they still kept her wrists trapped, the material hanging from them.

"You're going to be the death of me, you know that, right?" His voice was a hoarse growl as his hand slid down her arms, the calluses creating a friction that made her shiver.

This is a mistake, her brain screamed at her.

Then why does it feel so right? her heart argued.

Gia had no doubt both were correct. She dropped her arms, shirts and all, over his head and onto his shoulders, pulling him closer, pausing with her lips against his. "But what a way to go."

She knew the exact moment when Andrew quit holding back. It wasn't a change in his touch or in his kiss. The difference was in his eyes. They turned from dark brown to nearly black, filled with passion but just as full of relief, as if the effort to hold himself back had been slowly killing him.

"Gia," he whispered, capturing her mouth again.

She clung to him, longing to touch him, all of him. It had been so long, but she remembered. She hadn't been able to forget, even on those nights she'd so desperately tried.

His mouth didn't miss one inch of her from her neck to her shoulders. He lifted her arms over his head and tenderly removed the shirt from her wrists. Sliding his hands up her arms, gently massaging where the material left marks over her skin. Then his hands moved to cup her breasts.

Gia's head fell backward against the cabinet behind her and she reached for his butt, pulling him against her and wrapping her legs around his hips. Andrew's mouth moved lower, suckling her through the lace bra, teasing her with his tongue. The rasp of the material over her sensitive skin was erotic but not nearly as thrilling as the feel of his calloused hands gliding down her bared back and past the waistband of her jeans to cup her butt, his fingers digging into the flesh.

Her fingers sought the waistband of his pants, working the button open before he even realized what she was doing. Gia worked them down his thighs with her bare feet. She felt his smile against her skin just before he plucked at the curve of her breast with his lips, moving lower, tracing the line of her ribs with his tongue.

"Tricky," he murmured, nipping her sensitive flesh. "But want to see one better?"

With a quick flick of the fingers of one hand, he unbuttoned her jeans, and with the other managed to slide them off, pulling them down her legs and dropping them to the floor while his mouth never left her ribs.

Gia laughed quietly. "I don't even want to know how you learned to do that."

"Sweetheart, I've got so many tricks up my sleeve for you, but only if you promise not to ask." His hands slid up the inside of her thighs, inching closer to where she burned hottest.

"Mmm, just keep doing that and I'll promise anything."

His thumb moved over her, making her squirm again. He grasped her hips and pulled her closer to the edge of the counter, dropping down in front of her. The heat from his breath caressed her just before he pressed his lips over her lace underwear. Gia gasped, her fingers gripping his shoulders.

Andrew moved the wisp of material aside and touched his tongue to her. Gia lost sense of everything but the feel of him. Of his hands, his lips, his tongue, his heartbeat. He tormented her, teased her to a frenzy. The rest of her clothing fell away, although she had no idea when or how he removed it. Like a magician, it simply disappeared in the frenzy of touch, kisses and sighs of pleasure. Andrew carried her to new heights as the tension coiled in her, exploding behind her eyes, forcing her body to melt into him.

Andrew held her in his arms as she slid from the counter, her legs wobbly and unable to hold her upright. His laugh rumbled against her shoulder as he wrapped his arms around her waist. "Maybe we should take this into my room."

"I'm all for that," she agreed, trying to catch her breath, "when I can walk that far."

Andrew scooped her up and carried her down the hall. "Wait!" she said.

"Gia, shh." He smiled down at her, silencing her with a kiss that stole her breath and her reservations. "I didn't forget about Bella, but she's asleep, and I can only take care of one of you at a time."

"Then I'll walk." He settled her carefully on her feet, treating her like she was made of porcelain. Gia stood on her toes and slid her hand behind his neck. "Have I told you recently how much you surprise me?"

"Not in the past ten years. But I like the sound of it." He shook his head, the praise brightening his eyes.

"Go check on her," Gia said, "and meet me in the bedroom."

Andrew walked back into the living room wearing nothing but his boxer briefs and peeked in on Bella, still sleeping soundly in the playpen. Only in his wildest dreams would he have imagined himself checking on a newborn just before he made love to Gia, but he was oddly at ease with it. It felt right, like this was how it should be, even if it did have a surreal quality.

Heading back into his bedroom, he found Gia lying in his bed, the sheets pulled up around her breasts. He clenched his jaw at his body's response to the sight. Every part of him wanted her, wanted to be touching her, buried in her. He needed her the way he needed air to survive.

"She's still sleeping?" Gia's voice was soft but held that slightly breathy quality that let him know she wanted him as much as he did her. Without waiting for his reply, she pointed at his side of the bed. "I don't know how long she'll stay that way, so let's not waste time."

He hardened at the thought but shot her a cocky grin as he slid his knee onto the mattress, leaning over her. "Aw, honey, I don't do my best work when I'm rushed."

She ran a hand down his side, over his hip, and cupped him gently, laughing quietly, her eyes sparking with wicked humor. "Who are you kidding?" she asked, the fingers of her other hand playing over the ridges of muscle on his back. "We could half-ass this completely and it would still be better than with anyone else."

Andrew closed his eyes, savoring her touch. This woman got his blood pumping like no one else. While he knew it was completely true for him, he was shocked by her admission. Before he could even respond, she let the sheet fall completely, reaching for him, her fingers gliding down his back to his butt and dragging him down to her, nestling his body into the curves of hers. Even as petite as she was, they fit together perfectly, like they'd been carved from the same whole. He groaned as his hand slid down her side, catching the sheet between them and shoving it past her hips. Her fingers hooked into the band of his boxers and she pushed them down, releasing his throbbing erection to nudge against her heat, seeking release. Andrew reached for the drawer of the nightstand.

A mewling whimper from down the hall broke through the haze of his passion. His head dropped forward and he slid the drawer closed, rolling to one side. "I knew it," he groaned, draping one arm over his eyes, willing his body to calm the storm of need raging within.

Gia scrambled off the end of the bed, searching for something to cover herself. "It will only be for a minute." She looked at the end of the bed. "My clothes?"

"In the other room," he muttered, sliding from the bed and grabbing her one of the T-shirts from a dresser drawer.

Her arms wound around his waist from behind, her breasts pressing into his back and her fingers trailing over his abs, teasing him as they slid lower. His erection jerked in response and he couldn't stop the groan that slid past his lips.

"Not nice," he growled through clenched teeth, sucking in a hissing breath.

"We're not finished. She just needs to eat."

Gia slid the T-shirt over her head, and Andrew couldn't help but get turned on by the way it pulled tight over her ample breasts yet hung loose over her hips, reaching midthigh. As she walked out the door to prepare a bottle for Bella, she glanced back at him over her shoulder and winked. His mouth went dry as she flipped up the hem of the shirt, revealing the sweet curve of her butt cheeks.

Andrew reached for a pair of jeans from the next drawer down and slid them on, going commando for the moment. He tried adjusting himself but Gia had him rock-hard, and he had to be careful pulling the zipper closed.

Until Bella's mournful cry broke the silence of the bunkhouse. It was almost as effective as a cold shower.

Hearing the water in the kitchen, Andrew hurried to the playpen, scooping up Bella and holding her against his bare chest before he returned to his room and sat on the edge of the mattress. Bella immediately opened her mouth and rubbed it against his chest. He laughed quietly as Gia came back in, dropping her clothes in a pile at the foot of the bed and setting the diaper bag on top. She tipped the bottle against her wrist, testing the temperature.

"Here you go." She passed the bottle to him and cocked her head to one side, her hair spilling over her shoulder. "There is absolutely nothing sexier than a man with his baby."

Andrew's gaze snapped up to meet hers. "What?"

She frowned, looking confused by his reaction. "Nothing sexier than a man with a baby?"

Andrew closed his eyes and edged himself backward on the bed so that his back was braced against the wall.

He might have misheard her, but he had no doubt this was his conscience making sure he didn't mislead Gia.

"Come here." He patted the mattress beside him. "Let's talk while she eats."

She slid on the mattress beside him, her brow arching in question.

"Gia, I want you to believe me that I never cheated on you." Andrew felt her stiffen against him, and she started to move away.

"Fine." She scooted off the bed and made her way to her clothes, sliding her underwear back up her legs, looking incredibly pissed off. "Are we done talking?"

"We both know you can't leave until Bella's finished, so we might as well discuss this."

"I said I do. What more do you want?"

"You're lying." She gave him a half-hearted shrug. "I need you to believe me."

She turned her hazel eyes on him and they were hard as stone. "This isn't really about *your* needs, though, is it, Andrew?"

He clenched his teeth, realizing she was shutting him out. "No, it's not. Let's table this one for now and circle back to it." His voice was quiet, begging her to hear him out and just as concerned that she wouldn't. "I know Bella isn't your daughter."

"What makes you say—"

"Your father. He told me about what Lorena did to you."

She looked away, closing her eyes and taking a slow breath. "You don't know the half of it," she muttered.

When she opened them, she focused on the baby in his arms instead of looking at him, and Andrew could see the worry in her eyes. It was just as quickly replaced with the fierce determination that characterized Gia as she began to pace at the foot of his bed.

"Talk to me, Gia. You know I'll help you if I can."

"That's just it. You can't. Lorena left me with her daughter and ran off, but not before she gave *my* name to the hospital."

"She left you to deal with everything?"

"Doesn't she always?" Angry tears filled Gia's eyes as she forced herself to look at Andrew. "She even put my name on the birth certificate form."

"You're already planning on raising her, right? Why not just go with it?" She narrowed her eyes at him. "Your father told me," he explained.

"I swear, telling my family anything is like putting it on a billboard. Yes, I am, but what happens when Lorena changes her mind?"

"It doesn't sound likely."

"What if Bella's father finds out about her and decides he wants her? It's fraud, Andrew. And I have to turn in the form in a couple of days, but if I do and everything goes south . . ."

"Any idea who the father is?" He held his breath, waiting for her answer.

She threw her hands into the air. "Who knows? Lorena only tells me what she wants to. I'm assuming it's the guy she's with now, Bobby something. She said he never wanted kids, and she told him Bella didn't make it."

"What if he's not the father?"

"I don't know. What else can I do? Even if I could get Lorena to correct the documentation and I'm able to file for guardianship, the court will still need to find the father to see if he will sign off parental rights before I can adopt her. It's a risk."

Her tears slowly crept down her cheeks.

Tell her.

Andrew felt his gut churn, knotting with the fear that the truth might be what drove her away for good.

He looked down at the infant, sucking greedily on the bottle and staring up at him with wide, innocent eyes. He lifted her to his shoulder and rubbed her back to burp her the way Gia had showed him. In a perfect world, this baby would have been his and Gia's. They would have been celebrating her birth together, with their families. Instead, he was about to break her heart with the truth that there was a possibility *he* was Bella's father.

Gia took a deep breath, steeling herself and rolling her shoulders back. "I won't give her up without a fight."

"Bella might be my daughter, Gia," he said at the same time.

Andrew's gaze met hers. She lifted a hand and covered her mouth, shaking her head, her eyes wide with hurt and betrayal. She had every right to feel that way, but he had to explain, to make her understand.

"It was New Year's Eve and I'd just gotten off shift late—"

"So, you decided to ring in the new year with my sister?" she threw at him, reaching for her jeans and jerking them up her thighs.

He'd be lucky if she let him get any of this out.

"It's not an excuse, but Grant had just gotten engaged a few months before and Ben was off that night, so we decided to go to the New Year's celebration your parents throw at the restaurant every year. Maddie was supposed to be our designated driver, but she bailed on us and your sister—"

She spun on him, throwing her palm up. "I don't need the details about the *ride* she gave you."

Andrew clenched his jaw, trying to control his temper. "It wasn't like that. I don't even remember anything."

She rolled her eyes, clearly disgusted by him. "Well, that definitely makes it all okay."

"Gia, you and I weren't together. You'd avoided me for ten years. I'm not a monk." His voice was quiet but the message was clear. She couldn't blame him when she had been the one who dumped him years ago.

She pinned him with a look, bitterness clouding her eyes. "You're right, Andrew. But us being together didn't stop you ten years ago, did it?"

Chapter Ten

ANDREW OPENED HIS mouth to speak but nothing came out. He'd suspected Lorena had been the one to make the accusation, but hearing the extent of her lie numbed him with shock, until he was overtaken with white-hot anger. Rage poured through his veins. Normally he would have put his fist through a wall when he felt this way or headed in for DTAC, but since he was still holding Bella, there was no release. Instead he tried to hold it in, his hands shaking with the effort.

"I never touched your sister before New Year's." He ground his teeth together, his jaw popping with the pressure. "And I *never* cheated on you with her."

"That's not the way she tells it."

His chest heaved with the effort of controlling his temper. "I'm sure it's not, but since when has your sister been the poster child of honesty? Hell, Gia, you just finished telling me how she lied to the hospital about who she was so she could bail on you. I'm the one telling you the truth."

"So you claim. I suppose the other people who confirmed seeing the two of you together were lying too?"

He rose from the bed and carried Bella to her. He wanted her to stay and listen, for them to get past this, but he didn't want it to be because she felt like she *had* to stay. "Gia, listen to me. I have no idea what you're talking about. I have never touched your sister before New Year's Eve. There is nothing for me to gain by telling you any of this and I have everything to lose, especially if Bella isn't my child."

She glared at him. "You have *nothing* to lose."

"I'll lose you again."

She took Bella from him before crossing the room, snatching the bottle from the nightstand and throwing it into the diaper bag, then stuffing the rest of her clothes inside. She walked out, giving him one last look from the doorway.

"You can't lose what was never yours."

GIA FELT HER stomach twist in knots as she slipped her shoes back on and buckled Bella into the car seat. She'd trusted so many people and they'd all lied or betrayed her. Andrew, Lorena, her father, her mother . . . The names raced through her mind. She heard Jackson's voice from the other side of the door as he yelled to one of his siblings.

"Hey, I'll be right back. I forgot my phone. Calm your tits already." Jackson burst into the bunkhouse, nearly running into Gia, stopping short with his hands in the air. "Shit!"

"Sorry," she mumbled, taking a step backward before he bumped into the car seat. "I was just leaving."

Jackson smirked, lifting a brow. "In Andrew's shirt?"

Gia glanced down. In her hurry to escape, she'd forgotten to change her shirt or put on her bra. Then the devil himself came thundering down the hall.

"Just what the hell does that—"

"Hey, bro? Hope I'm not interrupting anything." Jackson crossed his arms and his grin widened, brightening by several degrees. Andrew glared at his brother, his fists clenching at his sides. "I guess that scowl means I am."

"We were just leaving." Gia tried to brush past, but Andrew reached for the handles of the diaper bag.

"I'll walk you to your car."

She shot him a look that, if he'd had even half a brain, should have sent him cowering in a corner.

"So that we can set up a time to discuss this concert," he explained. "You still need my help, right?"

Damn him, he knew she did. Just like he knew she wouldn't sit by and let her parents lose their restaurant because she felt betrayed by him. She was a grown

woman, and she would simply set her feelings aside—
again—to make sure she did right by her family.

"Concert?" Jackson looked doubtful.

"Linc is going to do a concert at the restaurant," she
explained. "Instead of the bachelor auction we talked
about."

Jackson nodded slowly. "And *Andrew* is going to
help? As what? A bouncer?"

Andrew clenched his jaw so hard she heard the snap
of his teeth and rolled her lips inward to avoid smiling
at Jackson's insinuation that he was all brawn and no
brain. Considering what he'd just told her, she had to
agree with Jackson's assessment.

"Shut it," he warned.

"Andrew arranged it with Linc, but I could use more
volunteer help, if you'd be interested," she suggested.

Jackson looked over at his brother again, taking note
of the displeasure coming off Andrew in waves. Gia
wanted to smack him. If either of them had a reason to
be upset, she had him beat by a mile.

Bella started to fuss, and she realized she'd missed
her window to escape without feeding her the rest of
the bottle. She rolled her eyes and sighed, turning back
toward the bar, lifting the car seat on top and jerking the
diaper bag from Andrew's hand. Unbuckling the infant,
she reached into the bag for the bottle, only to realize
that most of the formula had leaked onto her clothes
inside.

"Figlio di troia . . ." Gia bit back the muttered curse, opening the bottle and preparing to make another.

Jackson slid his hands to her shoulders and squeezed gently, working the muscles to release the tension building there, reassuring her that things weren't as bad as they seemed right now. "Relax," he whispered. "Don't let him get to you."

She knew exactly what he was doing, and while she appreciated the attempt at aggravating Andrew, she really wasn't in the mood to deal with the repercussions. Gia gave Jackson a quick nod while Andrew's back was turned.

Andrew tossed the phone at his brother. "This what you came back for?"

Easily catching it, Jackson slid it into his pocket. "Yep."

"Good. Now get lost."

Jackson slowly slid his gaze from Gia to his brother. "Excuse me?"

"We're kind of in the middle of something and don't need your interference."

Jackson stood tall, raising himself to his full height, and stepped up to Andrew. He was barely an inch shorter, but Andrew had him beat on sheer mass alone. She had to give Jackson credit—he didn't appear intimidated in the slightest.

"Sounds to me like you're in the middle of being a jackass, but then, that's nothing unusual, is it?" His eyes narrowed to slits. "If I'm not mistaken, Gia was on her way out when I came in."

As much as she didn't want to stay and listen to Andrew try to make excuses for sleeping with her sister, as much as she wanted to hate him for it, she knew how close Andrew was with his brothers. She didn't want to be the cause of conflict between them. Family was everything to the McQuaids. It always had been and was just one of the things they had in common. She wasn't about to tear his family apart simply because he might be a reason hers was in ruins.

"It's fine, Jackson." She laid a hand over his shoulder. "I'll leave as soon as Bella's finished."

She spoke to Jackson but kept her eyes fixed on Andrew, daring him to contradict her.

It was bad enough that she was forced to continue working with him to plan this concert. But it didn't mean she had to like it or that it would be here at the bunkhouse, where she was vulnerable to his charm. Where he stood in front of her without a shirt on, looking far too tempting. Where every second, her body continued to betray her, reminding her of how he'd sent her senses reeling in this very kitchen.

Her unspoken warning must have come through to both loud and clear, because Andrew moved to the refrigerator and retrieved the eggs he'd put inside earlier. Jackson shrugged and headed for the front door.

"If you need me, Gia, just call." He wiggled his phone. "I'll rescue you."

"You and what fucking army?" she heard Andrew mutter from where he faced the refrigerator.

"Please. You're so whipped I could kick your ass even if you cuffed me at the ankles." Jackson laughed as he slammed the door shut.

Once he was gone, silence hung in the room. The tiny kitchen clock ticked quietly, and the refrigerator's buzz seemed abnormally loud. The eggs sizzled as Andrew poured them into the pan and reached for the chopped ingredients they'd left on the counter. For the first time since her birth, much to Gia's frustration, Bella seemed content to take her time drinking her bottle.

She just wanted to leave, to turn around and revert to pretending Andrew didn't exist, the way she'd managed to do for ten years. Back to focusing on convincing Lorena to return to take custody of Bella again, to help their parents with the restaurant. All so that she could go back to her sad life where she was nothing more than a woman struggling to make her mark in the male-dominated world of corporate marketing. All in order to leave Hidden Falls behind again. Except the mere idea left an ache in her chest. She didn't want to leave again, even if that meant coming to grips with her past feelings for Andrew.

Past?

"I should have never gone to the party at the restaurant. You have every right to be angry with me, Gia."

Andrew's voice sounded like he'd been gargling gravel and his head hung forward. He looked defeated.

Lifting his hand to the back of his neck, he squeezed. She could see the tension building as the muscles of his back and shoulders bunched. As much as her initial response was to want to make him feel better, she was tired of giving everyone else what they wanted at the cost of her own happiness.

"You're right. I do." She swallowed back the bitterness that clogged her throat. "You fucked my sister."

There was nothing he could say that would lessen the pain. For years she'd believed he'd done something with Lorena but she wasn't sure what, other than her speculations. Visions of what they could have done hurt badly enough, but this—hearing his own confession—was unbearable. She couldn't seem to stop the images of them together—kissing, touching, sighing—the way she and Andrew had only moments ago. It didn't matter to her that they weren't a couple this time, that they hadn't spoken in years. She didn't blame him for going back to his player ways, but she'd never thought he'd jump in bed with her sister. She'd never forgotten how she'd felt about him, and it devastated her that he hadn't even considered how this might hurt her.

"Did you love her?"

"Gia . . ."

"Did you?"

Andrew turned to face her slowly. Bella finished her bottle, her eyes droopy as Gia lifted her from the car seat to burp her. She laid the infant against her shoulder, wishing for just a moment that she could savor the

feel of the child in her arms as her own, without realizing there was a good chance she was the product of her
sister's betrayal with the only man she'd loved. If Andrew's suspicions were correct, this could be one of the
last times she was allowed to hold Bella this way.

And she'd just given him the ammunition he needed
to take Bella away from her.

"No, Gia." His gaze locked with hers. "I've only been
in love with one woman in my entire life. I let her go
once, a long time ago. It was just the first of many stupid
things I've done since. Even if that one wasn't my fault."

A small burp rumbled from Bella. It wasn't great, but
it was enough. Gia couldn't stay here any longer. Not
when her heart was so conflicted—wanting to believe
him, unable to deny the feelings she still had for him, yet
unwilling to move past the agony at the thought of him
with her sister. She laid Bella into the car seat and buckled her in, tossing the empty bottle into the diaper bag.

"If you want to talk about the concert, you can find
me at the restaurant in the evenings. Otherwise, we
have nothing further to discuss."

She hurried to the front door, eager to finally make
her escape, unable to comprehend how the shattered remains of her heart were still able to beat in her chest.

"Yes, we do, Gia. Because if Bella is my daughter,
I'll be in her life."

She hadn't thought she could hurt any more than
she did a moment ago. She was wrong. The pieces of her
heart splintered even further.

"Then you'd better order a paternity test to prove it. Because as of right now, my name is on her birth certificate, and she's staying with me," she warned him.

Andrew shook his head as he took a step toward her. "That's bullshit, Gia." His tone was outraged.

"Story of my life," she pointed out, shutting the door behind her.

Gia prayed he'd let her walk away as easily this second time as he had the first. But she wasn't holding her breath.

Chapter Eleven

TWO DAYS, THAT was all. Two days of fear. Two days since she'd texted her sister, demanding the truth about Andrew and their New Year's tryst. Two days of silence. Two days before the sheriff's deputy, who was probably a friend of Andrew's, showed up at the restaurant to serve her with papers requesting a paternity test for Bella. Two days before there was a knock on her bedroom door and she felt the bottom drop out of what little sanity remained in her life as Lorena stepped across the threshold.

"Is that her? She's gotten so big!"

Lorena brushed her long, dark waves over her shoulder as she hurried toward the bassinet Gia had purchased for Bella. Instinctively Gia stepped in front of Bella, blocking Lorena's path.

Her sister stopped short, crossing her arms and cocking a hip. "What? You're not even going to let me see her now?"

"Why are you here?"

"You asked me to come, remember?"

Gia didn't trust her as far as she could throw her. "You didn't return my calls, didn't text me back. Nothing. Now you're showing up out of the blue. Why?"

"I was busy. Sue me." Lorena scooted around Gia and stood by her daughter, brushing her hand over Bella's downy hair. "She looks exactly like the baby pictures Mom and Dad have of us." Looking up at Gia, Lorena's eyes were dark and filled with regret. "Have you filed the paperwork yet?"

Gia's heart stopped and she held her breath. Lorena wouldn't ask unless she'd changed her mind, would she? It had always been a possibility, but Gia'd been so worried about losing Bella to Andrew the past few days that she'd forgotten Lorena could still demand her daughter back.

Damn it! This wasn't fair. She was the only mother Bella had known, even if it had been for just eight days. It had been enough for her to fall hopelessly in love with Bella.

"Not yet," Gia finally whispered.

Lorena threw up her hands in disbelief. "What the hell are you waiting for?"

Gia wasn't sure she'd heard her sister correctly. "What?"

"You're going to screw us both over if you don't

hurry up and file it." She glanced down at the sleeping baby again, but this time her face lacked any maternal expression, and the regret Gia had seen was gone. "Your text said Andrew was trying to get custody, right? How does it look if you haven't even turned in any sort of documentation for her? No birth certificate, no Social Security card."

"Lorena, my name is on those documents. Not only is that fraud, but I don't want to live that kind of lie." She grabbed the stack of papers from her nightstand. "Here, fix the birth certificate documentation and fill this out. At least do this. Then if you still don't want to be a mother in a few months, we can go to an attorney and I'll adopt her."

Lorena's laughter was bitter and hollow. "You just don't get it, do you? I don't need to wait a few months. I *know* I don't want to be a mother. I never did."

"But you carried her, gave birth to her." Her voice dropped to a near whisper. "You didn't have to."

Her sister rolled her deep brown eyes and shrugged slightly. "Okay, maybe I considered it for a while." She glanced down at her bare hand. "But it didn't get me what I thought it would."

Gia felt sick to her stomach. "You were trying to trap Bobby into marrying you?"

"Not exactly . . . I mean, I guess, technically." Lorena wandered over to the bed and flopped backward onto the mattress.

"What is wrong with you?"

"Oh, here comes the lecture from Saint Gianna." She rose onto her elbows and looked at Gia. "Can this wait until tomorrow? I'm tired too tired to listen to you bitch me out." She slid back down and tucked one of Gia's pillows under her head.

"Go sleep in your own room. Mom and Dad will be happy to have you home."

"Aw, sis, doesn't sound like you're thrilled to see me. You're cranky." Lorena braced her palm against her temple and looked up at Gia sweetly. "What's the matter? Not getting enough sleep? Is the baby keeping you awake? Maybe you should just find a man and get laid already."

Disgusted with her sister, Gia threw the legal paperwork and a pen onto the bed. "Sign the damn papers, Lorena. Fix your name on the birth certificate and award me full custody. Then you can take off again and do whatever you want. I'll deal with the repercussions from whatever happens with Andrew."

"Hmm, Andrew McQuaid," her sister sighed and flipped onto her back again, smiling up at the ceiling. "Now, there is a sweet slab of man meat. Makes my mouth water just thinking about him."

"So I've heard."

"What's that supposed to mean? You can't possibly still be mad about your engagement. That was years ago, and I was just a kid. I mean, it was Andrew McQuaid. If anything, you should thank me."

Thank her?

"You slept with my fiancé." Gia couldn't understand how her sister saw nothing wrong with what she'd done, if it had even really happened. After her argument with Andrew, she was beginning to wonder which of them was lying.

"I saved you from a life married to that cheating bastard."

"Andrew said nothing ever happened between the two of you back then."

Her sister's brows shot to her hairline as she quickly sat up. "Really? When did you talk to him about me?"

That was the part her sister was focused on? Not the fact that Andrew called her a liar. Gia also wasn't about to mention it had been just before they'd almost made love.

"We weren't talking about you, we were talking about Bella. And you just called him a 'cheating bastard.'"

"Just because he isn't good enough for you doesn't mean he isn't good enough for me." Lorena winked at her and wiggled her brows suggestively. "I'm not dumb enough to fall in love with a guy like him. I'm perfectly content with some fun handcuff action with Officer McQuaid."

Gia felt her insides recoil from the thought of the two of them together. It still felt like someone was carving her heart from her chest with a dull knife. Gia slowly inhaled, trying to remember why she needed to put family first, how she needed to be patient with her sister, who never seemed to think about anything before she let the words fly from her lips. She slid one hand to her temple, rubbing the ache forming behind her eyes and wishing she could ignore the ache in her heart.

Raw fury blossomed in Gia as she moved closer to her sister on the bed. "Is he Bella's father?"

"So, you heard about that." The corners of Lorena's mouth twitched, almost as if she were trying to hide a smile. Then it was gone and she shrugged apathetically. "Maybe. Maybe not. I don't know. I mean, I guess it could be possible."

"Just tell me the truth for a change." Gia glared at her sister when she didn't elaborate. "He told me about the New Year's party but said that nothing happened between the two of you ten years ago."

Lorena closed her eyes, looking bored with the conversation. "He's lying."

"After all these years, why would he bother?" Crossing her arms to keep from shaking her sister, Gia sighed. "I just want the truth, Lorena. You owe me that."

"Why do you even care?"

Gia opened her mouth to answer, to remind her sister that she was still trying to clean up the mess Lorena had left with Bella's birth certificate, when a humorless smile spread over Lorena's lips.

"I knew it. You're still in love with Andrew McQuaid. After everything he's done?"

Gia clamped her jaw shut and turned her back on her sister. "I'm not sure he's actually done anything, Lorena."

"Oh, my God!" Lorena jumped off the bed and hurried in front of her, blocking her path, letting loose a laugh. "You're such a pathetic idiot, Gia. He even admitted screwing me a few months ago and you're still chasing him?"

She wasn't ready to discuss her feelings for Andrew, not with Lorena and not with him. Hell, she shouldn't even *have* feelings for him. Lorena was right—she was a pathetic idiot—but regardless of how much she might want to deny it, she still cared about him, which made her furious with her own weakness.

Gia threw the manila envelope with the paternity documents at her sister. "*That* is why I need to know. Because he's insisting on a paternity test, and if Bella's his, he wants custody."

Lorena gave Gia a half-shrug. "So? Give it to him. You can move on with your life. I can move on with mine. Let him worry about the kid."

"That is your daughter you're talking about. Bella is your *child*, not a puppy. You are twenty-five years old. It's time to start acting like it and taking responsibility. You can't just walk away like she never existed. If you want to give her up, fine, but do it the right way."

"Don't talk to me about taking responsibility. You take on enough for everyone." She pushed past Gia and headed for the door. "We can't all be perfect like you, Gia."

"I'm not perfect, Lorena. I'm just trying to do the right thing for Bella."

Lorena laughed as she waved her hand at the paternity documents. "Yeah, well, if you'd just filed the paperwork like I told you to and kept her in San Diego, you wouldn't be dealing with that now. But you had to *do the right thing.* Guess what? It's backfired on you now."

"Lorena, you have to—"

"I don't have to do anything. And in answer to your question, yes, I fucked Andrew. I fucked him when you were engaged and again last year." She leaned close so that she was face-to-face with Gia. "Wanna know why? Because I was trying to prove a point. I did it for your benefit."

"For me? So, you were, what? Taking one for the team?" Gia didn't buy it. Lorena didn't care about loyalty, or family. "I don't believe you."

"I don't care what you believe." Storming from the room, Lorena headed down the hall.

"Lorena," Gia hissed. "We're not finished."

Her sister simply raised a hand to her shoulder and flipped Gia off. Before Gia could follow her, her mother appeared at the end of the hall in her robe.

"Lorena?"

"Hi, Mama. I missed you so much." Her sister hurried into their mother's arms, hugging her tightly.

"When did you get home?"

"Just now. I had a friend give me a ride from the airport."

Gia shook her head and went back into her room, shutting the door quietly. Of course their mother welcomed Lorena back like the prodigal child. She'd always been the daughter who could do no wrong in their mother's eyes. Gia tried to shut out her conversation with her sister just as easily. Lorena had left Gia with more questions.

Squaring her shoulders, she moved to watch Bella sleep. It didn't matter that her sister had come home. She had made her position clear. She wasn't changing her mind about giving up Bella, which meant Gia somehow needed to clear up the mess about the birth certificate and file the adoption papers tomorrow. *She* wasn't giving Bella up.

"Dude, you never actually had sex with Lorena," Ben said. "You know that, right? I was there that night. You were so drunk, you couldn't've gotten it up even if you wanted to."

"Could you say it louder?" Andrew asked, eyeing the other people surrounding them in the busy coffee shop. "I'm not sure everyone heard you."

While it was possible that he wasn't Bella's father, he should have never left the party with Lorena. Never should have gotten into the position where the potential of Bella being his was even a question. He saw the worry in Ben's eyes in spite of his easy dismissal of Andrew's concerns. He'd known his brother would understand his worry when he informed him that Bella was actually Lorena's daughter and did some quick calculations.

"I don't know that for sure. But if there's any chance that Bella is mine . . ." He ran a hand over the back of his neck, squeezing slightly.

Ben toyed with his coffee cup, twirling it slightly on the table. "You haven't said anything about this to Mom, have you? Because if she thinks she has a grandchild, she's going to go nuts with excitement. There'll be no stopping that steamroller."

"Hell, no!" Andrew lowered his voice, making sure no one else was listening. "I haven't told anyone but you. And Gia, she knows."

"You told *Gia*? That you slept with her sister?" Ben shook his head. "You're either very brave or very stupid, and you can guess which I suspect."

"Yeah, I know." Andrew rubbed a tired hand over his eyes. "Trust me, I know."

He'd barely slept in the past few days since Gia walked out of the bunkhouse angry. He'd weighed his options and, while he didn't want to hurt her, he wouldn't walk away from his child. This might not be the way he'd planned to start a family, but he wasn't about to turn his back on his kid. In the end, he'd asked a buddy on the force he knew would keep quiet to serve her the papers requesting the paternity test.

If the mother was anyone else, he would have simply asked. But Lorena wasn't exactly a straight shooter. She'd been the cause of more drama since she turned sixteen than any one person should have been in their entire life. She was troubled, to say the least.

He'd always known it, had seen the unreasonable jealousy she'd harbored against Gia back when they'd dated. Finding out now that she'd been the cause for their breakup didn't come as a shock, although it did piss him off royally. What she'd accused him of was ridiculous, and he still wasn't sure why Gia believed it.

Andrew had tried to stay as far from Lorena as possible, despite her overly flirtatious nature. For one thing, he'd loved Gia. For another, she was his girlfriend's sister. He'd never have done anything to jeopardize what they had.

Even after their breakup, after Gia had left town, he'd kept her at arm's distance, seeing her promiscuous nature and the drama she'd caused for other guys he knew. He didn't have the time or inclination for that. But she'd caught him at a weak moment.

Nine years to the day since his proposal to Gia. Although she'd managed to avoid him for nine years, luck had abandoned him and he'd literally run into her, Christmas shopping with her father. Over the next week, he'd let the memories crowd in around him. Too many he'd ignored for too long, too many dreams he'd had for them crushed. But partnering those with tequila shots had left him vulnerable. When Lorena offered to drive him home, he'd seen Gia's face, heard Gia's voice.

He should have just stayed at the fire station and slept it off with Ben when he'd offered. Instead, he remembered getting into Lorena's car and then nothing else until he woke in the passenger seat of her car the next morning with Lorena putting on lipstick in the driver's seat, a monster hangover and his pants unzipped.

"So, what did Gia say?" Ben jerked him from his reverie.

"I haven't heard from her since she walked out the other day." Andrew finished off his cup of coffee. "Shit, who could blame her?"

"Now what?"

"You know, you're kind of useless. I brought you here to offer me your brotherly advice, not point out that I have no clue what to do next."

Ben rolled his eyes and shook his head. "Fine, you want advice? Find Gia and tell her you love her, that you've always loved her and that you want to raise this baby together."

"Yeah, because that'll work."

Ben's brows lifted and his mouth twisted with humor. "Actually, I was kidding, but damn, you didn't even deny one iota of that. Shouldn't that tell you something?"

Andrew let out a sigh. This was not what he'd expected from Ben. As much as they liked to bust each other's balls, the two of them understood each other, even if they were opposites. "Ben, I know, okay? I've *always* known she was the one that got away. I don't need the reminder."

"Weren't you the one who, not so long ago, told me that you were the one-night-stand guy and I was the marrying guy?" Ben grinned into his cup. "Seems that was a facade and you were just talking out your ass again, huh?"

"Facade? Where'd you learn that one? Emma teaching you new words?"

"Word of the day toilet paper, dickhead." He drained his own cup. "Look, I get it. You want someone to wave a magic wand and give you the right answers. But let's face it, this situation is fucked up all the way around."

"Thanks for that. You're a big help." He stood, waving to Gina, who was working as the barista behind the counter for her mom again today. She nodded and hurried to prepare him a cup of his usual to-go.

"Hold up." Ben pushed the chair beside him with his foot to block his brother. Andrew slid back into the chair he'd vacated. "What I started to say was that you need to talk to Gia. Let her know how you feel, how you've always felt about her." Andrew shook his head in denial. "Don't start that." Ben waved his hand at Andrew.

"What?" He could feel himself growing defensive, the tension bunching the muscles in his neck and shoulders again.

"That denial, self-preservation thing you do. Talk this over with her. Even if it turns out you are the dad, maybe the two of you can work something out."

"She lives in San Diego. That's eight hours away."

"Do you really want to take this to court? Her job is nine to five. She can be there for the kid. You're a cop. It's a dangerous job for a single parent," Ben pointed out.

"In a small town?"

"Shit happens in small towns, too."

Andrew knew he was thinking back to the recent trouble his fiancée, Emma, had when someone had targeted her animal sanctuary and nearly burned the place to the ground.

"Not to mention that Lorena already gave her custody, or tried to. Just talk to her. You said you're setting up this concert with Linc. Use that to get your foot in the door and, for the love of all that is holy, do not threaten her with a paternity suit. Just tell her that you'd like to get the test done. Don't give a woman a reason to go on the defensive."

"I already did," Andrew muttered.

Ben sighed and rose, tossing his cup into the trash. "You're a lost cause, bro. I can't help you." He shook his head. "And you were supposed to be the one who had women all figured out. You're an idiot."

Andrew watched Ben head out the door of the coffee shop and back toward the fire station down the road.

He couldn't help but agree with his brother's assessment of him. He needed to figure out a way to get out of this mess he'd made for himself.

Chapter Twelve

GIA WATCHED HER mother serve Lorena her favorite breakfast of crepes with strawberry cream cheese filling and fresh whipped cream on top while Gia changed Bella's diaper and the second outfit she'd already spit up on this morning.

"Gia, I thought you were going to cover me for breakfast service this morning," her mother complained, giving her a warning look over her shoulder before turning back to the stove.

"I called Rusty. He went in early."

"That's expensive," she scolded. "You know your sister—"

"Could head in to the restaurant and help out," Gia said quickly, interrupting.

Her mother turned around and planted her hands

at her hips, glaring at her. "—is tired from her long trip home."

Gia glanced at her father, who rolled his eyes, shrugging slightly as if she should just let the argument go, and rose from the table. "I'll head in this morning and your mother can take the lunch shift instead."

"Don't worry, Daddy." She reached for his arm and scooped Bella from the seat. "I'll go, if Lorena keeps an eye on Bella."

Her sister dropped her fork onto her plate, letting it clatter loudly. "Are you serious? No way."

Bella instantly began fussing at the noise.

"Excuse me, young lady." Her father's voice deepened, sounding like he had when he'd corrected them as children. It was the voice that made sure they did their chores and homework and worked at Rossetti's every day. The one that didn't leave any room for argument.

"Daddy." Lorena's voice miraculously switched from angry to plaintive. "I'm so tired. I took a late-night flight just to get here to see you." She rose and came around the table, wrapping her arms around his neck and pressing her cheek against his. "I promise, I'll take the dinner shift tonight. I just need to get some sleep, and I can't do that if I'm watching a baby."

"Not *a* baby," Gia corrected her. "*Your* baby."

"Lorena Micheala," their father growled in warning. "It's not right leaving your sister to take care of your responsibilities. This is your child, not hers."

"Giovanni, stop it." Her mother slapped the spatula

onto the counter. "This isn't fair to do to her. She's only just come home. Give her some time to settle in before we start making demands."

Gia turned to her mother, her mouth hanging open in shock. She had been the one who'd had her life uprooted and thrown into chaos, her job put on hold, not her sister. She was the one her mother insisted return home, the one expected to figure out some way to get them out from under the financial ruin they now faced. Yet her desires were never even taken into consideration. Lorena smirked, and it took every ounce of self-control Gia possessed to keep from slapping the spoiled brat. Vicious words slid to her tongue, ready to be released, until her gaze fell on her father's pale face.

Instead she bit them back and carried Bella into her room to pack her bag for the day, shouldering her way past her sister and Lorena's cheesy, victorious grin.

"Never mind, Mama. I'll manage." Gia couldn't stop the bitterness from creeping into her voice.

"You always do, *tesoro*," her mother called after her, either not noticing or not caring about her frustration.

As usual, Gia would figure out a way to bear the weight of being everything to everyone once again.

AFTER SOMEHOW MANAGING to work through the breakfast shift and cover her mother's lunch shift, Gia was now two hours into the dinner service without a sign of anyone coming to relieve her.

Damn Lorena.

Gia glanced at the back door for the tenth time in the last hour. Her parents not coming was understandable. Her father had seemed especially weak this morning, whether due to stress or the tension in the house now that Lorena had returned. Her mother was busy trying to take care of him. It really wasn't fair to expect either of them to come in.

But her sister was a different story. She should have known better than to trust her sister to actually show up, let alone on time. She wasn't even responding to text messages.

"Hey, Gia, something's going on at the bar. I think Nick's going to need your help."

Heather had no more poked her head into the office before Gia was on the run for the bar area. "Watch Bella for a second," she called back. She froze as soon as she saw her sister talking to Andrew at the bar.

"Aw, you know you missed me, sweetie." Lorena's voice held that flirty complaining tone she had perfected.

"Get out of my way. I'm going to talk to Gia. Now."

Gia would know Andrew's angry growl anywhere but wondered when her sister had arrived and why she hadn't come back to relieve Gia. Spotting the two of them at the bar, she understood why.

"Humph, she wasn't the one you were looking for the last time we ran into one another."

Her sister ran her fingers down Andrew's chest and

smiled up at him coyly. Andrew grasped her wrist and lifted her hand, holding it away from his body.

"Don't. I still don't know exactly what happened that night, but I'm going to find out."

Lorena gave him a husky laugh, her eyes cutting toward Gia before meeting Andrew's gaze again. She stood on her toes, her mouth a scant inch from his. "You know *exactly* what happened that night. Which is why I have these for you." Lorena dropped a manila envelope on the bar and shoved it toward Andrew. "Consider this matter closed, for both of you."

Andrew turned to stare at Gia, his eyes taking on the regret he'd tried to convince her he felt. She wanted to believe him, but after being served the paternity documents yesterday, she couldn't let herself be swayed by anything that might risk Bella's welfare or Gia's custody claim.

"What're those?" Gia's voice sounded weak, even to her own ears. She wanted to reach for the envelope, to keep Lorena from having the satisfaction of causing a scene, but Gia's hand was shaking.

Andrew took a step back from Lorena, and Gia wondered if he was doing it because he wanted to, or to prove a point—that Lorena meant nothing to him. Unclasping the envelope, he pulled out a stack of papers, his dark eyes scanning them.

"Lorena, what did you do?" He shook his head, letting it fall forward as he held the papers out to Gia.

"Oh, no worries." Lorena laughed, waving her hand before reaching into her purse for another envelope and tossing it onto the bar. "I have another copy just for my dear sister. Here. Now everyone gets what they want. I have my freedom, you—" she looked pointedly at Gia "—can go back to San Diego, and congratulations, Andrew. You're a father."

Gia sought Andrew's gaze but he wouldn't look at her. Instead, he slid onto one of the stools with his head in his hands. Gia reached for the second envelope and pulled out the contents—a birth certificate with Lorena's name on it and Andrew listed as the father. Behind it were the documents signing off all parental rights of Bella, giving full legal and physical custody to Bella's father, Andrew McQuaid.

GIA'S FACE PALED as Andrew watched the papers fall from her fingers. He had no idea why Lorena would give up her daughter without a paternity test, but the look on her face was victorious and he knew exactly what her motive was.

This was just one more way for her to wound Gia.

He'd seen her do it more times than he could remember. There'd been the time Gia saved every dime she earned tutoring to buy a piece-of-shit car, only to watch her sister take it for a joyride without Gia's knowledge, and total it. Or the time Gia ran for senior class president and Lorena spread a rumor that Gia was offering blow jobs to any guy who'd vote for her. Jackson, who'd been in the same graduating class, had gotten to the bottom of that one and helped him shut that rumor down quickly, but not before she'd lost the votes from every girl in her class. Even after her sister had headed to college, Lorena had made sure people around here thought Gia was nothing more than a conniving bitch, painting herself as the victim, playing on sympathy whenever she could.

"Nick," Lorena called, circling her finger in the air. "I think we need some drinks at this end to congratulate the new father."

"Tell Gia the truth, Lorena," Andrew warned as Nick slid three shots of Jack Daniels onto the counter and hurried away.

She narrowed her gaze at him. "Fine, then I'll celebrate for all of us." She downed the shot in front of her before reaching for the other two and waving at Nick to bring another round.

"Why, Lorena?" Gia's voice was thick, and Andrew could hear her fighting back the tears choking her. "I told you I'd—"

"Let's go to your office," Andrew interrupted. "We can all talk privately in there."

Gia's hazel gaze cut to him, seething with rage, and Andrew knew she was about to unleash her infamous temper on him. It wasn't something he wanted seen publicly, for her sake as much as his.

"Gia, please. I'm still on duty."

Lorena snorted. "Begging isn't very becoming, *Officer* McQuaid. But then again, it's not the first time I've heard it."

She smiled broadly as Gia clenched her jaw and spun on her heel, leading the way through the doors to her father's office. Andrew started to follow when he realized Lorena was still in her seat.

"Come on." He grasped Lorena's upper arm.

"Screw you. You can't tell me what to do. We aren't a couple. You have what you wanted, no paternity test necessary."

"That's part of what I want to get to the bottom of."

Lorena threw back another shot. "Well, you two have fun with that. I've got a plane to catch now that I'm finished here."

Andrew leaned close, not wanting everyone in the bar to hear their argument. "Finished making your sister's life hell, you mean?"

Lorena smiled up at him. "Have fun trying to win her back now."

"Who said I was—"

"Please. The two of you aren't exactly subtle. You've both been making puppy-dog eyes at each other for ten years. It's pretty disgusting." She rolled her eyes. "I warned you when you woke up that morning not to think you could fuck with me and walk away, remember?" She stuck out her lower lip. "And then you wouldn't even call me."

"Your sister didn't have anything to do with that and you know it. Why do this to her?"

Lorena laughed, twisting the shot glass between her thumb and finger. "She kind of did have something to do with it. I'm tired of her being Daddy's fucking perfect daughter and getting whatever she wants while I get screwed. So, I decided to even out the score."

"By lying so she'd break off our engagement."

She shrugged. "I didn't have to do much. A little insinuation, a few people who 'saw us together.'" She used her fingers in air quotes. "I figured it would screw her up but, nope, Perfect Gia just threw herself into her studies and finished her degree early, then landed the perfect job. She got to leave and I was stuck here."

"You could have left at any time. You didn't have to ruin everyone else's lives."

Andrew couldn't comprehend the fierce hatred Lorena must have for her sister to want to hurt her so badly. He and his brothers might argue and bicker, but they would do anything for one another, no matter what. They would lay their lives on the line for each other, and had, but Lorena was doing whatever she possibly could to cause her sister misery. Gia had never done anything but try to help her.

"And New Year's? What could you have possibly hoped to gain?"

Lorena toyed with the last shot glass, chuckling as she stared at the amber liquid. "That was partially your fault.

You'd been going on and on all night about how you were just going to go to LA, like you'd always talked about. Dad had just pulled the plug on opening the second restaurant and I was going to be stuck here forever. You were my ticket out *and* a way to get even with Gia." She glared at him. "Until I realized the next day you were full of shit. You're a sad sack who's never going to leave this one-horse town. Technically, *you* lied to *me*."

Andrew clenched his jaw, his hands fisting at his sides. "Why didn't you just tell me you were pregnant?"

"Because you screwed me over. Instead of living in LA, I'm stuck following Bobby from gig to gig just to be out of this godforsaken place. I thought he'd want the kid when I told him she was his but . . ." She looked away, waving at Nick to bring her another round of shots.

"I never would have taken you. I'm not in love with you."

She glared at him. "Yes, I know. You love Gia. You've *always* loved Gia. Doesn't everyone? I knew she'd take care of Bella, but I hoped it would turn her life upside down, make my parents realize she wasn't as perfect as they think, that she couldn't keep her shit together either."

"It's still *your* shit, Lorena!" He rose from the stool to head toward Gia's office. "You're one sick, twisted bitch. I'll never understand why your sister does so much for you."

"No one loves me." Her face soured and she slammed back the last shot. "I didn't get what I wanted, and now

I've made sure neither of you gets what you want either. On that note, I have a taxi waiting to take me to the airport."

Andrew barely heard the words over the noise of the bar and restaurant dinner service, but before he could ask her anything else, Lorena was already up and heading for the front door, leaving Gia to take care of the crowded restaurant, shorthanded.

If anyone could do it, it was Gia.

The woman amazed him with what she'd been able to handle already. Taking care of a newborn, spending most days at the restaurant and now dealing with her irrational sister. He wasn't sure when or if she ever slept, but he wasn't going to make her life any more difficult than it already was. Somehow he'd figure out a way to make this work for them both.

He rapped on the office door lightly with his knuckle. "Gia?"

"Yeah? Come in."

Her voice sounded muffled and, as he entered, she lifted her face from her hands, brushing her hair back. He could see twin tracks from her tears running down her cheeks, even as she quickly tried to wipe away the evidence left behind.

"Aw, hell." Andrew hurried to her, reaching for her hands, careful not to disturb Bella sleeping in some chair contraption she was strapped into.

"What the hell did I ever do to her?" Gia pulled her hands from his and balled them in her lap. "I've tried to help her every way I possibly could. Ever since we were little. But she just seems to hate me more every time."

He sat back against the edge of the desk and tucked his hands into his pockets. "Your sister is a spoiled, entitled bitch. You didn't do anything wrong, Gia." Andrew shook his head, at a loss for what to say. "I have no clue why she's doing this other than she wants you to be as miserable as she is."

Gia narrowed her eyes as she looked up at him. "She didn't do anything different than you were doing." She pushed her chair back and rose, putting some distance between them. "You were planning on taking Bella away from me, too."

"No, I wasn't."

She shot him a dubious look. "Bullshit, Andrew."

"I wasn't taking her away. I wanted to know if she's mine and, if so, be responsible, Gia. That's what a father does. If she's my daughter, I *do* want to be a part of her life, but I never planned on cutting her out of yours."

"And just how is that supposed to work out?"

She reached over to adjust a blanket on Bella, but Andrew knew it was just an excuse. Bella grounded Gia, gave her something to focus on. She gave Gia a purpose. He could see it in her eyes. She loved that little girl like she was her own.

"Lorena was supposed to fix the birth certificate and sign off rights so I could adopt her," Gia muttered, more to herself than to him. She glanced up at Andrew, her eyes misting with tears. "You know you're responsible for her now. I have no right to keep you from walking out the door with her right now."

"I'm not taking her from you. We need to find a lawyer tomorrow. Come with me."

She turned her back on him, avoiding meeting his gaze. "I have to help my mom . . ."

"It's one day, Gia. They can manage. This affects you too." He reached for her hand, his fingers closing around hers tenderly, his thumb brushing over the racing pulse at her wrist. "I want you with me."

She closed her eyes, looking defeated. "Fine, who?"

"We need a family lawyer we can trust." At her look of disbelief, he corrected himself. "We'll go into Sacramento and find someone there."

Her hazel eyes met his and he could easily read the fear in them. "Can I trust *you*?"

He gave her a sad smile, one colored with all the remorse that filled his heart. There were so many things he wished he'd said to her, ways he wished he'd handled things differently, including the paternity suit. "I'd lay my life on the line for you, Gia. I swear. You can trust me. I won't hurt you again."

He probably shouldn't have made the promise, but now that he had, he'd do anything to keep it. Anything.

Chapter Thirteen

IT WAS BARELY ten a.m. when he pulled up to her house, but Gia was already waiting on the front porch for him. As soon as she saw the car, she hurried down the steps, the diaper bag and purse bouncing against her right hip, with Bella sleeping in her car seat held in her other arm. He jumped out and took the bags from her while she buckled the car seat into the back.

"I told you I'd be here at ten thirty."

Her gaze flickered to his, then back to the baby as she struggled to make the car seat fit properly. "I know."

"Maybe we should take your car if the car seat won't fit right. I can drive if you want."

"No," she said, finally clipping the buckle into place. "I don't want Lorena to know I am gone, let alone where."

"I thought she said she was flying out."

The run-in with Lorena last night had been more

than enough to last him a while. He had the documents she'd signed in the car, and he'd already had a brief consultation with an attorney over the phone, filling the lawyer in on their current predicament. The man's first piece of advice was to avoid any further confrontation with Lorena or Gia if he wanted this entire matter to go smoothly. More than anything, Andrew wanted this to go smoothly for Gia. He just prayed she was as optimistic as he was about what the attorney would propose.

"She was, but after last night, she decided it would be more fun to stay and gloat. She was waiting up for me when I got finally home from the restaurant."

"Shit," he muttered, holding her door as she slid into the passenger seat. "Are you okay?"

"Apparently it's not the first time she's used you to hurt me." She gave him a pointed look before tugging the door closed.

Your breakup, moron.

Andrew made his way to the driver's seat and climbed inside, glancing into the back seat at Bella as he dropped the car into Reverse. He was going to make up for the past to Gia, both his own mistakes and those that had been made by other people where Gia was concerned.

"She admitted that she lied ten years ago, and that she convinced people to lie for her as well. Ten years, Andrew." She closed her eyes slowly, keeping him from seeing the depths of her sorrow.

He reached for her hand. "Gia."

"But that doesn't change where we're going and why now."

There was a sharp *thud* against the front of his car. "What the hell?"

Lorena banged her hand against the hood one more time for good measure. "Just where are the three of you going, looking so cozy?"

"Just go," Gia muttered to Andrew. "It's not like she's going to chase you down the street."

"I wouldn't actually put it past her." Andrew looked over at Gia as Lorena hurried to the driver's side, reaching for the door handle.

"Sitting here isn't going to help matters either. Go."

Andrew let the car roll backward down the driveway and into the street, making sure Lorena was several feet away when he put the car into gear. He gunned it when he saw her jerk one of the walkway lights from the ground and throw it at them.

The light shattered as it hit the rear bumper. "Hey!"

He caught a glimpse of something else in her hand as she cocked her arm back again. Andrew wasn't waiting for anything else to hit his car. "You're sister's a real piece of work."

Gia pursed her perfect lips and rolled her eyes, turning toward the window. "I wasn't the one who slept with her."

"Not that you want to hear it, Gia, and I'm not trying to make excuses, but I really don't know what happened that night. I was drunk. One minute she was giving me a ride home and the next—"

"She was riding you?" There was no mistaking the sarcasm dripping from her voice.

"I woke up with a killer hangover." He glanced in her direction but she was looking out the window. "I was upset."

She sighed, turning toward him as she rolled her eyes. "Well, I'm sure she made you feel better."

"Damn it, Gia. How many times do I have to apologize?"

"Until I believe you." She looked out the window again. "Until it doesn't hurt anymore," she whispered.

Andrew guessed that she didn't realize she'd said the last part aloud. It cut into his heart like a jagged wound. And in truth, he deserved the pain after what he'd done to her. Any penance she decided she wanted from him, he'd gladly pay.

Gia remained quiet for most of the ride to Sacramento. Even when he tried to talk to her, she rewarded him with either a dirty look or a one-word answer. He had no clue how to draw her out anymore. At one time, they would have talked about sports, movies, music or books. Now a shrug seemed to be her go-to answer for any question from him. There was only one thing he could think of that might get her to start talking.

"Linc said he'd make the arrangements for the sound system and have the equipment delivered to the restaurant the Thursday before the concert."

She pulled out her cell phone and pressed some buttons. "That should work. I'm going to hire a couple extra people this week, so they should be fully trained by then."

"Have you thought about where you want to advertise? I'm sure I could talk to Missy over at the printers and see if she'd donate some posters. I bet Linc already has some sort of media package they send out at the various venues whenever he performs."

She twisted her lips to one side, frowning. "There is probably a fee to use those graphics. I've got a good photo editor on my laptop. I could put together a poster image and tickets if you think you could convince her to print them."

"She'll do it."

Gia rolled her eyes, instantly tense again. "I don't even want to know why you're so certain, although I'm sure I can guess."

"Gia, if you're going to guilt-trip me about every woman I've dated, that's going to be a heavy burden to bear."

She threw her hands up. "Oh, sorry. I had no clue the number would be so vast. I'd forgotten what a he-ho you are."

"A what?" he said with a laugh. "Did you just call me a he-ho?" She rolled her eyes again and sighed, not amused at his attempt to make her laugh. "Look, I've dated my fair share of women, but it's not like it's a crime. I'm a twenty-eight-year-old man. You can't tell me you haven't dated since you left."

She didn't answer, crossed her arms and kept her

face toward the window. He could see her eyes shift toward him in her reflection, and her silence was as telling as her rigid posture.

"You haven't dated?" He couldn't keep the awe from his voice.

"Depends on your definition of *dating*. Instead of sleeping my way around San Diego the way you have been here, I've been busy building a career," she pointed out. "I'm the youngest associate VP of marketing my company has ever had."

"Damn," he muttered, impressed by her accomplishments but more than a little pleased with the fact that it sounded like she hadn't found anyone she'd been serious about since she'd left Hidden Falls.

"'Damn' is right. I've worked hard to get where I am. You can't expect me to just walk away from it."

Andrew frowned. "Why would you?"

She glanced into the back seat and lowered her voice, as if Bella might understand. "I took four weeks of leave to come here and get everything settled. I need to go back to my real life. I have an apartment and . . . and . . ."

His brows lifted, waiting for her to expound on what else she had in her life, other than an empty apartment. Her words fell flat and she sighed, as if the reminder of how little life she was really living disappointed her. She had so much more here—her parents, the restaurant, him. He hated the loneliness that echoed in her voice. Here in Hidden Falls he had his job, his family, friends, their ranch, hobbies. She was caught in limbo.

"No cats?" he asked, trying to lighten the mood. She glared at him and he didn't even bother to hide his grin. "Maybe a plant or two that need watering?"

"You're not funny."

"Tell me you at least have a DVR that needs to be updated."

"I actually do, and it's filled with *Supernatural* episodes and *House* reruns."

"Cheesy horror and a type-A doctor . . . No reality TV for you?"

"I think I get enough drama without that, thanks."

He bobbed his head to one side in deference to the comment about her sister. "Yeah, you do."

He turned off the highway and headed into town, slowing as he reached a park.

"So, what's the plan?" she finally asked, breaking the silence.

"I talked with the guy this morning, and he's fitting us in between cases today at the courthouse. I explained a bit of what's going on—"

"That my sister abandoned her baby to my care, then changed her mind and is giving her to a man who may or may not be the father, just to spite me?"

"In a nutshell, yeah." He pulled into the parking lot and turned off the car, turning in his seat to face her. "This isn't easy for either of us, Gia, but we have to consider what's best for Bella."

"*I* am what's best for her."

"All I ask is that you keep an open mind and we hear

what he has to say." Andrew didn't tell her that the lawyer had already suggested he go through with the paternity test, for his own sake.

As a sheriff's deputy, he'd seen enough shady dealings to know that there were plenty of women who lied about the paternity of their kids to get child support. The problem was, Lorena wasn't coming after him for money. But after their conversation last night, he didn't trust that she wasn't doing this just to hurt him and Gia. Hell, Lorena might just be doing this to watch them self-destruct for her own sadistic pleasure.

"Fine." She reached for the car seat, but he unbuckled it from the other side and pulled it out. Watching him, she pinched her lips together. "I can do it."

"So can I. Grab the bags."

As she came around the truck, he slid a hand to her lower back. His fingers instantly heated as a sizzle traveled up his arm and a feeling of déjà vu came over him. This was what his life should have looked like. This was what he'd wanted before Lorena had snatched it away with a lie. Maybe, just maybe, he could use Lorena's latest scheme to retrieve what should have been his a long time ago.

GIA PREPARED A bottle for Bella as they waited for the attorney to finish with his clients who had just exited the courtroom. They looked thrilled with the outcome of their case as one of the two men lifted the boy into his arms. Gia couldn't help the little bubble of hope that swelled in her heart as she watched the happy couple. However, reality crashed in just as quickly.

You don't know why they're here. Maybe they just took that child from someone who loved him.

Desperation gnawed at her mind as a harried-looking man in an ill-fitting, rumpled suit hurried toward them. She rose as he motioned them to a side room.

"I'm so sorry I only have a few minutes, but we can use the mediation room for a bit." He slid his briefcase onto a long table and popped it open, tugging out a bright yellow legal pad. "I'm Erik Masters."

Andrew leaned across the table to shake his hand. "I'm Andrew. We spoke this morning. This is Gia and Bella," he said, motioning toward them.

He shook her hand with a firm grip, and she remained standing to feed Bella in the car seat.

"Please, Gia, you have this room as long as you need it. Go ahead and get comfortable." He glanced at his watch. "I, however, need to be back in court in twenty minutes, so I apologize for getting right to the heart of the matter."

Gia lifted Bella into her arms and slid into one of the chairs. A knot of anxiety curled in her stomach. Usually holding Bella relaxed her, but right now, she felt like she had a death grip on the child. Bella noticed as well and began to fuss. Andrew slid a hand to the back of her chair, letting his thumb brush against her shoulder reassuringly, and Gia took a deep breath.

"Mr. Masters," Andrew began.

"Oh, call me Erik," the lawyer said with a wave of his hand. "I tend to be a bit less formal with cases that are as simple as this one."

"This is simple?" Gia asked.

"Technically, yes." Erik pulled a file folder from his briefcase, and she could see copies of the documents she and Andrew had received from Lorena. "Because your sister has already listed Andrew as the father on Bella's birth certificate, it's assumed to be true, unless he wants to contest paternity."

They both looked at Andrew expectantly. Gia wasn't sure what would happen if he did contest it, but she suspected it gave her a far better opportunity to prove that she should raise Bella. He simply glanced at her before turning his attention back to the lawyer.

"If he doesn't, because she's already signed off her parental rights and given full legal and physical custody to Andrew, Bella would become his legal responsibility. You could contest it, Gia, of course, but you would need to prove why he is unfit to be her parent and, I have to say, it would be pretty difficult to do." He rocked his head from side to side. "He's an upstanding member of his community, sort of a local hero being an officer of the law, and has family support nearby. Not to mention, the mother of the child is saying he's her father."

Gia felt like her world was crashing down around her. "And if he does contest it?" Her question came out in a rushed breath.

"Then a paternity test would be performed, at the cost of the person contesting, of course. If he's shown to be Bella's father, he would again have full custodial rights as her father. If he's not, she would enter the foster care system, and anyone wanting custody would then go through getting approval. Later, after every attempt was made to find her biological father, you could proceed with the adoption process."

"So, it's possible I could lose her to someone other than Andrew?"

Erik glanced at Andrew then back to Gia. "If Andrew isn't her biological father and someone else comes forward proving paternity, then yes, it's possible."

Gia felt her entire body trembling, but she remained rooted to her chair as she finished feeding Bella. She wanted to get up and pace the room. She wanted to punch a wall—or, better, her sister—for putting them all in this position. In the span of just a few moments, she'd gone from hoping Andrew wasn't Bella's father to praying he was. At least with him, she might be able to convince him to allow her visitation. Who knew what a stranger might do?

"As of right now, the matter is pretty simple. If you believe you are Bella's father, Andrew, you should acknowledge paternity and accept custody. You would have all the rights and responsibilities as her father, the same as any single parent." He glanced at Gia. "Which would also include deciding who your daughter spends time with and any visitation she might be allowed with her aunt."

"If I don't?"

Erik Masters leaned forward, steepling his hands in front of him. "If you don't, you could both lose her."

Chapter Fourteen

GIA WALKED BACK to Andrew's car silently. She was grateful he didn't press her to discuss their options but, in truth, he was really the only one who had any. She had none. Lorena had eliminated them the moment she wrote Andrew's name on the birth certificate and filed the document. When she'd shown up at Gia's apartment nearly two weeks ago unexpectedly, Lorena had left Gia with little choice but to drop everything to care for Bella. Then, just as quickly, she'd jerked the baby away from Gia, with no explanation.

Gia watched as Andrew struggled to buckle the car seat into the truck and pinched her lips together, moving to his side. "I'll get it," she said quietly.

She slid the buckle into place and moved around to her door, her eyes misting again.

Damn it!

Gia pressed her knuckle to her eye, stemming the tears. She hadn't cried this much in years. Not since she'd found out about her sister and Andrew, when she'd broken off their engagement. More of her sister's lies.

He opened her door, studying her as she dropped into the seat. Glancing her way as he moved around the back of the car, Andrew slid behind the wheel. She could see his concern for her but she didn't want to talk, not yet. Discussing it would make the fact that she was losing Bella real, and it was about to get real soon enough.

Once they returned to her parents' house, she would need to pack Bella's things and let Andrew take her home. To *his* home. She doubted he'd force her to, but there was no sense in dragging this nightmare out any longer. It would break her heart regardless of when she did it, so she might as well get it over with sooner rather than later.

Andrew eased the truck through a nearby coffee shop drive-through and placed his order. "What would you like?"

"Nothing," she mumbled.

She wasn't working at the restaurant tonight, so maybe once she had sent him and Bella on their way, she'd just crawl into bed, pull the blankets over her head and try to forget everything.

Fat chance.

"This isn't finished, Gia." His voice was tender, and he reached across the center console for her hand. "I have a suggestion."

She didn't want to acknowledge the hope that suddenly blossomed in her at the kindness in his voice. It seemed like each time she did, something new fell apart on her. But what if . . . She wouldn't let herself follow the fanciful train of thought. Turning back to the window, Andrew ordered another drink, slipping the money to the barista before heading into the lot of a park near the courthouse.

"Come on," he said, turning off the ignition. "Let's find a quiet place to sit."

Andrew slid the diaper bag over one of his broad shoulders and unbuckled the car seat, taking both, leaving her to grab the coffee cups. Under normal circumstances, the sight of Andrew McQuaid, manly-man cop, with his bulging biceps and massive chest, carrying a diaper bag covered in teddy bears would have made her smile. She paused for a moment to watch as he carefully selected a picnic bench along the edge of the water but still under the shade of several trees. He settled the car seat as Bella fussed slightly, and Gia couldn't stop the way her heart clenched when he made playful faces at Bella, retrieving her pacifier and helping her calm back down. As he sat, he didn't bother to remove his hand from where it rested beside the baby.

He was a natural and he was going to be a great father.

Gia's heart tightened at the thought of not being there to see it. She suspected that Bella was the first baby he'd been around. Or perhaps he was just good with kids because of his job. The truth was, it didn't come as a surprise that Bella liked him. As tough as Andrew always liked to believe he was, he was a big teddy bear himself.

He turned back toward her. "You coming?"

She was dragging her feet, wanting to delay this as long as possible. She wasn't ready to discuss how and when he was going to take custody of Bella.

Andrew stepped onto the seat and sat on the table top, beside the car seat. Gia straddled the bench in front of them and off to one side, holding his coffee out to him.

His eyes darkened as their fingers connected. "Gia, when I filed for that paternity test, I was only trying to get answers. I never planned on taking Bella from you."

She stared down at the cup lid, letting her dark hair tumble forward, hiding her face from his intense scrutiny. She was afraid of what she might see there. Afraid that she couldn't hold it together in the face of his empathy.

"I guess some things just don't work out the way we plan."

Her voice cracked on the last word. So many things hadn't turned out as planned. Their engagement, her lonely life in San Diego, her return home . . .

"We can work something out."

She glanced up at him, doubtful. "How?"

He shrugged and shook his head, looking lost. "I don't know, Gia. I guess I thought that we'd cross that bridge if we came to it." He reached over to run a finger against Bella's hand. Her tiny fingers immediately curled around his much larger one.

"I think we're standing at that bridge now." She took a sip of the coffee, letting the sweet taste of caramel coat her tongue. Unfortunately it didn't lessen the bitterness she felt.

"I want you and Bella to come stay at the ranch."

Gia choked on her coffee, covering her mouth so she wouldn't she spit it into his lap. Hope soared as she looked up at him and cleared her throat. "What? In the bunkhouse?"

Her hopes crashed just as quickly. She couldn't do that. According to her sister, she hadn't even managed to hide her feelings for him when she barely saw him around town. It was going to be difficult enough to plan this concert with him and pretend that she didn't still want him. There was no way she could do it while she was living in the same house.

"No, you can stay at Mom and Dad's. They've got two extra bedrooms right now and would love to have you. Plus, it will make the transition easier for Bella to have you there, and it would give me time to get accustomed to being a father."

He didn't need help. She'd seen him with Bella already. He was going to do fine and she was tempted to tell him so. Gia felt her lungs constrict as she tried to take a breath. Agony flooded her soul. This was really happening. She was going to lose Bella.

"Give me custody, Andrew," she whispered, her voice pleading. "She's all I have."

"That's not true," he pointed out.

"Yes, it is." She sighed. Maybe if she told him the truth, told him everything, he'd take pity on her. "I may never be able to have a child."

"What?" His shock was evident in his wide eyes.

"I've known for a long time that I might not be able to conceive."

He took a deep breath. "Are you okay?" His posture stiffened and he narrowed his eyes at her.

She nodded. "I found out about seven years ago, during a doctor's visit. I had no idea before that," she clarified, wanting him to know she hadn't misled him. "I can't just let her go. I've had her all to myself since she was born. You could just sign over rights—"

"Gia, I can't." He set the coffee aside and slid down to straddle the bench in front of her, their knees touching. Cupping her face in his palms, he tipped her face up so she was forced to look into his eyes. "If she's my daughter, I can't just . . ."

He closed his eyes for a moment, and she could see his heart written on his face clearly. He was torn.

"But what if she's not? There's that possibility." His eyes bored into hers, and she could see the fierce determination in their depths.

"I'm doing this as much for you as for myself and Bella. Your sister fucked this up all the way around. Now that my name is on the birth certificate, it's assumed I *am* her father. If I contest it, you'll win the battle but risk losing the war. You'll be forced to find her real father. Are you prepared for the possibility of losing her completely?

"Come to the ranch. You can stay as long as you want to." He reached for her hand, and his thumb brushed over the back of it. "Or get a place in town. It's your choice, although I'm assuming you'd rather be closer to her."

Gia tried to look away and he tipped her chin up again. "And if she's not yours, Andrew? Could you really do that? Raise her as your child, even knowing that someone else might be her father?"

Gia watched Bella as the baby stared up at the sky, her blue eyes bright and inquisitive. She could understand her own desire to raise Bella. It was her niece; Gia wouldn't be able to have children. But apparently, she'd mistakenly assumed he'd want to keep his freewheeling bachelorhood. He couldn't do that with a baby.

What kind of man raised a child born of a one-night stand? One that might not even be his?

A good one.

One thing was clear—he wasn't willing to walk away, any more than she was. And Gia had no claim on Bella now. As wonderful as it was that Andrew was offering to let her stay at the ranch for a while, she needed to head back to San Diego soon.

Unless you don't go back.

The thought wasn't foreign. She'd often gotten homesick in San Diego, and if being back home had proved anything, it was how little she had in her life other than her job. But she couldn't minimize the success she'd fought for either. Gia wasn't sure she could walk away from what she'd worked so hard for. The problem was that everything she wanted was here—the restaurant, her parents, Bella and Andrew.

As if sensing her wavering resolve, Andrew dipped his head to look at her. "Gia, you needed my help to save the restaurant. Now I need yours. I have no clue how to take care of a baby."

As if on cue, Bella began to cry and they both stood. Gia unbuckled her from the seat and lifted her out, making her decision.

"I have two weeks left before I'm supposed to go back to work." She held Bella out to him. "First task, taking over poopy diaper duty."

"I THOUGHT YOU were staying here, to help me with your father." Gia's mother stood in the doorway of her room, looking from Gia back toward Andrew with a scowl. *Che cosa ha mai fatto per voi per aiutare lui in questo modo?*

What's he ever done for you to help him this way?

How could her mother hold a grudge against Andrew but not against her youngest daughter for what she'd managed to put Gia through? It made no sense, but there was no point in arguing with her when she was like this.

"Mama, Lorena says he's Bella's father and we decided yesterday, he should get to know his daughter." Gia urged her mother out of the doorway with her hands on her shoulders, making sure to stay between her and Andrew. She wasn't sure her mother wasn't going to beat him with the empty laundry basket she held under her arm. "And this concert at the restaurant was his idea," Gia pointed out, hoping to gain Andrew at least a small measure good will.

"*Stronzo*," her mother muttered, glaring at him as she walked away.

"*Mama!*" Gia scolded, casting him an apologetic smile, grateful he didn't seem to remember the Italian word for *asshole*. She motioned to the baby gear on the floor beside her bed. "I think that's the last of Bella's things."

Andrew looked around at the small box of baby clothing, blankets, diapers, miscellaneous supplies and ointments. Folded beside it were the portable bassinet and playpen. On the bed was Gia's single suitcase with her clothing and toiletries.

"This is everything?"

"What can I say? We travel light."

He lifted the playpen onto one shoulder and wrapped his other arm around the box. "I'll be right back for the rest."

"I can help, Andrew."

She reached for the suitcase but he shook his head. "Your mother already thinks I'm an asshole. I'm not giving her any other reasons. Why don't you load Bella into the car? I think the sooner I get out of here, the safer my hide will be." He glanced at the direction her mother had taken. "Plus, who knows if your mother's actually going to kill me or whether that's something she'd rather wait to do with your sister when she comes back?"

"A better question would be, *if* Lorena's coming back." Gia rolled her eyes. "Supposedly she's at the restaurant until my shift tonight." She looked around her at the meager belongings and bit her lip nervously as she began to second-guess her decision. "Are you sure you're okay with doing this? And that your parents don't mind?"

"You're kidding, right? My mother is over the moon at the thought of you guys staying in the house." He took a step closer, staring at her mouth, and for a second, she thought he might kiss her. "She always liked you, Gia. As a matter of fact, she was pissed when we broke up."

She lifted her gaze to meet his and gave him a weak smile, feeling the butterflies in her stomach take flight. "You do realize that's not reassuring, right?"

"She was pissed at *me*," he clarified with a chuckle. "She wanted to know what I'd done to screw it up. And the fact that you're bringing her granddaughter . . . you're her new favorite person."

Andrew loaded up his car with their things but suggested she drive Bella in her own car. When both of her parents came out to the porch to send her off, her father shook Andrew's hand, giving him a nod and an odd smile. Her mother, on the other hand, looked like she'd just swallowed a lemon. Her mouth was pinched tightly.

When that didn't work, she sighed loudly, several times, making her displeasure evident without saying a word. Gia almost caved and changed her mind but reminded herself that she was doing this for Bella, the only person in this entire web of lies who was innocent.

"I'm just living a few miles out of town, Mama." Gia hugged her mother. "You'll see me at the restaurant every day, and it'll be easier to get the concert planned this way."

She gave Gia that look she'd used so often when they were children. The one that said she didn't believe her for even a second. "Humph! I thought this was supposed to be about making the transition easier for Bella."

Gia sighed, sadness filling her. She'd already had this conversation with her mother. Twice, actually, since returning from the courthouse. She lowered her voice so Andrew didn't hear. "It is, but I'm hoping Andrew and I can figure out some sort of compromise about the custody."

Her father ignored her mother's reprimand and pulled Gia into his arms, hugging her tightly. "You do what's best for you and Bella, *piccola*. That man is doing what a good father should."

"I know, Daddy," she whispered against him, pressing her cheek to his chest and feeling the steady pound of his heartbeat. He'd been her rock for years. "I'm just a phone call away, okay? If you need anything."

She felt his smile against the top of her head just before he pressed a kiss there. "I know, *dolce mia*, but it's time you live your life for yourself. Find what makes you happy."

Her father released her, looking at Andrew. "I'm glad to see I was right about you."

"Yes, sir."

Gia's mother huffed loudly and stormed back into the house.

"Just do right by her," Gia's father said.

"I'll take good care of your granddaughter, sir, and you both are welcome at the ranch anytime. You know that."

Her father arched a dark brow, shaking his head as he turned back toward the house with a soft chuckle. "I think we both know I wasn't talking about my granddaughter, son."

Chapter Fifteen

"GIA, WILL YOU RELAX?"

Andrew could see the tension in her shoulders as she unpacked Bella's things in the smaller of the spare rooms. She'd refused to take both rooms for her and Bella, opting instead to keep the baby close to her. He didn't push. He knew the past few days had been a shock, and over the next two weeks, he hoped they'd adjust and find some balance. He was bound and determined that they would figure out some sort of arrangement that would be in Bella's best interest and simultaneously make them both happy.

Her gaze shot nervously toward the open doorway. "Are you sure your parents are really okay with this?"

"As soon as I told my mom you agreed to stay for a few weeks, she rushed out to go shopping. She's at the store now, picking up who knows what for her first granddaughter. I'm sure she's trying to make up for lost time so, yeah, it's safe to say she's excited."

"What about your dad, though? And your sister's room is just down the hall. I don't want Bella to wake either of them."

He rolled his eyes. "If that happens, we'll move you into Grant's old room in the bunkhouse. Right now his stepson, James, is the only one using it, when he has sleepovers with us guys."

"I can't stay in the bunkhouse."

"Trust me when I promise you that you wouldn't want to." He reached for the tiny clothing she was folding and refolding as she stood in front of the empty dresser drawers. He eyed the shirt and felt his gut twist as he realized he'd be trying to figure out how to dress Bella in this soon. He'd be the one staying up nights with her, feeding and changing her, holding her when she cried.

And unless he could convince Gia to stay, he'd be doing it alone.

As much as he wanted to, Andrew knew there were flaws in the idea. Gia had walked away from him once already, thanks to her sister's machinations. But there was more hurt between them now, especially if Bella really *was* his daughter. It all kept coming back to this one simple fact—both of their futures were dependent on whether Bella was his. If she was, he didn't think Gia would ever forgive him. If she wasn't, he might be able to salvage what they'd once had, but he would lose the one thing that connected them now.

DINNER WITH THE McQuaids wasn't anything like Gia had expected. Instead of returning from a day in the saddle exhausted, Andrew's father, Travis, had been energized, especially when he realized that the entire family—minus Linc—was home for the meal. He couldn't wait to fire up the grill with the kebabs marinating in the refrigerator. Gia, on the other hand, would have liked to beg off and hide in the guest room with Bella, but Andrew's mother, Sarah, was having no part of that. She hadn't released Bella from her grandmotherly clutches since arriving home with her arms laden down from shopping.

"Gia, you realize you're going to have to move into the other spare room once the furniture arrives." Sarah was talking to Gia but making faces at Bella. "There won't be space for the bed once we get the crib, changing table and dressers in there. No, there won't," she cooed at the baby, her voice climbing an octave higher. Bella yawned at her grandmother's singsong tone.

"I should probably put her down." Gia rose from the lawn chairs where everyone had gathered, waiting for the food.

"Nonsense," Sarah stood up and danced her way toward the back door. "I'm happy to do it. You stay and visit with everyone."

"But . . ." Gia shot a pleading glance at Andrew but he gave her a half-shrug of defeat. She slid back into the lounge chair as Sarah headed into the house with her only excuse for escape.

"Gia, how do you like San Diego?" Madison asked. "I've always wanted to go. That's where the navy SEALs train, right?" The young woman's eyes gleamed wickedly and she wiggled her brows.

"Ugh, Mads, stop," Grant ordered. "You're grossing me out."

Bethany, Grant's fiancée, bumped a shoulder against him. "Leave her alone. She's twenty-four. I think she's allowed to move past the guys-have-cooties stage at this point."

"Thank you, Bethany." Madison nodded in the other woman's direction.

"So, spill it? How often do you get to watch them training on the beach? Are they shirtless all the time? And, please, *please*, say they wear Speedos."

Grant jumped up and flailed his hands. "Okay, I'm out. Come on, little man," he said to Bethany's son, James, his fingers moving in sign language as he spoke. "Let's go throw the ball around."

"I'm up for that." Jefferson leapt from his chair, then nudged Jackson with his foot. "You too?"

"I don't know." He glanced at Andrew watching the group quietly from near the grill beside their father. "Depends on whether Andrew's coming or not."

"Not. Unless you want these things burned." Andrew motioned at the grill.

Jackson frowned. "Can I trust you alone with Gia? The last time she was here, you got into a fight with her." Shooting her a quick look, Jackson winked.

The damn troublemaker! He's trying to start shit again.

"Well, this conversation just got interesting." Emma Jordan, Ben's fiancée, scooted forward on her chair.

"Last time? When?" Madison's neck swiveled to pin Andrew with a scowl. "What did you do?"

Andrew laughed as he held up his hands. "What makes you think I did anything? Maybe it was Gia fighting with me."

"Right, Andrew," Emma chimed in with a laugh. "You picked a fight with me and you didn't even know me, remember?"

Gia leaned back in the chair, trying to hide her smile as she basked in the laughter and camaraderie of this family unit, including the two new women who seemed to fit right in. It had been a long time since her family had felt this way—connected and whole—and she couldn't help but wonder how long her sister had been playing her and her parents for fools.

Andrew still insisted that he'd never touched Lorena before New Year's, and her gut told her to believe him. While he was many things—a cocky, arrogant flirt being at the top of her list—he'd never been a liar.

It made her sick to think that she'd turned her back on what they should have had together because she'd so easily believed a lie. If only she'd questioned her sister, pushed for more details, asked Andrew about it up front . . . something. Looking back, the people who had come forward to corroborate Lorena's story were probably friends of her sister. She hadn't known them well, only that they were a few years younger. Yet she'd been so shocked and hurt by Lorena's accusation, she'd readily believed when they told her they'd spotted Lorena leaving the patio with Andrew, her shirt barely buttoned and his hand down her pants.

They'd never spoken to her again afterward. Never so much as waved hello when she'd been home. Gia felt stupid. She'd been played, so easily conned, and her entire future was destroyed because of it.

She had no doubt had it not been for the lie, she and Andrew would have stayed together. They'd have been married. He would have never slept with her sister and they wouldn't be in this mess right now. It was her fault, because she'd trusted in the family loyalty she assumed her sister had.

"You okay?" Andrew leaned over her shoulder to hand her a plate with several steak kebabs.

She looked up at him and her heart was filled with so much regret that it made her physically ache. She'd lost out on so much because of her sister's lies. But she couldn't tell Andrew the truth about how she was feeling. Her thoughts were still too jumbled, too messy, to make any logical sense of them.

"Yeah, I'm okay. At least, I will be. Just tired," she confessed. "Your family's a little crazy."

"You act surprised, but it's not like you didn't know

that," he pointed out as he settled himself at the foot of her lounge chair. He narrowed his eyes, studying her. "Are you sure you're okay?"

Gia nodded, pasting on the best fake smile she could muster as his father approached with plates for himself and his wife. Gia looked anxiously at Sarah when she came back outside. "She's all right?"

"Happily fed, changed and now asleep."

"So, Gia," Travis began, handing his wife her plate. "I understand why the name Bella was chosen. After your mother. But what's Bella's middle name?"

"Maria, why?" She caught Andrew's eye roll and his mother's groan. "What?"

"Travis, give it a rest." Sarah reached over to pat his hand. "You cannot ensure that every child born into this family is named after a historical figure in American history."

"Why not?" Travis sat straighter as he defended himself. "There is nothing wrong with paying homage to the people who made this country great."

His wife patted his knee but Gia didn't miss the patronizing smile she cast his direction. "No, dear, there isn't. But you had your opportunity, and I'm sure our seven children are thrilled with your choices. However, you don't get to name their children."

"I know that," he huffed, and Gia couldn't help but laugh at his crestfallen expression.

"If it makes you feel better, she was named after Mary Todd Lincoln," Gia offered.

"Really?" He sounded surprised but extremely pleased. "You see? Someone else appreciates tradition and history as much as I do."

Andrew leaned close to Gia. "Really?" he whispered.

"No. She was named after my grandmother, but it makes him happy so don't burst his bubble."

Sarah must have heard because she shot Gia a conspiratorial wink. "Travis, go tell the rest of the boys dinner is done." She pushed her husband toward their sons still playing football on the grass. When he left, she ruffled Andrew's hair before patting his knee. "Don't you let this one slip through your fingers again, you hear?"

"Doing my best, Mom," he said, shooting Gia a wink that had the butterflies in her stomach rioting.

Gia almost said something, desperately wanting to set the record straight with Sarah, but Andrew gave her a look that told her it was better to let the woman entertain her fantasies.

The problem was that the fantasy was becoming more real to Gia as well, and she wasn't sure her heart could take it.

ANDREW DIDN'T MISS the panic in Gia's face when his mother assumed they were a couple again. He wanted them to believe it, wanted the entire family to believe it, because the simple fact was that he wasn't letting Gia go again without a fight. He'd managed to keep her at ease during the rest of dinner, but once his mother kicked everyone out of her kitchen, Gia looked slightly lost.

Bella was still sleeping, and the rest of the crew was heading to the bunkhouse for their regular Friday night poker game. It was a family tradition and now they'd included Bethany and Emma. Gia watched nervously as the group headed through the back door.

"Aren't you coming?" Andrew fought the urge to reach for her hand, sliding his into his front pockets instead.

"I don't think so." Glancing back down the hall toward the bedroom she shared with Bella, Gia twisted her mouth to one side. "I think I'll just turn in. Bella will be up soon to eat."

"Come on. When was the last time you had any fun, Gia?"

"Scoot," Sarah said. "I'll take care of Bella. Go have a good time." Sarah urged Gia toward the door by her shoulders. "And take as much of their money as possible. They cleaned me out last weekend."

Gia rolled her lips inward over her teeth, still looking uncertain.

"Or I could take you out to see Jackson's horses." Andrew hadn't forgotten how much she'd loved riding when they'd dated. It was something they'd done for most of their dates. They would just saddle up the horses and head through the pastures for a picnic.

Her eyes brightened. "I can't even remember the last time I've been around a horse."

"Then we need to remedy that."

Andrew held open the back door, letting Gia lead the way. He knew it was his best option if he wanted her to let her guard down. He'd hurt her and was going to have to earn her forgiveness by proving he wouldn't do it again. It was going to take time, the one thing he had a limited supply of, but until then, he was going to have to respect her hesitancy and let her take the lead.

They walked to the barn in silence, but as soon as he slid open the main door and flipped on the lights, several horses whinnied a greeting. The soft *clomp* of their hooves echoed down the aisleway, and a few leaned their heads out of the stalls to see the visitors. Andrew chanced a glance at Gia and was rewarded with the childlike wonder she'd always had when they were around the animals. She moved toward a jet-black mare who tossed her head, demanding attention.

"She's gorgeous."

Her voice held every bit of the awed pleasure he'd hoped for. Gia ran a hand over the mare's cheek and down her sleek neck. Before he could say anything, a high-pitched whinny sounded.

"Oh! She has a baby."

The smoky-colored foal pranced into the stall from the run attached to the outside of the barn as his mother nickered quietly at him, more interested in Gia's attention. Andrew leaned against the side of the stall as the mare slipped her head under Gia's hand, giving him the opportunity to watch Gia freely. This was the woman he remembered. She was vulnerable and happy, trusting and open to experiences. There was a lightness to her now, as if being around the mare had miraculously lifted the thousand-pound weight life had dropped around her shoulders.

"We could go for a ride tomorrow," he offered, moving around to the other side of the mare, rubbing his hand over her broad face.

"Really?" Her eyes lit up like he'd just given her the moon before quickly looking disappointed. "I can't. Bella," she said, as if that explained everything.

Andrew arched a brow and laughed. "You really think that my mother will let you do anything tomorrow? We're going to have to pry her fingers off that child."

Gia frowned again, her face shadowing with her dark thoughts. "I thought that's why I was here. To help you adjust."

Unfortunately he'd brought her full circle, to her lack of trust in him.

"Give her a few days, Gia. She's been pestering all of us to get married and give her grandkids for years. James wasn't a grand*baby*. Now that she has one . . ." He shook his head in wonder. "She's happier than I think I've ever seen her."

The mare, bored with them, turned back into the stall to nudge her foal, and Andrew closed the distance between him and Gia. His palm landed on the door of the stall but his thumb brushed over her hand, igniting a slow, burning desire in him.

"Go for a ride with me tomorrow."

"I have to work at the restaurant and we're supposed to be planning a concert, remember?"

"We'll do it. Tomorrow. I promise."

Gia's scrutiny was intense. Her dark eyes stared into his, as if she was trying to read his thoughts. "Okay," she finally conceded.

It had been a long time since he'd felt excited. So long, in fact, that he barely recognized the sentiment at all. She'd awakened all kinds of emotions in him he'd stopped experiencing after she left town. Looking down at her, the one that struck hardest and burst to the surface was the love he'd once felt for her. The corner of his mouth twitched, lifting in a smile. Andrew ducked his head, unable to resist kissing her.

Gia's hand planted square in his chest and she took a step backward, shaking her head, the movement tossing her hair around her shoulders. "*That* is not what I'm here for."

Damn.

It had been a while since he'd taken a hit this hard to his ego. Of course, it had been a long time since he'd cared about a woman enough to have his ego involved.

Andrew hung his head slightly but shot her the cocky grin that seemed to work magic when he used it. "I guess it's just wishful thinking on my part."

Gia frowned at him. "Maybe we should join that poker game after all."

She still seemed hesitant, but at least there was a hint

of a smile on her perfect lips. "Why, Gia? Are you feeling lucky tonight?"

He realized exactly what he'd said at the same time she did. However, his laughter only made her blush even more.

Chapter Sixteen

EVERYTHING FROM HER neck upward heated, and Gia she wished she could drop through the floor of the barn. Andrew had no way of knowing how badly she'd wanted him to kiss her, or how she'd almost leaned in and kissed him herself. Somehow she'd managed to hide her longing beneath a mask of indifference all evening, but his comment had broken through that facade like a sledgehammer.

His shit-eating grin only solidified the fact that she wasn't fooling anyone about her inability to hide her feelings for him. He knew exactly what he was doing to her, and what dirty thoughts were suddenly taking up residence in her mind. Instead of answering, she turned on her heel, prepared to walk away, until her stubborn pride refused to allow him to have the last word. Gia pivoted back toward him, stepping up to him, her hand landing against his abs.

"As a matter of fact, I *am* going to get lucky, and leave you crying while you kiss the last of your cash goodbye."

Not her best comeback, but with her pulse throbbing through her veins and the thought of climbing him like a vine in the forefront of her mind, it was the best she could come up with. However, that fact only made her feel like a sad, pathetic excuse for a modern woman, especially considering everything that she had recently discovered about him.

Gia stormed out of the barn, determined to take every penny from him tonight, even if she had to cheat to do it.

"Hey, Gia," he called on a laugh, still standing by the stall. "Maybe next time you should think about what you want to say a little longer. That one wasn't very good."

She faced him and flipped up a very modern single-finger salute as she backed out of the barn. His laughter followed her as she hurried to the bunkhouse. Andrew managed to catch up to her at the front porch, reaching for the door just before she could do it herself. He paused with his hand on the knob.

"You shouldn't write alligator checks your bunny rabbit ass can't cash."

She pinched her lips together, refusing to cave to her longing for him. And she wasn't about to let this flirtatious banter get the better of her. She could face her temptations and not give in, even if those temptations took the form of one aggravating, painfully sexy cop. She was a grown woman, *damn it*.

Maybe if she continued to keep repeating that like a mantra she'd eventually believe it.

"You have no clue what my ass is capable of." As she realized her blunder, her blush returned, twice as furious.

The slow, confident smile that spread over Andrew's lips infuriated her, as did the lazy way his gaze slid over her, heating areas of her body she refused to acknowledge. "Actually, I do, and while it's a mighty fine ass, I'm thinking you probably haven't learned any new tricks."

Common sense told her to stop this game now, while she could. Pride, however, told her to make sure the next words out of her mouth wiped the smirk from his arrogant face. Ignoring her better sense, she gave him the most coy smile she could muster and ran a hand down his chest, following the indentation between his rockhard abs.

"Ten years is a long time. I've got tricks that would make a magician proud."

His eyes instantly changed, going from teasing to hungry, as if she'd just flipped a switch. His inhalation caught in his chest. Andrew looked at her like she'd just unleashed a hungry beast.

The point of her comment was to make the bold statement, then walk away, but the desire she could easily read in his eyes had her rooted to the ground, afraid to breathe. As if wading through cement, Gia forced her feet to move and shouldered past him to open the door for herself.

The shouts from the group already gathered inside masked her yelp of surprise as Andrew smacked her rear as she walked past.

His arm was firm as it wrapped around her waist from behind, his voice hot and gravelly as he leaned to whisper in her ear, his five-o'clock shadow brushing her skin and causing goose bumps to break out on her flesh. "Don't make promises you won't keep, Gia. That's just cruel."

SEVERAL HANDS OF poker and nearly one hundred dollars up, Gia slid all her chips into the pot as she confidently smiled at Emma across the table. The other woman narrowed her eyes in response.

"I don't think I like you very much after all, Gia," she said with a laugh, throwing her cards facedown onto the table. "I'm out. You two are killing me tonight. If Ben hadn't left for work, he would have whipped you both."

"Sorry, Emma." Gia really didn't want to take anyone's money but Andrew's, However, with luck like she was having tonight, she should have forgotten holding a concert and joined a poker tour. She was on fire. "Blame Andrew for shooting off his mouth and practically daring me to take his money."

Andrew arched a humored brow at her from across the table but remained silent as Grant scrutinized both of their expressions. "Normally I'd stay in just for spite, but you two are getting out of control." He tossed his cards onto the pile of chips in the middle of the table. "There has to be at least three hundred in that pot," he pointed out.

"I'm out," Jefferson proclaimed.

Jackson, Madison and Bethany had all folded in the first round of betting, leaving Andrew and Gia as the only two left with a stake in the game. She eyed him. "That means it's between you and me, again."

Andrew nodded slowly, perusing the cards in his hand and twirling a chip on the table. "But I'm the one with the chips and you're all in," he pointed out.

"Only a coward would bet higher just to knock me out of the game. Besides, that not how it's really played."

"True." He tapped his chin with the chip. "But those are the house rules."

"Come on, Andrew, bet or fold." Jackson rolled his eyes. "Stop dragging this out forever."

"I don't know." He scrunched up his face. "I have a good hand, Gia. I'm pretty confident I'll win."

"You're confident because you cheat," Grant pointed out.

Andrew took the ribbing in stride and focused on Gia, which made her nervous. "What do you think you could add to sweeten the pot? Since you're out of money," he clarified.

She wasn't giving in that easily. "What do you want?"

Jackson and Jefferson both laughed as Bethany shot

Grant a look that said she had no doubt what Andrew would ask for.

Emma shook her head sympathetically. "Oh, Gia, you're just asking for trouble now. Fold before we all get grossed out."

Madison, on the other hand, looked smugly thrilled as she leaned back in her chair and crossed her arms, content to watch the drama unfolding before her.

"I'm just laying down one ground rule," Grant said as he rose. "There will be no stripping at this table. I do not want to see that naked." He waved a hand at Andrew. "I'm getting a beer, if anyone wants to join me in escaping."

"I do." Bethany jumped up, followed closely by Emma, who tugged on Madison's arm.

Andrew continued to stare at Gia from across the table, patiently, but looking like he was ready to devour her all the same. Madison nudged Jefferson. "Come on," she muttered.

"Aw," Jackson complained as he pushed himself to standing. "Just when everything gets fun."

"Shut up, nerd." She shoved the twins into the kitchen, where Gia could see them over the bar, milling around the refrigerator, pretending to discuss the merits of Andrew's latest home brew while pretending they weren't watching the two of them from across the room.

"So? What's it going to be, Gia?"

She shrugged. "Again, what do you want?"

"You."

His answer was so matter-of-fact it shocked her. Her entire body seemed to flush with a flood of deliciously acute lust. Her heart stopped, just before it kicked into high gear. Gia wasn't sure if the kitchen had really gone silent or whether she'd simply blocked out everything but Andrew's sultry voice. She wanted him to be telling the truth, almost as much as she wanted to agree, to call his bluff, but she couldn't catch her breath, let alone find her voice. She bit her lip, her hand hovering with her cards over the pot.

"Too rich for me," she whispered.

He didn't hesitate. "Okay, how about you trust me completely until you head back to San Diego?"

"Why are you doing this?"

"All you have to do is promise to trust me, like you used to, until you head back. That's what? A few weeks?"

"I thought you said not to make promises I couldn't keep," she reminded him, glancing toward the kitchen. The six people inside had crept to the edge of the bar and immediately jumped back, acting as if they hadn't been eavesdropping.

"So don't. Keep it." He moved a hand over the stack of chips. "Are you in?"

"I'll give you five."

"Seven," he countered, his eyes gleaming with mirth.

"Six," she offered.

"Six and a kiss."

Gia knew he was playing her, knew he had something in mind for the next six days if she said yes, but she couldn't figure out what it was. She'd already agreed to stay here for the next two weeks to help him acclimate to being a father, and it wasn't like he would ever force her into anything. He was actually the one doing her a favor by letting her stay with Bella a little longer. What harm could it do to pretend she trusted him?

And a kiss. Don't forget that.

Gia stared at his mouth. The perfect mouth that just a few days ago had nearly brought her to tears of ecstasy. Just the thought of kissing him again made her squeeze her thighs together under the table in an effort to contain her desire. His smile broadened, as if he'd read the direction of her thoughts. But it was that same overconfident smirk he got when he was bullshitting that gave her the push she needed to agree. Because if she won this hand, she'd walk away with her pride and a few hundred dollars of Andrew's cash.

"I'm in . . . if you go all in."

SHE THOUGHT HE was bluffing. Andrew could see it in her eyes.

She was still seeing him as the young man he'd been, but he'd learned a lot after she'd left. He'd learned how to con a con man. He'd learned how to convince criminals he was their friend. He'd gone undercover more times than he could count. He was more than accustomed to deception and was good at it when he chose to be. But he wasn't lying this time.

He wanted her and he had a winning hand.

Andrew hesitated when Gia made her demand, acting as if he was contemplating folding, as if the full house of aces over ladies wasn't enough to win. "I don't know, Gia. That's pretty stiff."

She cocked her head to one side and arched a brow at his innuendo. "Nice."

The corner of his mouth inched up even higher. "It will be." He shoved the four piles of chips to the center of the table. "I'm in."

Gia flipped her cards over and leaned back in her chair, crossing her arms. "Full house. Kings over nines."

"Yes!" Jackson shouted from his spot in the kitchen, leaning across the bar to watch them.

Andrew shot his younger brother a glare, irritated with his family watching his love life play out like it was some sort of sporting event.

"Ooh," Jackson groaned. "Nice try, Andrew. You almost got her."

Gia wiggled her brows at him, leaning forward to collect her winnings, but Andrew stopped her with a hand over the pile. "Yeah, it would have been . . . if I wasn't sporting the same hand but with aces over queens."

"Oh!" came the yell from one of his brothers in the kitchen.

"Holy shit!"

"That cheating son of a bitch," Emma yelled.

"How?" Gia stared at him in disbelief, glancing from his face to the cards and back again. "Did you cheat?"

Andrew leaned backward and crossed his arms behind his head. "Gia, is this the way to start our six days of trust? With you already questioning my integrity? You need to learn to trust, honey."

She closed her eyes and shook her head, still mildly in shock.

"Well, that's a night, guys. I'm quitting while I'm ahead," Andrew informed them.

"Yeah, me too," Jefferson said on a yawn. "Dad's already warned us he wants our butts on horses at seven, ready to head out."

"Speaking of which, Jackson, do you mind if we take a couple of your horses out for a ride tomorrow?" Andrew began clearing the poker table.

"Go ahead. Take Ruby and Slick. They both need the exercise." He gathered up the empty beer bottles and set them to one side for Andrew to clean and reuse later.

The group had the house put back into a semblance of order quickly, and Grant and Bethany took Emma home. The twins headed to their rooms, leaving Madison, Andrew and Gia in the living room. Maddie eyed Andrew, silently questioning whether he wanted her to offer to walk with Gia back to the house. He gave her an almost imperceptible shake of his head. She rolled her eyes, and he knew he was going to owe her, again.

"Oh, damn, I forgot. I'm supposed to help Jefferson with that . . ." Maddie paused, trying to find some sort of excuse, which pretty much made her the most unconvincing liar of all time. ". . . résumé."

"Résumé?" Gia's brows shot up dubiously. "At midnight?"

"Yes. He's applying for a job with the school I work at and needs to turn in the application tomorrow."

Andrew gave her a thumbs-up just as Gia turned to look at him, shooting him a sardonic look.

"Come on," he said with a chuckle. "I'll walk you back to the house before Maddie comes up with an excuse worse than that one. Thanks a lot, Maddie. Good thing you're quick on your feet."

"We can't all bluff like an undercover cop, you douche."

Chapter Seventeen

GIA COULDN'T BLAME anyone but herself for the mess she was facing. Damn her pride. It never failed to get her into one mess or another.

She knew she was overreacting. She'd agreed to trust Andrew for six days. Less than a week. It wasn't really that bad in the grand scheme of things, and she was planning to head back to San Diego right after the concert anyway. Whether to return to her lonely existence and make it the life she wanted or to quit her job and tie up the loose ends before returning to Hidden Falls was still undecided.

A knot of fear began to bunch in her stomach at the thought. When she'd left Hidden Falls permanently ten years ago, it had been with the intent of making something of her future, and that centered on the premise that her future didn't have Andrew in it. She'd sealed that decision the day she gave Andrew back his engagement ring. Never once had she planned on returning to Hidden Falls. And coming back with nothing to show for her time away except a job where she was easily replaced.

Yet now she was back, regardless of her detailed plans, and even worse, she was practically living with the man who'd derailed her plans the last time. There was no getting away from Andrew now, not if she wanted to remain a part of Bella's life. Unless she wanted to challenge his paternity, Gia would have to make nice with Andrew, and that meant playing along with this stupid bet she'd lost.

Refusing to look at him as they walked back toward the house in silence, Gia saw him glance in her direction occasionally, as if he wanted to start a conversation. For one reason or another, he remained quiet. Reaching out, he opened the back gate. In the distance, one owl called to another and the crickets chirped, adding to the melodic nighttime symphony. Ahead of her, the pool sparkled beneath the moonlight as frogs croaked in harmony.

She wanted to talk to Andrew but wasn't sure what to say. There was so much that had gone on in their past, so many beautiful memories that she'd forced herself to forget after what she believed was his betrayal. Finding out that it was likely a lie caused them to come rushing back, overwhelming her, flooding her with melancholy, even as hope trickled into her heart.

The fact that he wanted her to trust him again could be the start of a new chapter for them. But she wasn't sure whether he wanted to forget their past and start new, or build on what had happened, mistakes and all.

"Andrew?"

"Hmm?" He stopped as they reached the back door of the house. His mother had left a light on in the kitchen, and the soft glow filtered through the small window in the door, shadowing his face and making his expression unreadable, but not his posture. With his hands in his pockets and his shoulders slightly hunched, he was uncertain. This confident man was unsure with her.

She wanted to ask him why he'd made the bet, what he was hoping to accomplish in the next six days, or where he saw this tentative friendship going, but she couldn't bring herself to form the words. Instead, the question she heard fall from her lips surprised her.

"You swear you didn't sleep with Lorena while we were together?"

He inhaled deeply and glanced to his right, as if the answer could be found in the distant darkness. He took a step closer, and the light cast a glow in his dark eyes. His hands slid up her arms, resting on her shoulders.

"I swear to you that I never even looked at another woman after you agreed to go out with me. I fell for you hard and fast, Gia. While we were together, I never touched another woman. When you broke things off, I went a little nuts. That's why I went into the police academy early. It gave me something to focus other than the fact that I'd just lost the only thing that mattered to me."

"I'm sorry," she whispered, her gaze falling to his Adam's apple as he swallowed.

Andrew pulled her into his arms, holding her close, enveloping her against the hard wall of his chest. She inhaled the scent of him, letting herself relax into his embrace, realizing for the first time that she wasn't the only one who'd been cut deeply by her sister's lies. Instinctively she wrapped her arms around his waist, her fingers gliding up the lean muscles of his back. She felt him press his cheek to the top of her head, his hands winding in her hair.

"You have no reason to be sorry, Gia. You didn't do anything wrong. You thought I betrayed you."

"I should have asked you. I should have trusted you." Her admission fell against his chest where his heart beat beneath her cheek, steady and strong like the man in her arms. "If I had . . ."

"Shh." Andrew pressed his lips against the top of her head. "It wouldn't have changed anything." His voice was sad, as if the realization was painful.

She looked up at him. "You don't think so?"

Andrew shook his head, his eyes shadowed from within now. "We obviously had issues that we hadn't dealt with. If it hadn't happened then, it would have eventually. Either while you were away at school or while I was in the academy. We both needed to grow up."

"We've both done that."

"Well," he said, giving her a mischievous grin, "you have. I don't think I ever will."

The sweet face of the baby inside the house filled her mind, and her heart swelled with adoration. "Bella will help you do that."

She felt the tension in the muscles of his back at the mention of his daughter. Andrew nodded but didn't say anything more about the subject. She wondered at the sudden change but was too self-conscious to ask about it. At one time, she wouldn't have hesitated to ask him anything. He'd been an open book to her. But she didn't know his thoughts anymore, and didn't have a right to ask. They'd become different people.

She slid out of his embrace. "I should head inside."

"I'll be in for breakfast and we'll pack a lunch before we head out."

"Okay, night."

"Sweet dreams, Gia."

It had been what he used to say to her when they were younger, the way he would sign off their late-night phone calls. She found comfort in the familiarity and felt a blossom of hope spreading in her chest. The memory of the way she'd always answered bubbled to the surface, and she debated remaining silent. Maybe they could maneuver their way through the labyrinth of their mistakes. Making her choice, she opened the kitchen door, bathing them in the light from inside.

"Only because they'll be about you."

She could barely make out his faint smile as she closed the door behind her.

ANDREW WOKE THE next morning with a smile on his face. He hadn't slept this well in years and knew it had to do with Gia's parting words last night. It had felt so right holding her that when he wished her good-night, he hadn't even realized what he'd said until she responded. It also made him realize that there might be a chance Gia would forgive him, a glimmer of hope that he could convince her to give their relationship another try.

He hopped into the shower, careful not to wake Ben, who'd come in after his shift at the fire department sometime after six a.m and had another shift today. However, Andrew had the next two days off, which meant his dad was going to expect him to help out around the ranch, unless he could convince him there was something more important that needed to be done.

And there was. He needed to convince Gia to return to Hidden Falls, permanently.

By the time he entered his kitchen for a cup of coffee, Jefferson was already dressed and waiting for Jackson. "Morning," he grumbled.

"Morning," Andrew greeted him, taking a mug from the cabinet and pouring himself a cup. "Where are you guys heading to today?"

Jefferson rubbed his eyes. "Dad wants to start moving the cattle farthest out closer to the house today. Tomorrow he's planning on all of us being there to bring them in for sorting."

"Shit, tomorrow?" Andrew asked. Jefferson nodded slowly. Sorting was a family affair and took every member, plus a few neighbors, to get done. "I totally forgot."

"Well, you better un-forget, because Dad isn't going to listen to any excuses, not even when it comes to having a new baby. He'll just give you some bullshit about how he ran herd with one of us on his back or something."

"Do we even have enough people?" He'd planned on worming his way out of any work this weekend to spend whatever time he could with Gia and Bella. "Maybe I can convince him to put it off until next weekend."

"Next weekend, Ben will be working and you only have Saturday off, which is why we planned on tomorrow. Everyone is here." Jefferson narrowed his eyes at his brother. "Are you trying to wiggle your way out of this? Because I will personally kick your ass."

"Who's kicking whose ass?" Jackson sauntered into the room looking far too dolled up to spend his day working from horseback. His hair was styled with some sort of product making it stand up in spikes, and he'd put on a brand-new denim shirt instead of one of his usual raggedy faded T-shirts. Andrew had no idea when his brother had bought the dress boots he wore, but he was positive they'd never seen a day's work.

"Where the hell are you going?" Jefferson asked with a guffaw.

"I'm going to saddle Ruby for Gia, why?"

Andrew nearly choked on his coffee. "No, you're not."

"In that getup?" Jefferson snorted. "You look like you just stepped off the cover of some Western wear catalog."

Jefferson could barely contain his laughter as he rose and made his way to his twin, pressing on the spikes of hair, which sprang back into their original position as soon as he removed his hand. "And what the hell is in your hair?"

Jackson scowled at Jefferson before turning his attention to Andrew, casually sipping his coffee. "You going to stop me?"

He didn't even bother to meet his brother's gaze. "Yep." He wasn't about to give Jackson the satisfaction of getting a rise out of him again. "Gia and I are just now back on amiable ground. I'm not going to let you screw that up."

A wide grin split Jackson's face. "Good."

That got Andrew's attention. His gaze snapped up to Jackson's. "What do you mean, 'good'?"

"I mean, good." Jackson turned around and started walking back down the hall toward his room. "That means I can get these awful boots off and quit busting your balls. It's about time you fixed things with Gia."

"I never had a problem with her," Andrew pointed out, feeling the irritation with his brother's meddling creeping over him. "She had one with me."

Jackson came back into the kitchen. "Dude, you slept with her sister."

"Allegedly," Jefferson pointed out, much to Andrew's relief. At least there was someone taking his side.

"I think your kid sleeping in the house takes 'allegedly' out of the equation."

Andrew sipped his coffee, unwilling to engage in this conversation with his youngest brother. What had or hadn't happened between him and Lorena was none of his business. If not for the fact that Lorena had made the entire matter a family issue by publicly declaring him the father, he might have been able to keep this quiet until he found out the truth. Because the more he thought about that night, the more he realized Ben was right. The likelihood of him being Bella's father was complete bullshit.

Not that it mattered now. He'd signed the acknowledgment and accepted custody. But if Bella wasn't his daughter, he could sign off his parental rights to Gia.

The first thing he needed to do was to get a paternity test—not one that would end up on the records, either—one that was simply for his benefit, to satisfy his own need to know.

"What's got your dick in a twist this morning?" Jackson kicked a foot at the leg of the chair.

"You're just talking out your ass, and I don't feel like dealing with it." He rose and headed for the front door. "I'm going for a ride with Gia today, and we'll deal with the past as needed, including what's best for Bella. It doesn't concern you."

Jackson followed him. "Gia's my friend, Bella's my niece and you're my brother. We're family and they're part of our family now. It concerns all of us, Andrew. Stop trying to be such a lone wolf."

Andrew paused with his hand on the door, realizing

his brother was right. They were a close-knit family and when one person was in trouble, they all pulled together to help. He might take issue with Jackson's methods for getting him to step up with Gia, but he couldn't deny that it was effective.

"He means well," Jefferson pointed out, jerking a thumb at Jackson. "It's not his fault he got the looks and none of the brains."

Andrew faced his brothers. "I appreciate the sentiment, but for right now, there's nothing you guys can do. There's nothing *I* can do. The ball's sort of in Gia's court."

Jackson shook his head. "Well, be careful, because I'm not sure she'd decided yet whether she'd rather play ball or bust them," he warned.

GIA HELD THE small soft-sided ice chest with the lunch Sarah was still busy packing for her ride today with Andrew. She'd already put in four turkey sandwiches, brownies, potato salad and some fresh strawberries. How much more could Andrew possibly eat? She'd already seen the man with no shirt on and there wasn't an ounce of fat on him. Where in the world could he possibly put that much food?

"Oh, here." Sarah handed her the container with the leftover kebabs from the night before. "He'll probably eat these too."

"You've got to be kidding!" Gia hadn't meant to blurt it out, but the bag of food weighed more than Bella.

"Nope. That son of mine can pack away the food. That's why this kitchen looks like it feeds an army." Sarah laughed.

"Because each one of those brothers of mine can eat as much as one," Maddie explained, glancing down at Bella, sound asleep against her chest.

"Are you sure you don't mind me going?" Gia asked the pair for the fourth time this morning.

"Go," Maddie insisted. "I'm happy if I can get her away from her grandmother for ten minutes so I can cuddle with her myself."

Sarah shot her daughter a warning look and wagged her finger. "You watch it, miss. Until someone else in this family has another baby, you guys are going to just have to make due with me spoiling the grandchildren I finally have."

"Cut me some slack, Mom," she teased. "I'm still paying off my college loans. Maybe once I have my own place and, you know, a husband, then you can worry about me having kids."

"Then I guess I'll just have to continue spoiling Bella and James for a while." Sarah winked at Gia as the back door opened and Andrew entered, looking extremely sexy in his tight Wranglers and a dark T-shirt stretching over his chest like a second skin.

Gia felt her breath catch at the sight of him, but when his dark gaze caressed her, she felt every part of her from the waist down turn to Jell-O. This man could turn her on like a light switch, and the thought wasn't exactly conducive to keeping her wits about her when she was near him.

"Morning." He directed the comment at the three of them, but his gaze never left Gia's face.

"Okay, Princess. Time for you to go see Daddy." Maddie rose and walked toward him, slipping Bella into Andrew's arms without waiting for him to ask.

Andrew took his daughter and cuddled her close. Bella blinked, staring up at him as the movement jarred her from her nap, but she didn't protest. Gia watched the pair connect with a simple look, and when Andrew lowered his face toward the baby's, her heart lurched slightly. As touching as it was to see them together, it reminded her that her time with Bella was short.

"Well, good morning to you too, Sweet Pea." He pressed a gentle kiss to the top of Bella's forehead. "Next time we'll take the truck so you can go with us."

"We could do that now, if you prefer," Gia offered.

"Today is for you, Gia. It's been a long time since you were able to ride, and I remember how much you used to love it. Trust me."

She questioned whether he heard the innuendo in his words. Logic assured her that he would never be that bold in front of his mother and sister, but his hungry gaze made her second-guess her assumption.

Desire swirled in her belly, hot and languid, and she could practically hear the sizzle of their connection. It vibrated between them like a living, breathing entity that threatened to consume them both. Gia licked her lips, staring at the man who had long ago awakened the passion in her and wondered where she'd ever gotten the strength to walk away from him, because right now, he made her feel weak-kneed.

Maddie cleared her throat quietly, breaking the silence that must have grown awkward between them. "I'll take her back so you can go saddle the horses, Andrew."

Sarah eyed the two of them with a calculating smile on her face. "Why don't you *both* go saddle the horses. I'll finish packing the food and bring it out to you." She pressed her hand into Gia's back, forcing her to move toward Andrew. "Go."

With little room left for debate, Gia followed Andrew out the back door and toward the barn, feeling slightly like a lamb being led to slaughter. "You're not going to kill me and leave my body for the coyotes, are you?" she teased.

Andrew chuckled. "I was actually just wondering if you, Maddie and Mom had been planning the same thing for me."

Chapter Eighteen

ANDREW WATCHED GIA in the saddle. She'd always been a natural, taking to riding like a pro, but he'd never realized quite how seductively her hips rocked in the saddle. Or how her long hair curved in dark waves over her back, swaying in time with the mare's steps and making him remember all the times he'd run his fingers through those tresses, or how satiny they'd felt when she'd fallen asleep on his chest.

"This way, right?" She glanced back at him over her shoulder as she pointed toward the creek. The sound of the gently gurgling water was barely noticeable through the stand of pines as the horses' hooves snapped the branches, pinecones crunching where they littered the ground. "The trail sort of diverges right here. See?"

She pulled the mare to a halt and waited for him to ride up beside her. The trail split into four different directions, created by various paths of cattle. He knew that they all led to the same place, but Gia wouldn't know that. He pointed to the one on the right.

"That one will take us around the trees, but it's a straight, flat route. These—" he pointed to the two on the left "—will take us downhill and around the bend. They're steeper paths and slightly rocky, so they're a bit more dangerous, but that one—" he pointed at the one that continued straight ahead "—will head directly toward the creek. It's not as troublesome as the two on the left but not quite as easy as the one on the right. Your choice."

She twisted her mouth to one side, looking adorable as she tried to decide.

"You do realize this isn't a life-and-death decision. We'll get to the creek whichever way we choose."

She arched a saucy brow at him and bumped her horse in the ribs lightly, directing the mare straight ahead. "Let's take this one."

He gave her a lopsided grin. "Splitting the difference?"

"Something like that."

Andrew knew Gia had never been much of a risk-taker, and even choosing the middle path was a bit of a gamble for her. It was also the reason he'd been sur-prised when she'd taken him up on his bet. But once she made up her mind, Gia stayed her course, as if changing her mind made her seem irresponsible. He supposed it was that steadfastness that made her so reliable for her

family, but he wondered if anyone else realized the toll
it took on her.

They rode the rest of the way in silence. It was too
difficult to hold a conversation when he was behind her,
but he could see the tension leaving her. The farther
they rode away from the house, the deeper her breaths
became. The more distance between her and the troubles connected to Bella, the more her brow smoothed as
she took in her surroundings.

Squirrels leapt through the branches overhead, following their path, barking like tiny sentinel guard dogs.
A scrub jay swooped down and landed on a low-hanging
branch ahead of them, squawking a warning as they
rode beneath it. When they came out of the thicket, the
sunlight shone brightly over the meadow, highlighting
the rich green grass. Two mule deer does with fawns at
their sides paused their meal to stare at the intruders.

"Let's go to the other side and leave them plenty of
room," Andrew suggested.

He led the way to a cozy area, sheltered from the glaring sunlight but only partially shaded. He dismounted
and tethered his horse to a nearby branch, loosening the
saddle. As she walked her horse up to him, he repeated
the process on her mare.

"You hungry?" he asked, glancing down at his watch.

"Not really, but feel free to eat if you are. Your mother
loaded a ton of food into that pack."

She wandered closer to the water, finding a rock that

hung over what was, in reality, a narrow, slow-moving river tributary, even if they'd grown up calling it a creek. She slid her boots and socks off, setting them to one side of the rock and dipping her toes into the water. It was lower than normal due to the recent drought conditions, but it still had plenty of water to pool and create a couple of swimming areas. That was more than most people had on ranches around here. When the rains came, it would flood its banks and saturate the meadow, creating the lush grass that would feed the cattle over the summer, as well as the wildlife that visited regularly.

Gia leaned back on her palms and tipped her face skyward, the light filtering through the trees and dappling her face with golden light. She inhaled deeply, releasing it slowly. The long waves of her hair fell over her arms, the tips just reaching the top of her hands, swaying as she shook her head, letting the whisper of a breeze feather over her face.

Andrew felt his heart stop in his chest as he watched her, forgetting the soft-sided cooler in his hand. She looked like a wood nymph caught in the midst of sunning herself. He was afraid that any movement from him might break the spell.

"I don't think you ever brought me here before." Gia glanced back at him, frowning when she saw his face. "What?"

Andrew swallowed past the lump that formed in his throat. "Nothing."

He shook his head, trying to clear it slightly from the

vision of her that had rendered him nearly speechless. "I did, once. It was right after we'd started dating, but it was late spring and the water was pretty high." He dropped the cooler behind the rock she was on and leaned his hip against it. "As a matter of fact, this rock was probably partially underwater then."

"Really? I don't remember it." She smiled and it lit up her eyes, making her look young and carefree again as she took in the woods across the creek. "It's so peaceful here. You're lucky, you know."

Gia turned back toward him, still smiling softly. It was the first time he'd seen her completely open and vulnerable since her return. It was also the first time he'd seen her happy. Unable to stop himself, Andrew reached a finger forward and brushed a strand of her hair back from where it was caught between her lips.

"I used to be," he agreed. "But I took things I shouldn't have for granted."

"Andrew," she protested, looking back at the water with a sad exhalation, making him wish he'd kept quiet. "We both did. We were too young and naive. We thought what we had would just last forever."

He wanted to kick himself for being the reason her smile disappeared. "You don't think it would have?"

She rolled her eyes as she looked in his direction again, but her lips spread in a sardonic smile and she sat up, pulling her knees to her chest and wrapping her arms around them. "Please. I've heard the gossip about *the* Andrew McQuaid over the past ten years. People like talking about you McQuaid boys, and from what's been said, you've given Linc a run for his money in the woman department."

Andrew knew people had talked about how often he'd dated. He'd been the McQuaid to tame, right up there with Linc, who was constantly on the cover of some rag intent on speculating about his love life. But Andrew wasn't famous like his brother. His exploits had been Hidden Falls' favorite fodder for the small-town gossip mill at its finest—barely based on reality at its core and wildly exaggerated for drama.

"I haven't exactly been sitting at home," he admitted, "but don't believe half of what you hear. What about you?"

She shrugged half-heartedly. "I've been pushing forward in my career so long that I didn't stop to think I might be missing out on anything."

"You never met anyone at work?"

"There have been a few, but it's kind of hard to date men when you're their boss. It sort of creates a conflict of interest."

"What about clients?"

She shook her head. "Nope, not allowed. Not that I would have anyway. Most of the clients I deal with have all been very, very old men with their hands tightly gripping their corporations' finances."

"A bunch of money-grubbers, huh?"

She shrugged again. "Not really, but cautious, especially when you try to convince them that social media is a legitimate marketing pool. Some are really old-school, which made being a woman in the business difficult. Regardless of how well I might prove myself or my ideas."

Andrew fought the grin that tugged the corners of his mouth at the thought of several old men in suits trying to argue anything with Gia. She was a pro when it came to debating. She could be as passionate as a politician and as conniving as a con man when she knew she was right.

"What?"

"Just trying to imagine anyone telling you no."

"It didn't happen often," she said, returning his grin.

Andrew's heart lurched in his chest. God, he wanted this woman.

Not just physically, although fighting his desire for her was becoming exhausting. He missed the woman who'd been his friend. He'd missed the connection they'd shared where something as simple as a look spoke volumes, and how her smile made him feel like he'd been kissed by angels.

Andrew didn't want her to see his reaction, so he bent to retrieve two water bottles from the cooler and passed her one. She took the bottle, their fingers barely touching. He wondered if she felt the same electric shock he did at the contact. If so, she didn't show it.

"Thanks."

He took a long gulp. "So, did you like it? Your job?"

"Yeah, I do." Her tone belied her words. The lack of

enthusiasm was clear; Gia was lying. Andrew just stared at her, arching his brow in question. "It's okay," she clarified. "Parts get old, but I've worked too hard to just walk away and start over. I mean, my parents need my help now, but for how long? Once the restaurant is back on track . . ."

And that was really the crux of the issue. She'd spent the last ten years working toward a career that wasn't fulfilling her. Now she had Bella and, between her and the restaurant, an excuse to leave it all behind, but Lorena had stripped that away from her just as quickly as she'd given it. At every turn, Lorena was working so hard to make her sister miserable, but without intending to, she was giving Gia exactly what she needed—a reason to return. Now he just had to give her a reason to stay.

"Life's too short to do anything that doesn't make you happy, Gia."

"Is that what's worked for you? Doing what feels good?"

She wasn't accusing him, but the guilt pulsed through his veins all the same. "Touché. I guess my method isn't foolproof either. We're a pathetic pair, aren't we? Maybe we should form a support group."

She laughed. "The Great Fakers, huh?"

"I've never had to fake anything with you."

Her gaze jumped up to meet his again, and he saw her eyes go soft and dark. "Andrew . . ."

He wanted to confess everything to her. How he'd

been trying to forget her memory for the past ten years. How no woman had ever measured up to her. How he'd never stopped loving her.

But he could see remorse in her expression, the look in her eyes that told him she wasn't ready to hear those things. She wanted to believe he'd moved on, that she'd moved on, that what they had was dead, or at least mostly dead. He couldn't hurt her again by dredging up the past that she thought was over and buried.

Instead, Andrew cleared his throat and moved back to the cooler, pulling out a sandwich for himself and holding one up to her. Unfolding herself from the protective embrace she had around her knees, she took it, careful not to touch his fingers this time.

"So, what are your plans now?" He slid down to a boulder near hers but lower to the ground. "Have you considered the idea of moving back here? It wouldn't exactly be starting over."

"It's crossed my mind," she admitted. Andrew tried to temper the hope that soared at her confession. "Especially with everything going on. I'd like to be closer for my dad in case he needs me." Gia shook her head. "I don't see how he's going to be able to focus on getting better and run the place the way they used to without help."

"I don't think it's possible, Gia. Your dad should be focused on his health, not which entrée to put on the menu this weekend."

"Which is what Mom says and why she wants to sell. They'd be set financially if they did."

"And the problem?" If that were the case, Andrew didn't see why there would be any question as to the right decision for her parents.

"Dad would be miserable. Rossetti's is his life. Rusty says he's actually gotten worse since he quit working at the restaurant." She ran her hand over her eyes. "I don't mean to lay my issues on you. You've got enough on your plate now."

Andrew reached his hand out and squeezed her knee. "Gia, that's what friends are for, and regardless of what's happened, we *are* still friends, right?"

Chapter Nineteen

A FRIEND WOULD want to see him happy, even if it was with someone else. A friend would wish him the best, even at the expense of her own desires. A friend wouldn't have to think twice about calling herself a friend, but, the truth was, Gia didn't want to be his friend.

Did he have any clue what he was asking of her? How was she supposed to forget the fact that she would always see Andrew as the love of her life, the one man she'd have given up anything for? Even worse, how was she supposed to forget that he'd slept with her sister? Not only had he slept with her but they had conceived a child, one she'd almost raised. In the face of both situations, she didn't have it in her to turn him away.

The sad fact was that Gia still loved him. She'd never stopped, even when she'd broken off their engagement. Finding out that Lorena's accusation, as well as her proof, had been a lie had only made her feel like a fool for believing her sister.

She couldn't even fault him for sleeping with Lorena on New Year's. Sure, it had been stupid, but he'd simply made the same mistake she had—putting her trust in the wrong person to do the right thing. However, there was nothing either of them could do to change the situation now, and she sure as hell couldn't be *just* a friend to him.

"Of course we are," she assured him, praying that the lie sounded convincing as it slipped out.

"Then you can drop whatever burdens you need to into my lap anytime."

He smiled at her and she could see the dimple deepen in his cheek. Gia's heart flipped in her chest and pounded heavily against her rib cage, like a bird attempting to escape.

"Glad to hear it." She sat up straighter, trying to control her emotions. She needed to get away from these dangerous topics. "I really need concrete plans for this concert. I'm thinking of holding a VIP show on Friday with some of Dad's best recipes. Linc could perform an 'unplugged' concert for a select group of about two hundred."

"But will that bring in enough money?"

"No, but it would bring in Linc's die-hard fans. And, at one hundred dollars a ticket—"

"That's twenty thousand dollars, before expenses. It would make a dent," he finished her thought. "What about the next two nights?"

"The ballroom can only hold about four hundred people, which is a plenty for local events and weddings but not for a concert. We'd have to break it into at least two concerts." She bit her lower lip. "Unless you think we could convince him to add a third?"

"Might be pushing the limits of his voice. But we could ask him. I'll call him when we get back and the three of us can do a conference call. You're going to need to hire more bartenders," he pointed out. "And wait staff. Rossetti's will be booming as soon as people start getting wind of what you're planning."

She hadn't considered that. Once she started advertising the concert, more people would begin showing up, even if they didn't come to the concert. It was the underlying purpose—to drive more traffic to the restaurant, thereby boosting her parents' income and making selling an unnecessary option—but finding staff and hiring and training them took time, something she had little of.

"I could probably recommend a few people, or maybe you could hire temporary help from a catering company. I have a friend, Charlene, who worked as a waitress for one, and they are always looking to pick up more hours."

It was a fantastic suggestion, but Gia hated the fact that his idea wasn't the part she'd honed in on as she read between the lines.

"A girlfriend?" She arched her brow in question, feeling slightly satisfied when he had the good sense to look sheepish.

"Not really. We went out once," he clarified. "Why? Jealous?" he teased, wiggling his brows.

But she couldn't deny the jealousy that flashed through her. It was safer for her to simply remain silent. Luckily he took that as encouragement to go on.

"Anyway, I just thought it would give you the extra hands you'll need without the added expense and time of training new employees. I'll call Missy over at the printers and confirm that they'll donate the tickets and posters for you too."

"You're doing all the heavy lifting for me," she pointed out before biting into her sandwich. Sourdough and roasted turkey made her mouth water and she groaned out loud. "Holy crap, is that pesto?" The taste of basil and pine nuts exploded on her taste buds. She looked inside the bread at the ingredients Sarah had added. "And provolone?"

Andrew laughed. "Mom makes a killer turkey."

"I'll say." She sighed with bliss and took another bite, chewing slowly and closing her eyes. "I have to find out her secret and convince Dad that we need this on the lunch menu."

She opened her eyes and saw him staring at her. The second sigh that had been about to escape caught in her throat. He had a hungry look in his eyes but it wasn't for the food his mother had packed. Her body instantly imploded, her pulse racing while every inch of her skin tingled with anticipation.

Which was ridiculous, because she couldn't act on

her desire for Andrew. She'd made that mistake last week and look how badly that had turned out.

But she wanted to.

"Don't look at me that way." Her voice was barely a breath, but her plea was loud and clear.

"What way?" He set his food aside and rose, moving closer but stopping when he was directly in front of her with his hands on either side of her legs.

"Andrew." She felt like she was always scolding him or warning him off. This didn't sound like she was reprimanding him now. She sounded like she was begging him to continue.

"You mean, like I want to kiss you until you beg me to stop? Or to hear you say my name with a sweet sigh like the one you just let out over a sandwich?" His eyes gleamed and his voice turned husky. "Or that I'd like to taste you instead of any of this food?"

Gia couldn't catch her breath, and her chest constricted tighter with every word that slid from his lips. Her mind spun with reasons she needed to keep her distance, but the pounding of her heart drowned them out. She wanted only one thing and he was standing right in front of her, waiting for her to give him any indication that he could proceed.

"Gia, you are the only woman I've ever wanted." Andrew lifted his hand and brushed her hair back from her face, letting his fingers linger over her cheek and gently touch her jaw. "The only woman I still want."

Andrew leaned forward slowly, giving her plenty of

time to move away. Instead, she met him halfway, her fingers curling at the back of his neck. She opened to him, yearning engulfing her as he slanted his mouth over hers. His mouth seduced her as their tongues danced, her hands finding the knotted muscles of his biceps before sliding back up, over his shoulders.

Her reservations seem to flit away like the scrub jays. She no longer cared about what happened between them in the past, or what he'd done since. She didn't even care about what the future might bring. She cared about only one thing—right now. With Andrew's lips caressing her neck, his hot breath brushing over her skin, his teeth grazing her shoulder, Gia refused to give up one more moment of bliss.

"Andrew?"

"Hmm?" He withdrew slightly, just enough for her to see his dark eyes gleam with hungry desire.

She began unbuttoning her shirt. "Are we going to do this or not?"

Gia shot him a smile that made it clear what she wanted as she tugged on the buttons at her wrists, not wanting a repeat of her last attempt seduce him. Laying her hand against his chest, Gia slid from the rock, landing on her bare feet in the grass. She made her way carefully to the edge of the water, dropping her shirt along the way and tugging her camisole over her head before letting it fall to the ground as well. She unbuttoned her jeans and slid them down her thighs, letting them pool at the edge of the creek.

Wearing nothing but her bra and underwear, she glanced backward at him and arched a brow, shooting him a mischievous grin. "Coming?"

Andrew shed his shirt silently, but he didn't need to say a word. His eyes said more than he'd want her to know. In them, she could read his desire for her. But there was so much more: hope, remorse, longing and worry. He unbuttoned his jeans and kicked them off, walking toward her confidently in nothing but boxer briefs.

The sight of him was intoxicating and made her mouth suddenly dry. He was the kind of male perfection that inspired sculptures. Chiseled muscles rippled as he walked toward her, the light dancing over him. His erection pressed boldly against the material, and she couldn't help staring, her tongue sneaking out to lick her lower lip as longing shuddered through her.

Andrew wound his arms around her from behind, his palm splaying over her bared belly, his lips caressing the back of her shoulder, and he breathed her in. "You sure you want this?"

He was giving her a chance to change her mind, to pull away again, but it was the last thing she wanted to do. His body was feverish against her back, scalding her with his ardor, and she surrendered to the temptation of him. His hand moved against her skin, and she found herself wishing he would lower it just a few inches and extinguish the inferno raging in her.

"I am."

"And tomorrow?" His voice was a tortured sound,

but as he spoke, his mouth touched that spot that sent shivers down her spine to center between her thighs.

"We'll face that later," she whispered, turning her head to give him better access to her shoulder. He tugged the strap of her bra down, nipping at the sensitive flesh before he licked any pain away, his body rocking into hers, his length pressing against her. Gia's head dropped backward against his chest, reveling in the sheer devastation he wrought on her senses.

"Make love to me, Andrew."

He spun her in his arms, lifting her up as she wound her legs around his hips and he turned back toward the rock.

"Wait, where are we going?" She tightened her arms around his neck.

"Darlin'," he drawled, "that water is freezing, and I seriously doubt I could . . . uh . . ." He leaned his forehead against hers. ". . . perform at my own high standards," he finished.

She laughed. "Are you trying to say it's too cold for you to—"

"Yes."

"Well, then where?"

He paused, looking from where they stood at the edge of the water toward where the horses calmly grazed. "Horse blankets?" he suggested.

"Itchy."

"We could spread out our clothes."

She loosened her hold and crossed her arms behind

his neck, smiling at him. He rolled his eyes and sighed heavily. "I seem to recall you being far more adventurous in your youth, Mr. McQuaid."

Andrew groaned and looked back at the creek. "Man, I hope that water isn't too cold."

Gia leaned toward his ear, nipping the lobe with her lips. "If it is, I promise I'll warm you up."

His erection swelled against her, sparking her need into a wildfire. Her eyes widened even as he grinned, and she sighed, dropping her forehead to his shoulder and losing herself in the sensation. "See? I think you'll manage just fine."

He frowned. "I don't have any protection."

Now *he's worried about it?* Gia cast the thought aside. She wasn't going to let their past invade this time.

"It's okay. I've been on the pill for years for other reasons."

"I'm good, Gia," he assured her. "I've been tested."

"I trust you." When his brows shot up in disbelief she almost laughed. "Wasn't that the bet?"

Andrew frowned again. "Gia, this isn't about the bet. I don't want you to—"

She cupped his face in her palm. "Shh, I'm not, okay? It was a joke." He didn't look entirely convinced. "You know, I'm growing old waiting for you to make love to me." She brushed her mouth over his, sucking his lower lip between hers.

"Damn, woman, I don't remember you being so demanding."

"I don't remember you being so talkative," she countered.

Andrew took a step into the water, and she almost laughed out loud at his sigh of relief. He looked toward the sky. "Thank you, God! It's warm."

She didn't wait for him to say more, plundering his mouth with her own. His moan rumbled against her chest where her breasts pressed against him. As the icy water hit her feet, she realized he'd been full of shit.

She sucked in a breath. "I thought you said it was warm?" she squeaked.

"It's warmer than I thought it would be." Andrew nipped at her jaw, his hands seeking the curve of her breast, sending hot spirals of pleasure through her limbs. "Don't worry. I'll warm *you* up."

Chapter Twenty

THE WATER SHOULD have been cold enough to freeze his balls off, but with Gia in his arms, Andrew felt like steam was coming off him. He was on fire, his body a raging inferno of desperation and need. He could barely even feel the frigid water as he walked her into one of the deeper pools.

As kids, he and his brothers used to swim here, so he knew which were the deepest. Even then, the water came only to the middle of his ribs, but that was enough for it to just cover Gia's breasts where they bobbed against the surface of the water, tempting him, the black lace clinging to her. She cupped her hands and let water fall over his chest, her fingers following the path the droplets took, moving lower. Andrew sucked in a breath.

"See, it's cold," she scolded. Even now her voice was thick with passion.

He reached for her wrist. "It wasn't because of the water."

Andrew dragged her against him, his hands reaching down to cup her butt. She tangled her legs around his waist again, letting the water hold her buoyant. The small movement was agonizingly seductive. He used a thumb to ease his briefs down, barely noticing the chill of the water any longer. Dipping his head, he used his tongue to sweep the exposed flesh at the top of her breast. Gia grasped his arms, arching her body into his, and leaned backward with a whimper of need, succumbing to the complete euphoria of their lovemaking. The movement also had the gloriously agonizing effect of pressing her heat against him.

He'd waited almost ten long years to be with her again. All he wanted was to bury himself in her, but he also knew the perfect elation that would be found with patience. Andrew slid his hand up her back, letting her float on his arm, brushing his thumb over the taut peak of her breast through the lace, watching reverently as it beaded and her legs tightened around his waist. Gia reached behind her and unclasped the garment, sliding it down her arms and holding it up to him. The audacious smile she gave him made his entire body throb. He reached for it and flung the scrap of lace onto the bank.

"You're incredible." The words slipped from his lips before he could stop them, and her eyes flickered with hesitation, her arms coming in front of her chest to cover herself. "Don't you dare."

Andrew lifted her so that her breasts were rubbed against his chest, letting her hold herself up against him as he slid his hand between them, brushing his fingers over the last scrap of material she wore. His thumb slipped beneath, finding the nub of her pleasure, and she gasped.

"Holy shit." Gia's eyes widened in passion. Andrew slowed. "Please, don't stop," she whispered.

He was sure his smile could be seen from outer space. He knew this woman. Knew how to drive her wild, knew where to touch her, and knew exactly how much she would let him torment her before she demanded release. Andrew slid a finger inside her, teasing her until her breasts swayed, the waves of water sluicing between them as he plundered her mouth. She bucked against him.

"Andrew. Oh, Andrew . . ." Gia buried her face against his shoulder as her release washed over her, leaving her hanging on to him weakly.

She dropped to her feet, slid her underwear down her thighs and cast them aside, near where her bra had landed on the bank. Andrew barely had a chance to reach for her when her hand closed over him.

"Your turn."

"I don't think—" he protested, stilling her.

Gia arched a brow. "Good, don't."

Her fingers traced the length of him, and he clenched

his jaw to keep from responding like a fourteen-year-old boy. He'd never fought for control before, but Gia had a way of making him do things he'd never thought were possible.

"Gia," he growled. She laughed quietly as his eyes fell closed, his entire body trembling with the battle to hold back. "I can't wait any longer. I just can't."

Gia lifted herself over him, settling him at the entrance to her body. "Neither can I."

Andrew gripped her hips, guiding her down his rigid length, growling in ecstasy as she sucked in a quick gasp.

The fantasy of making love to Gia had nothing on the reality. He might know her, but she knew him just as well, and her body excelled at driving him over the edge. Gia moved on him, rolling her hips, her hands clutching him, giving in to her passion. Andrew's fingers clenched her thighs as he drove himself into her. She urged him on, her body molding to his until they were one—one movement, one breath, one heartbeat.

His climax came before he could stop it, roaring through him like an earthquake, his entire body tensing and, for a moment, he thought he might die from the sheer gratification of it.

"Gia," he whispered against her hair. "I love you."

He slid his arms around her, holding her tightly to him, still buried within her, not wanting to ever release her. Andrew swore to himself that he never would again.

GIA TRIED TO contain her shiver, but despite their scorching lovemaking, the cold water eventually seeped into her bones. Andrew must have felt her tremble.

"Aw, shit, Gia. You're cold." He looked at the bank as if realizing for the first time that they didn't have any way to dry off. "Come on."

He picked her up, tucking his arm under her legs and wrapping the other around her back, curling her into his chest, keeping her warm with the heat emanating from his body. The gesture made her feel cherished, as if her needs came before his own.

"I *can* walk."

He settled her on one of the large rocks that had been in full sunlight. After the chill of the water, it was heavenly. She tried not to think about the dirt that would probably smudge her butt when she stood, and prayed that was that worst thing that ended up on her rear.

"You could, and I would love the view, but this is far more gentlemanly of me, don't you think?"

She watched him retrieve her clothing, admiring every lean play of flesh in the light, every stretch of sinew and flexing muscle. He was the poster child for man-candy.

He turned toward her and caught her staring. Arching a brow high on his forehead, he shot her an arrogant, lopsided smirk. "You see something you like?"

He was far too confident for his own good. Then again, he had every reason to be.

"Maybe," she teased.

"Maybe?" He stalked closer, plucking her shirt from the grass as he reached her. "What do I need to do to make that a yes?"

A thousand ideas flitted through her mind, each one more erotic than the last. His gaze turned hot and wicked as if he were reading her thoughts. As much as she wanted to deny it, to keep the truth hidden from him, she couldn't help the way her heart lurched at how much she loved him.

She chewed at her lower lip, wondering if he knew that he'd said as much to her while they were in the water. She doubted it. It had been one of those "heat of the moment" things that he'd regret as soon as he realized what he'd said—*if* he ever did. Or maybe it was something he said to every woman he had sex with now.

Doubt crept in on her. This man was a known player—at least, that was how people saw him. Even by his own admission, he hadn't been lacking female companionship over the past ten years. He still had his bad-boy reputation for a reason.

The grin slowly dropped from his lips, and she was certain he could read her mind.

She fixed an impish smile on her face but it felt strained, like she was suddenly playing a role for him. "I might need some time to come up ideas."

"Don't ever quit your day job to play poker, Gia."

He settled her clothes on the rock beside her, disappointment clearly written in his eyes. Turning away, he retrieved his jeans and slid them up his legs, zipping them but leaving the button undone, letting them hang low on his hips.

She hurried into her own clothes, hating that she couldn't just let herself savor this moment of bliss. She was at a remote creek with a naked man who would make any woman's pulse skyrocket and he wanted her, had just brought her to the best orgasm of her life. He'd even said he loved her.

But she couldn't trust him. Not the way she needed to in order to completely give herself to him.

She could give him her body—celebrate it, even—but she couldn't give him her heart again. That would signal a disaster for her because she knew she couldn't survive losing him and Bella. And now they were a package deal. It left her with only one option.

She let out a long sigh. "What do you want from me, Andrew?"

"I want you to trust me."

She shoved her arms into the sleeves of her shirt and rolled them to her elbows. Sliding her feet back into her boots, she walked over to him, letting her hands rest on his stomach. "So do I, and I'm trying."

He raised his hand to cup her cheek, his eyes dark again. She could see the anguish in them, wished she hadn't been the cause of it. Maybe she wasn't entirely to blame, but she'd been shouldering the responsibility for everyone else's shortcomings so long that she accepted the blame readily.

"We should head back," she suggested. "I have to work at the restaurant tonight."

He nodded but instead of letting her go, he pulled her into his embrace, pressing his lips to the top of her head. "I gave up too soon last time. I should have fought for you." He tipped her chin up and looked into her eyes. Gia could read the fierce determination in them. "I won't make that mistake again."

She pinched her lips together. They couldn't go down that road twice. *She* couldn't do it. But she also knew the look in his eyes. It was the one that said, "Dare to tell me no."

"We have a lot more baggage now than we did when we were younger," she pointed out.

"Good thing I'm stronger now and can carry a lot more." His eyes gleamed and she knew, despite her attempt to do the opposite, he'd just taken her comment as a dare.

Damn it.

GIA SHOWERED AND left for the restaurant right after they returned. As much as he wanted to spend the time with her, Andrew quickly made plans for the rest of his afternoon. But before he could finalize them, he needed to get Maddie to cooperate with him.

"Hey, Mads!" he greeted her as he knocked on her bedroom door, leaning against the door frame. His sister was sprawled on her bed, reading a romance novel. He tugged the book from her hands and glanced at the pages. He saw the words *throbbing erection* and threw the book onto the bedspread. "Why do you read that crap? You know that's not real life, right?"

She sat up and snatched her book back from the bed. "Thanks, Captain Obvious. I couldn't have figured that out from this." She pointed where the spine labeled it *fiction.* His sister rolled her eyes at him in exasperation. "What do you want, Andrew?"

He tucked his hands into the front pockets of his jeans. "I need your help."

"You barging in here then acting like a douche isn't the way to get it."

"It's Bella," he went on as if he hadn't heard her warning.

"What's wrong? Is she okay?" Maddie jumped up from the bed, reaching for her shoes.

He placed a hand on her shoulder. "She's fine. I want to have a paternity test done, and you've worked with enough doctors to know one who could do it but keep it on the down-low."

She crossed her arms over her chest, arching a brow in question. "Explain."

"I don't trust Lorena."

"Duh. You'd be stupid if you did." He tipped his head in her direction in agreement. "But you've already signed the paternity acknowledgment. Why would you do that if you aren't sure if you're . . . Oh, Gia." Maddie shook her head. "I take it back. You *are* stupid."

"What? Why? I'm trying to help her."

"No, you're trying to trap her. You're a bigger douche than I realized." Maddie glared at him, her dark eyes glinting with malice.

"I'm not trying to trap her. If it turns out that I'm not Bella's father, by declaring I'm her father, I can sign over custody to Gia, which is what should have happened in the first place."

Maddie narrowed her eyes. "So you're going to lie?"

"No," he argued.

"What would you call it?"

"Lorena didn't want Bella and told Gia that her boyfriend didn't either. Supposedly she told him she was stillborn."

Maddie's eyes glistened and she shook her head sadly. "That poor baby. What if Lorena never even told him she had her?"

"How would he have not noticed she was pregnant? If he'd wanted that baby, he'd have asked questions."

Maddie lowered her voice and leaned closer. "I still don't see why you ever slept with her in the first place."

"Well, there *was* someone who had promised to drive us home that night, but she flaked."

"I got sick!" She glared at him.

"Uh-huh. Anyway, I'm not sure I did. The more I try to remember that night, the more I don't think it happened, but it's too fuzzy to be sure. Hence, the paternity test."

"Okay," she said with a sigh, pulling her cell phone

from where it was charging on the nightstand. Her fingers began tapping at the screen. "I have a friend I'd trust in Placerville."

"Can she fit me in today?"

"Boy, you don't ask for little favors, do you? I'm not a miracle worker."

Andrew reached out and tousled his little sister's blond hair, making sure it tangled in front of her face.

"Hey! Jerk," she yelled, shoving him toward the door.

He laughed. "When you're finished, I'll be on the phone with Linc if you want to talk to him."

She shot her thumb in the air as she concentrated on the cell phone screen. "She says she can fit you in at four." She glanced up at him, blowing her hair out of her eyes. "Just do me a favor and don't screw this up?"

"How would I screw up a paternity test?"

"Not the test, moron. Don't screw this up with Gia again."

Crap. Why did everyone keep telling him that. The problem was that he wasn't sure how to *not* screw it up.

Chapter Twenty-One

GIA HURRIED THROUGH the back door of the restaurant, into chaos. Rusty was yelling from the kitchen and she barely made out his threat to quit before her mother began cursing at him in Italian.

"Oh, shit," she muttered.

It was never good when her mother resorted to her native tongue, and the fact that Rusty was yelling back didn't bode well for anyone. Gia ran into the kitchen to see her father sitting at the counter with his head in his hands, while Rusty stood on one side of the stove, scolding her mother, who stirred a boiling pot of soup.

"That is *not* the way Giovanni does it and you know it," Rusty said.

"It's cheaper this way."

"Cheaper does not equal better, Isabella. This place is

known for its authentic *zuppa toscana*. You're going to kill Rossetti's reputation."

"*Coglioni*," her mother threw back at him. "*Sta zitto, capice?*"

"You know damn well I don't *capice*." Rusty slammed the spoon on the counter and started for the door. "I'm cannot work with you."

"Good. Go back to bagging groceries," her mother responded.

"Enough, both of you, please." Her father's voice was weak, and Gia could hear the exhaustion. "Isabella, Rusty and I will fix the *zuppa*. Go tell Lorena to take care of the front of the house and to stay out of the kitchen."

"She was helping," her mother insisted.

Lorena caused this fiasco?

"Mama, I'll take care of this." Everyone turned to look at Gia, standing just inside the kitchen doors. "Why don't you just take Lorena home?"

Her mother pursed her lips and frowned at Gia. "It's about time you showed up. How was your night off?"

Her mother didn't really want the truth; it was a question meant to make her feel guilty for taking some time for herself instead of giving yet more of her life to her sister. It was a jab at Gia for not coming in the night before, leaving Lorena to fill in for her.

"Gia." Her father's face brightened as his mouth curved into a weak smile. "How is Bella?"

She hurried to her father's side and kissed his cheek.

"She's good, Daddy. I think Sarah McQuaid is going to spoil her rotten," she said quietly as she gave him a hug.

"They're good people. All of them are."

Her mother narrowed her eyes and crossed her arms over her ample chest. "Well," she huffed. "I'm so sorry that we don't have the money to buy frivolous things. Giovanni, are you coming with me now that Gia's here?"

"Mama, that's not what I meant," Gia tried to cajole her mother.

"You go on ahead," her father said with a wave. "I want to visit with my daughter for a bit."

Gia wouldn't have thought it possible for her mother to look angrier, but her father's words managed to accomplish the task. Her mother pursed her lips tightly and turned on her heel, shoving her way through the metal doors and storming out of the kitchen. Her reaction had been almost frigid.

"What happened?" Gia asked as she turned back to Rusty and her father. She didn't miss the fact that her father looked pale and his eyes seemed sunken. "Daddy, are you okay?"

"Yeah, I'm just tired, *piccola*."

"I swear, I'm not sure which of them wants this place sold more." Rusty hurried over to the stove and grasped the soup pot, dumping the contents into the sink. "We're going to have to let the waiters know we won't have the *toscana* tonight. Only the minestrone."

"Make the *ribollita*. I'll tell the wait staff," Gia suggested. Her father looked at her, the pride in his eyes making her heart swell. "What, Daddy?"

"You're a smart girl, *piccola*. You run this place like you love it as much as I do."

She smiled at him and shrugged. "It means everything to you, so I do."

He cocked his head to one side and stared at her for a moment, making her feel like he was trying to figure out a puzzle. "What's the matter, Daddy?" She was an open book. All he had to do was ask. She'd give him a straight answer.

"Why don't you come home? Is it Andrew?"

"I did come home."

He shook his head slowly and she knew what he meant. "Permanently."

Shit! She didn't want to answer *that* question. "Daddy, I have a great job—"

"That's eight hours away." He eyed her. "There's more to it than that. You think I don't know what goes on, but I see the way you still look at him, Gianna, and I don't miss the way he looks at you. That man is *innamorato*."

In love.

"He's right, Gia," Rusty chimed in.

"What would you know about it?" her father asked with a tired laugh. "You never leave this kitchen. If you did, you'd know that Heather is getting sick and tired of waiting for you to give her a baby."

Gia's brows shot skyward. "A baby?"

Her father chuckled. "You've been married nearly seven years. That girl wants a family, Rusty. Better quit stalling or she's going to find someone else who'll give her one."

"I'm not good with kids," he muttered as he began chopping the onion and carrots for the *ribollita*. "What if the kid hates me?"

Her father's eyes brightened as he laughed at the nervous man standing at the counter. "Well, sir, I can pretty much guarantee that having your kids hate you at one time or another is just the sign of being a good father."

Gia looked at her father, his eyes bright as he teased Rusty. He rose and made his way to the soup pot, directing Rusty on how best to make the soup. Since her mother's departure, he seemed to have gotten a second wind. The truth was, Rossetti's was where he was happiest, contrary to what his mother might think. When he wasn't trying to put out fires his sister had started, her father looked younger, happier and healthier. Rusty was right; selling the restaurant would be the worst thing for him.

Her cell phone chimed in her pocket and she tugged it out. The nervous flutter in her stomach and the rush of heat through her limbs when she saw Andrew's name shouldn't still have surprised her, but they did.

Linc's ready and says your plans are perfect. Two guitarists are ready. Arriving Friday @ 10 for sound check.

The nervous flutter grew into a hurricane in her stomach. This concert had to work. It had to sell out in order to bring in enough money for her parents to pay down their medical debt. Her phone *ping*ed again with another notification.

Missy is a go for posters & tix. She's ready when you are. Charlene has four people lined up to serve. They want tix in exchange. I said you'd do that.

Andrew could charm a Tasmanian devil to dance. She'd never have been able to get both women to donate their services as well as four experienced servers for the concert.

Or he promised something more than the tickets.

Gia didn't want to think about what else he might have offered the women, one of whom he'd already admitted was an ex-girlfriend. Not that she had any say in the matter.

She'd already made it clear that she couldn't give him more than friendship. Friends and nothing more. She pushed her jealous thoughts to the back of her mind and texted that he was a lifesaver.

"Okay," she announced to her father and Rusty. "The concert is a go. We have extra wait staff and tickets, and the posters will be printed as soon as I e-mail the mockup to the shop." Her father's bushy brows pinched together. "You're not happy? I thought you'd be glad."

"It's not that."

Gia laid a hand on her father's arm, but he shook it off and wandered out of the kitchen without explaining his reaction. She started to follow him but Rusty stopped her.

"He doesn't want people to know, Gia."

"Know what?"

"No one realizes quite how sick he's been, at least in his mind. If they find out the concert is to help pay for his medical expenses, they'll realize he messed up."

"There's nothing wrong with asking for help," she pointed out.

"No," Rusty agreed, dropping the pancetta into the soup pot. "But your father is a proud man and very old-fashioned. To him, this must feel a little like begging."

This town knew Rossetti's and her parents had kept this town on the map. They were more than willing to show her parents appreciation for it. Part of the reason people would come was to help her parents out. If they didn't feel like they were doing a good deed, they weren't going to pay the premium ticket price.

"He was the one who ran the article in the paper," she pointed out.

"Yeah, and that article barely mentioned his illness. Most of it was about how that big warehouse store was pressuring him to sell. It made your dad look like an underdog fighting to keep himself and this town safe from corporate bullies. And you know how everyone loves an underdog."

"An underdog," she murmured, wondering how best to play up that angle instead of his illness.

Rusty was right. If her father felt like he'd been painted as a weakling, he'd refuse to come to the concert. She had to make sure she showed him to be a fighter, a warrior standing up for a cause, and that the town could stand behind him. But it would mean getting her mother and sister to play along, and right now, neither seemed too inclined to listen to anything Gia had to say.

ANDREW ARRIVED HOME just as his mother was finishing up the dishes from dinner. His brothers had scattered, leaving her with the mess, again. "Go sit, Mom. I'll take care of these." He settled the car seat with his sleeping daughter on the kitchen table.

"Where have you been?" his mother asked, unbuckling the baby and lifting her from the seat. "Is it dinnertime for her yet?"

Andrew glanced at the clock on the wall. "Almost, close enough."

"You finish the dishes and I'll feed my granddaughter," she agreed with a wink.

Andrew knew better than to deny her the pleasure and gave her a smile. "Yes, ma'am." He handed her the diaper bag and headed toward the sink, piled with dishes to be loaded into the dishwasher.

"So?" she prompted again.

He'd hoped that she'd forgotten the question. "I went into Placerville," he hemmed, not really giving her an answer.

"Why?"

Leave it to his mother to be direct.

"I doubt you want all the details, Mom."

She laughed quietly. "Andrew, as much as I adore all of you kids, I know your faults better than anyone else in the world. You had a baby show up on your doorstep and her mother gave up custody. Your father and I know you kids are all adults and we try not to pass any judgments on the decisions you kids make, but I doubt where you've been is any more questionable than what has led up to this point."

"I went for a paternity test."

She frowned at him. "I stand corrected."

"I don't want anyone to know."

"You don't think Bella is yours?" He saw the disappointment flicker in her eyes and she cuddled the child even closer, as if afraid someone might take her away.

Andrew shrugged. "I don't really know. That's why I had the test done. It's possible she is, but it also seems fishy. I have a feeling Lorena lied."

"But you *did* sleep with her."

"That's the assumption, but the more I'm able to remember, as I keep trying to piece together the fragmented memories of that night . . ." He shook his head. "I'm beginning to second-guess whether anything actually happened."

"Why?"

Andrew almost smiled. He and his mother were a lot alike. They both thought through every problem with logistical prowess. The same ability that had made him a good cop had seen her through raising seven children while running a ranch. She saw every situation in terms of statistics and logical probabilities. It was that very aspect of their personalities that had him questioning Bella's paternity.

He wasn't about to tell his mother the gory details of his memories of kissing Lorena. He didn't even want to relive them in his mind. And he certainly wasn't about to tell her how he woke up partially undressed. But there were other clues that gave him pause.

"Ben is sure I didn't. According to him, I was too drunk that night to even walk. He said he practically carried me to her car."

"Ben is too close to the situation," she pointed out. "And he always sees the best in everyone, especially you." She shook her head with a slight smile. "You'd have thought I had *two* sets of twins."

The corner of Andrew's mouth quirked. He and his brother Ben were a lot alike. Both had a stubborn streak, both had entered public service, and they loved to give each other crap. But in truth, while their personalities were as different as night and day, they understood one another better than anyone else could. Ben was the yin to his yang or, as his mother used to say, the Tweedledee to his Tweedledum.

"Take his opinion and alcohol out of the situation," she instructed, giving him a disappointed roll of her eyes. "What else makes you question it?"

Andrew finished loading the dishes and turned back toward her, leaning against the kitchen counter and rubbing his temples. "I don't know. It's just a gut feeling, Mom."

"Stop and think. You're a good cop, Andrew. What would you look at if this was a crime scene?"

"You've been watching too many *CSI* reruns." She scowled at him and he held up his hands. "Okay, okay."

Andrew took a deep breath and thought back to when he first arrived at the party. While on shift, he'd run into Gia shopping with her father and it had messed him up for the rest of the week, making him rethink his past, his choices and where he'd gone wrong. When Ben met him at the station on New Year's Eve and mentioned that he was going to Rossetti's for the New Year's party, Andrew figured he needed to go, if for no other reason than to prove to himself he was over Gia. Sort of a hair-of-the-dog situation, but in the back of his mind, he'd been hoping she'd be there.

Instead, he'd found Lorena behind the bar mixing drinks and looking so much like Gia that after a few shots, he'd begun to wonder if he wasn't hallucinating. Ben and Jackson had tried to slow him down but Lorena kept the shots coming, most of them on the house. Maddie had bailed early, even though she was supposed to be their ride, claiming she wasn't feeling good, but he suspected it had more to do with him being a dick to everyone.

He couldn't remember why he'd been so mad, but the last thing he remembered was his brother suggesting he sleep it off at the fire station, which was where Ben headed. Instead, he'd danced out the door with Lorena when the bar closed.

Somehow he managed to get to her car. Although he didn't remember any of it, Ben informed him that he'd helped drag him. The next thing he remembered was waking at sunrise in the passenger seat of her car up on Fool's Hill, the local make-out spot for lovers too cheap to get a room. Lorena had been smiling at him from where she sat in the driver's seat, putting on lipstick using the rearview mirror while his head pounded like a jackhammer had been turned loose inside it.

"The seat," he murmured, trying to picture the scene the way it would have looked to a detective.

"What about it?"

"It wasn't pushed back. My knees were crammed against the glove box. And it wasn't reclined."

Lorena drove an small Mazda two-door. It would have been difficult enough to have sex with the seat reclined and slid backward into the farthest position. It would have been impossible from the position he'd woken in. His mother looked at him expectantly, waiting for him to explain his sudden silence.

"Thanks, Mom." He ran over to her and kissed her cheek, running into the hall.

"Wait, where are you going now?"

Andrew skidded to a stop, realizing he couldn't just take off. He had Bella to take care of now. He shot his mother a pleading look.

"Oh, go," she said, waving him away. "But make sure you get this cleared up without ruining your chances with Gia."

What was it with his family and Gia?

Chapter Twenty-Two

ANDREW ARRIVED AT Rossetti's as the late dinner rush swarmed, but Gia wasn't in the front of the house, acting as hostess as he expected. Instead Giovanni greeted him, wide smile beaming and color in his ruddy cheeks again.

"Well, hello, Mr. McQuaid. To what do we owe this pleasure?" he asked, his accent thick, the way it was whenever he got excited.

"I'm looking for your daughter, Mr. Mancuso." Andrew eyed the dining room behind the older man, hoping to see Gia running around.

"She's in the office. Is she expecting you?"

"No," Andrew admitted. "But—"

Giovanni chuckled low in his throat. "Then by all means, head back there and surprise her. But do try not to scare my patrons, okay?"

Andrew didn't miss the sparkle in the man's eyes. "You realize I'm in love with her, don't you?"

Giovanni laughed. "Son, this entire town knows it. Just don't take another ten years to finally marry her. I'd like to walk her down the aisle."

"You can plan on it, sir. I don't make the same mistakes twice."

Andrew hurried past Giovanni and headed through the kitchen doors, turning left toward the office. Just before he reached the door, Lorena came out of the storage room and looked up, spotting him. She narrowed her eyes and tipped her head to one side, a smirk tugging at her lips.

"Well, well, look who's here."

He stopped, unwilling to get any closer to the she-devil. "I'm here to see Gia."

She pursed her lips, pouting. "There's no reason we can't be friends, Andrew. This is no way to treat the mother of your child. I mean, after all, we've been—" she shrugged "—so close in the past."

"Are you sure about that? Or maybe that's just one more of your lies."

She crossed her arms and cocked her hip to one side. "You think so?"

"We never had sex, did we?" Lorena's dark brows lifted but she remained stoic. "You wanted it to look like we did, you told people we did, but it didn't happen. I was too far gone. But that wasn't going to stop you from using it to hurt your sister, was it?"

"Oh, Andrew, what an imagination you have."

Her expression was patronizing but he wasn't about to be swayed. He knew he was right, knew it the way he'd always known the spark between him and Gia hadn't died. He wasn't letting this go.

"Why? Your sister and I weren't together. What made you think she'd even care?"

She shook her head and sighed. "To tell the truth, it wasn't even that memorable for me." Lorena shrugged. "You have this reputation with the ladies, but I'm afraid you just fall a little . . ." She held her thumb and first fingers up, separating them about two inches. ". . . short."

Andrew laughed out loud. "Now I know you're lying. Thanks for the confirmation."

She glared and took a step toward him. "Here the deal, Andrew. You think you're sly, moving my sister to your ranch. But things will never go back to the way they were for you guys. You three are not going to be some cute little family." She clasped her hands under her chin, batting her eyes. "I'll make sure of it. I will never let Gia have her happily-ever-after. Not with you, that's for damn sure."

"What the hell do you have against me? Or your sister, for that matter?"

"You both think you're so damn perfect. Perfect couple, perfect relationship, everything working out like a fairy tale. Guess what? I deserve a fairy tale too."

"Then go find it. Why ruin ours?"

"Because I can, and I will." She shoved past him and opened the door to the office. "Prince Charming is here,

Gia," she announced. "And since, thanks to you, I'm not allowed to help in the kitchen anymore, Mom says you can take my shift tomorrow."

Gia glanced up and Andrew could see the exhaustion in the fine lines around her eyes. Even with the dark circles under them, she was gorgeous. But there was no way she was going to be able to continue working both her own and Lorena's shifts at the restaurant while trying to plan the concert. She rubbed her eyes, resigning herself to the relentless task of making up for her sister's lack of responsibility.

"Fine." She shot a glance at Andrew and he saw her corners of her eyes crinkle, as if she was pleased to see him but trying to hide it. "Hi."

"Hey." His voice softened, and he would have forgotten Lorena was still present if she hadn't cleared her throat. "Do you mind?" He saw the surprise in Gia's face, but he refused to discuss why he'd come in front of Lorena.

"Actually—" Lorena rolled her eyes at him "—I need a couple of things from in here. Gia, where are those invoices from the alcohol vendor? I think we're missing a few bottles of some of our good stuff."

"Which ones?"

"Patrón, and at least three bottles of Grey Goose. I need to double-check the whiskey too. I haven't even started counting the wine yet."

Gia rose and pulled a file from the cabinet. "I think these are the two latest ones, but you might want to check it against the closing inventory from last year. It's in here somewhere."

While Gia's back was to them, Lorena moved closer, leaning toward him with her hand on his shoulder, making his skin crawl where she touched him.

"Tell her the truth and I promise to make sure she never, ever speaks to you again," she whispered. "I'll make her life hell."

He shoved her hand from him. "You won't do anything."

"Let's see. A small-town cop who takes advantage of young women, abusing his power? Sounds like a great article for the paper. Think carefully," she warned.

Andrew didn't have to think about it. The news was littered with stories about police abusing their powers and crossing lines. He'd always prided himself on his integrity. Not to mention that any bad press would reflect on Grant and Linc, most likely causing the tabloids to seek them both out again. And that didn't even take into consideration what sort of domino effect it might have on the concert for Gia.

He'd talk to Gia, tell her the truth, but it wouldn't be here. Not where Lorena might try to exact her sadistic revenge. Gia turned back toward them, holding the file out to her sister, looking from one to the other suspiciously.

Lorena smiled broadly, confident that she had them both exactly where she wanted. "Thanks." She plucked the file from her sister's hands and headed for the door, poking her head back inside. "Oh, and Andrew, it was nice reminiscing about our good time."

Andrew clenched his jaw, hearing the laughter in Lorena's words. She knew what the reminder would do to Gia, as well as the fact that she was ruining any desire Gia would have to talk to him. She'd be on the defensive now, not knowing the truth, and far less likely to want to listen now that she'd been reminded of how much Andrew had hurt her.

Damn Lorena.

GIA FELT LIKE she'd just been punched in the stomach. Her breath caught in her chest, and she pressed a hand against where her heart should have been beating. She'd been in the office, fantasizing about Andrew like a lovesick schoolgirl, wondering if they might not be able to make some sort of relationship work for Bella's sake, when he'd come in, almost as if she'd conjured him from her thoughts.

But then Lorena had gone and reminded her of what had happened between them. She had no doubt it was deliberate, but the knowledge that her sister was trying to hurt her didn't lessen the anguish the thought of them together caused. She turned away from him, dropping back into the chair and rubbing her fingers against her temples, trying to ease the pain building behind them.

"What can I help you with, Andrew?"

Exhaustion overtook her and every muscle in her

body felt weak, but none as much as her heart. It ached, feeling pierced and bleeding. Facing him, Gia could see the trepidation in his dark eyes, something she'd only seen in his face once before—on the night she broke off their engagement. It was gone just as quickly, replaced by the cocky, self-assured persona he typically clothed himself with.

"I just needed to see if you were going to be around tomorrow, but I guess I have my answer. I'll be helping my dad and brothers with the cattle."

"You just need someone to stay with Bella?" He nodded, but she saw his eyes cloud.

He was hiding something, she was sure of it. She wanted to ask him about it, but then she remembered that they were testing out their renewed friendship. It was still tenuous and she had no right to pry. "It's fine. I'll just bring her to the restaurant with me."

Andrew nodded, looking as if he wanted to say more but wasn't sure how. He shoved his hands in his pockets, and she saw the muscle in the side of his jaw clench several times. Andrew took a deep breath and let it out slowly. Gia just lifted her brows in question.

"All right then." Pivoting, Andrew headed back to the door.

"You came all the way to town to ask that? If that were the case, why not just call?" There was something on his mind and she wanted to give him the opportunity to get it out.

Pausing with his hand on the knob, he turned back

toward her. "Gia, how are you going to be able to manage two shifts tomorrow with the baby and still plan the concert?"

His concern was touching and sent a few butterflies spiraling upward toward her heart. Concern was the first step to caring, wasn't it?

"I'll manage." She gave him a tired smile. "It's what I do."

"Have you hired any new staff yet?"

"We did. I have six new people: four wait staff, a hostess and another bartender. Nick will be training her tonight. It should take some of the pressure off now that we're open all day again. Actually, I was in the middle of setting up the schedule for next week when you came in."

"Okay, well . . ." He glanced down the hall again, as if he didn't want to leave. "I should let you get back to work. I'll see you tonight at the house, right?"

"Eventually." She gave him a wry smile. "It'll be after we close at midnight and depends on how long it takes me to shut everything down."

He frowned. "Everyone will be up early tomorrow for the roundup, probably no later than six, and I'm sure Mom will have breakfast in the house, but I'll do my best to get them to keep the noise down."

"Don't worry. Bella will probably have me up by then to eat. I'm used to it."

"I should be the one getting up with her."

It didn't seem possible, but his frown deepened, and

she wished she dared ask him about it. Gia summoned her courage and sought the least prying question she could think of.

"Are you okay?"

"Yeah." He sounded distracted. Suddenly his eyes cleared and he focused on her, his deep brown gaze tender but intense. "Gia, do you still love me?"

His point-blank question left her mouth open, but no words emerged. She wanted to tell him the truth—that she'd never stopped loving him—but her pride wouldn't allow it.

No, it wasn't pride. She had to admit the truth to herself. She was afraid.

For all she knew, this was just a game he was playing, the way her sister was. A sick power trip of some kind. First he got custody of Bella, and now he could break her completely. She didn't think she could survive another heartbreak.

Andrew walked back to her, tugging her hand and drawing her to her feet. Against her better judgment, Gia leaned into his arms. One of his hands dove into her hair while the other wrapped around her waist, pulling her to him. His touch was gentle as his mouth slanted over hers, seeking the answer she couldn't voice aloud. Her entire body seemed to melt into him, molding against him, and a soft sigh escaped her as she gave in to the longing that she couldn't deny.

Her fingers slid up his arms, her nails playing over the flesh of his biceps, and she felt goose bumps break out over his skin. It was heady, the knowledge that she could affect him the way he did her and that his body responded with the same yearning. Her hands slid to the sides of his neck, up to cup his face, and the rasp of his whiskers tickled her palms sensuously.

She did love this man.

No matter how she'd tried denying it for the past ten years, she'd never stopped. Maybe that was why she'd never found anyone else. Maybe that was why she'd thrown herself into her work. She'd managed to bury the love she had for him, deeply, but it had never died. She couldn't deny it any longer. She was helplessly, hopelessly in love with Andrew McQuaid and always would be.

She'd been kidding herself to think they could be friends and nothing more. To think she could make love to him and not have it chain her heart to him once again. She'd been a fool, but who could blame her? Andrew was a force of nature, as wild and hypnotic as a lightning storm. And just as dangerous.

The taste of him teased her senses, the scent of him surrounding her. His kiss was as complex as the man behind it, strong but tender, demanding but giving even more, confident yet vulnerable. His tongue danced with hers, toying with her and teasing her into a writhing mess of longing in his arms. His lips found the hollow of her neck, nuzzling and sucking, and Gia trembled against him.

"Andrew," she begged.

"Tell me."

"I—"

The door slammed open and Lorena came inside. "So, there's . . . What the fuck?"

Lorena launched at them, but Andrew stood between them as Lorena pummeled his back, trying to claw her way past him. "What the fuck is wrong with you? You're supposed to hate him!"

Gia's eyes widened in shock as she stared at her sister. "Why would I hate him? He's not the one who has lied to me repeatedly. What did I ever do to you that would make you hate me this much, Lorena?"

"You told her?"

Andrew turned toward the raging woman, grabbing her wrists to subdue her. "I didn't say anything," he growled as she squirmed to get out of his grasp.

"Then how does she know?"

Gia felt like the room had tilted. She was dizzily trying to follow the sudden turn of the conversation even as her heart lurched in her chest.

"She knows nothing," Andrew growled quietly through clenched teeth. "Get out."

Gia took a step back, looking from one to the other. What didn't she know? Was this why Andrew had been acting so strange?

She'd been played again, by both of them this time. The pain in her chest nearly took her breath away as she replayed Andrew's words in her mind. They confirmed that he'd been a part of her sister's scheming.

"Both of you, get out."

Her voice was weak, and it hurt so much to speak. Her eyes filled with unshed tears, threatening to spill over, and she tried to shore up the dam quickly. She refused to let either of them see how much they'd hurt her, again.

Gia slid into the chair behind her desk and took a deep breath before looking up at them. Andrew still held Lorena's wrists, but her arms hung loosely at her sides now. She was no longer fighting him, and they both seemed surprised by Gia's calm reaction. It steeled her pride, and she squared her shoulders.

"What? You two seem to have things to discuss, and I have work to do." She cleared her throat, praying that her voice sounded more confident than she felt. She waved her hand, dismissing them both. "Find somewhere else to argue."

"Gia—"

"Save it, Andrew. I've heard enough."

Chapter Twenty-Three

"Aw, COME ON, Andrew." She laughed, chasing after him. "What's the matter? Are you going to cry? Did your little girlfriend give you the brush-off again?"

Andrew stormed down the hall of the restaurant, heading for the front door. If he stopped, he might actually murder Lorena. Gritting his teeth, he shoved through the door, slipping on his sunglasses.

"You know this isn't over, right?" Lorena stopped at the edge of the asphalt.

Don't stop, don't say anything.

"I warned you but you think you're smarter than I am. Just like my sister. Guess what? Not this time. I'm going to win this time around. I'll make sure of it."

Andrew stalked back toward Lorena and leaned close, his face only inches from hers. "You're one sick, twisted bitch. You do realize that I could run your ass in right now for threatening a police officer, right?" A slight shiver of fear flickered over her face and her smile faltered slightly. "Why don't you just do everyone a favor, Lorena, and leave town again? You're not happy unless you're making everyone else miserable."

Lorena's hand brushed over his chest, as if she were wiping something away. "And you, *Officer* McQuaid, think you're untouchable." She looked up at him and gave him a sly smile. Andrew froze as she stood on her toes and pressed her lips close to his ear. "You're not. I know your weakness."

Without another word, Lorena turned and disappeared through the front door of the restaurant, leaving Andrew to try to contemplate her veiled threat.

ANDREW DIDN'T WANT to head home. His mother was waiting for him to return with news of how his conversation with Gia had gone, and he wasn't ready to admit his defeat to her. He needed a sounding board and, though he could talk to his older brother, Grant had been on the road with his team when everything had gone bad with Gia. He didn't know Andrew's history with her the way Ben did.

Flipping a U-turn, Andrew pulled into the driveway of the fire station, letting the Challenger skid to a stop, taking his resentment out on the asphalt. He saw Ben in the doorway of the small firehouse, waiting for him to reach the entrance.

"Wow, bro, your dick is so huge," he said, sarcasm dripping from his voice. "Now that you've gotten that ridiculous display of male ego out of your system, what brings you by on your day off? Wishing you'd taken the fireman's test again?"

"Sure, then you guys would have someone who could actually save people instead of just cooking, cleaning and working out." The familiar banter between him and Ben released some of the pent-up frustration he'd been feeling.

"Says the guy who has to wear a body camera to defend his actions."

Andrew couldn't help the way his mouth tugged upward into a lopsided grin as he jerked a thumb at his car. "So, should I grab my laundry for you to do or what?"

"Shut up and get your ass in here." Ben chuckled, clapping him on the shoulder and shutting the door. "I didn't think I'd see you until tomorrow. I thought you were taking Gia for a ride today?" Ben wiggled his eyebrows suggestively.

"We went to the creek this morning, but she's at Rossetti's handling the dinner shift now."

"And you're in town stalking her?"

"Not exactly, although—" His phone ringer sounded, and he recognized the number from the clinic performing the paternity test. "Hang on." He held a hand up to his brother as he answered the phone.

"Mr. McQuaid? This is Dr. Alvarez. We spoke earlier. I have your test results."

"Already?" He was surprised since she'd warned him not to expect the results for a few more days.

"Yes, well, it was slow today and Maddie's a good friend. She mentioned you wanted these ASAP. I'll mail out the expanded results Monday but wanted to let you know that you are *not* the father of little Bella."

She didn't offer condolences or congratulations. In fact, Dr. Alvarez's voice was emotionless. Andrew wished that was how he felt. His entire being was in turmoil. Part of him wanted to celebrate the fact, but there was also a part of him fighting disappointment.

"I appreciate you rushing the order."

His mind spun. He knew what this meant but wasn't sure how to break the news to Gia, especially now that she was pissed at him. As he thanked the doctor again and hung up, he could see the concern in his brother's face.

"News you weren't expecting?"

Andrew sighed. "Actually, exactly what I *was* expecting. I'm not Bella's father."

"Isn't that good news?"

"It is for Gia. I have no reason not to sign off custody to her."

"Shouldn't that be good news for both of you? You're off the hook, then." Andrew scrubbed his hand over his face, unable to hide his misery from his brother. "But you don't want to be off the hook, do you?" Ben guessed.

Andrew shook his head. Ben ran a hand through his short hair. "Damn." He headed toward the kitchen and took two cans of soda from the refrigerator, sliding them onto the scuffed table in the center of the room. "Damn," he repeated. "When you fuck up, you do it royally, don't you?"

Andrew popped the top, letting the fizz clear from the top as he sighed. "How about a little help instead of stating the obvious?" He shrugged one shoulder. "At least this backs up the fact that I didn't actually sleep with Lorena."

"Well, I could have told you that." Angie, one of the few women on the fire department, walked into the kitchen. "How ya doin', McQuaid? Choke on any doughnuts?"

Andrew smiled at her. He'd always liked Angie. Ben had dated her for a short time, but everyone had known they were completely mismatched. Ben was as straight as an arrow and Angie was a wild child, or had been until recently.

"Not today. You save any foundations lately?" he joked back.

"Just one." She winked at him. "As far as Lorena is concerned, you probably don't remember me stopping to make sure you were okay."

Ben's brows shot up and Andrew frowned. "When?"

"We got a call about three in the morning, New Year's Day, that some kids had a bonfire up by Fool's Hill. I saw her drive up. Then she took off. It was weird, but we were kinda busy at the time." She pulled a bottle of iced coffee from the refrigerator. "Once we got the fire out, I spotted someone—you—out cold in the passenger seat."

"You didn't even leave the restaurant with her until after two," Ben reminded him.

"The engine was at Fool's Point until almost six when she came back."

"Back?" Andrew narrowed his eyes, rubbing his chin with his thumb thoughtfully. "Back from where?"

"Who knows?" Angie shrugged. "Some grungy guy dropped her off and sped out of there. I think we made him nervous. I would have waited around, but I saw you were coming to and she said she was taking you home, so I figured you were fine. I mean, you *are* a cop. Maybe I gave you too much credit."

"Angie, I need to get my answers and advice from you instead of this worthless piece of crap from now on." He jumped up and wrapped his arm around her neck, kissing the top of her head. "Thank you!"

She shoved him off and retrieved a sandwich from the refrigerator. "Duh. Why would you ask Ben anything? He's got his head up his ass most of the time," she teased. Ben reached for the towel near him, throwing it at her as she blew him a kiss, running from the room.

"So, now what?" Ben turned back to Andrew, picking up the conversation where they'd left off. "You should just tell Gia the truth."

"Yeah. Hey, Gia, I know what your sister says and what the rest of the town says, but I didn't really sleep with your sister."

"And that you love her and want her to stay," Ben filled in for him.

"I did tell her I love her."

Ben smiled. "Really?"

"Yeah."

"So, why do you look so miserable?"

"She said nothing."

"What do you mean, 'nothing'?" He gulped the soda.

"I mean, she didn't say anything. Then when I asked her, she kicked me out of her office."

Ben exhaled slowly, looking at his brother with empathy. "I guess you have your answer, then. I know you love her, man, but you know you can't hold onto her by pretending to be this kid's father."

Andrew slammed his hand on the table. "Why does everyone assume that's what I'm going to do? Shit! You and Maddie both."

Ben folded his hands and leaned forward calmly. "Maybe because we all know how hung up you've always been on her. Maybe because we all know she's the one that got away, and now you have a way to convince her to give you another chance, to be close to Bella. Any normal person would think about it, Andrew."

"Would you?"

Ben leaned back in his chair. "I'm the guy who does everything by the book. Boring. You're the rule breaker, remember? Your words, not mine."

"Past tense. I'm a cop."

"Yeah, well." Ben laughed. "Tiger not changing stripes and all that crap. You still push the boundaries. You want to stay for dinner?"

"No, I'm going to head back to the house. I need to talk to Gia but she's pissed. Either way, I have to tell her the truth, especially after this." He wiggled his phone.

Ben shook his head. "Do I even want to ask what you did now?"

"I confronted Lorena and she threatened me if I told Gia the truth. I think Gia got the wrong impression. I need to make sure she didn't misunderstand, and she needs to know about Bella."

"Are you going to be okay when they leave?"

Andrew could see the concern in his brother's eyes, but he didn't speak for a moment. His thoughts were in turmoil. Like he'd told Giovanni, he didn't make the same mistakes twice. He wouldn't lie to her, but he was going to fight for her this time.

"I love her too much to watch her walk away again. But I love her too much to try to make her stay."

"So, no?"

Andrew shook his head. "I don't think so."

GIA MADE SURE to stay at the restaurant until as late as possible. By the time her Lexus crept up the driveway to the ranch, the entire house and bunkhouse were dark. She flipped off her headlights in an attempt to not wake anyone and slowed to a crawl the rest of the way, parking her car and managing to slip out almost silently.

The moon glowed bright orange in the sky, lighting

the way as she climbed the steps to the porch. As she reached for the door handle, she realized she didn't have a key, and Sarah and Travis had likely locked the house long ago. She tried the knob but it barely moved.

Locked out, damn it.

She turned away, weighing her options. She would try the back door, but if that was also locked, she'd just sleep in her car. There was no way she'd try the bunkhouse. She wasn't taking any risk that might put her face-to-face with—

"Home later than you planned?"

Andrew.

Gia swallowed, spying him sitting the railing in the darkened corner of the porch. She was too tired to have this confrontation with him now. Too hurt after what she'd heard between him and Lorena.

"Yeah, it was a long night. I should check on Bella and turn in."

She managed to make it down only the first step of the porch when his voice stopped her. "Gia, we need to talk."

She held up a hand and sighed heavily. "I don't want to talk, Andrew. I'm tired."

He rose and crossed the porch, stopping just short of touching her. Leaning against one of the railings. His gaze slowly caressed her, making her insides quiver and her legs feel weak. In the stillness and her exhausted state, she wanted to pretend that today had been nothing more than a bad dream. That she could fall into his embrace and let the fantasies he brought to life there become her reality.

"You're hiding from me. Why?"

His husky voice dragged her back to the present. There was no sense in her denying the truth. "Because I don't want to think about you and Lorena together. I don't want to think about how I'm being lied to and toyed with. After today, you both made it clear neither of you is being honest with me. I don't know exactly what happened between you two, but it's not the bullshit that either of you is telling me."

She hurried down the rest of the steps, putting some distance between them, making it easier to catch her breath and not be taken in by the spell he wove around her.

"I thought you were going to trust me. Six days, that was the bet, wasn't it?"

The bet? This wasn't a game; this was her life. She stopped, pausing her retreat, but refused to look at him. "And I thought you were going to give me a reason to. All you've done is prove to me again why I shouldn't."

"That's not fair, Gia."

She spun on him. "After today, that is more than fair. What are you hiding, Andrew? You said you hadn't told me something. What was it?"

She'd tried to get the answer from her sister earlier, but Lorena had simply burst into tears Gia doubted were real and claimed she needed to go home, leaving Gia shorthanded again. It hadn't lessened the churning fear in her stomach. Even now, Andrew opened his mouth to speak but let out a slow breath instead of confessing the truth.

"Good talk."

Gia was tired of being lied to, kept in the dark and treated as if her feelings weren't important. She walked around the side of the house toward the gate, praying the back door would be open and she could finally escape into the house.

"I didn't sleep with Lorena," he blurted out quickly.

Shock rooted Gia to the spot. She tried to process the information quickly, but he reached her before she could, gripping her shoulders and turning her to face him.

Questions spun in her head at a dizzying speed, like being caught on a roller coaster she'd never wanted to be on. Why did he tell her he had? If he didn't sleep with her, how could Bella be his child? Was this just another lie, and to what end?

"Did you hear me?"

She nodded dumbly, staring up at him. "Bella?" she asked quietly.

Andrew dropped his head forward, hiding his face from her, making it impossible to read his expression. "She's not mine."

"Then, why . . ." Gia took a step away from him and threw her hands into the air, not even finishing the question.

"It's a long story."

What was that supposed to mean?

"A long story you don't want to tell, you mean. Was this just some game you and Lorena cooked up?" The repercussions of their actions hit her hard. "How long have you known about Bella? Why would you tell your mother she had a granddaughter—"

"I just found out today." He ran a hand over his short hair. "Look, will you please just sit so I can explain?"

"Did you know when you came to the restaurant today?"

"Not about Bella, but I was coming to tell you my suspicions about the rest."

She rolled her eyes. She didn't believe him. She wanted to. Desperately. She wanted to believe that was what had sparked the argument between him and Lorena, but that wouldn't have sent her sister running away. Her gut told her there were more secrets, far too many convoluted details. Yet no one was telling her more than minute snippets which made her distrust them all.

He reached for her, his hand finding the curve of her jaw, and for a moment, she wanted to lean into the strength of him. To let go of this fear and judgment and doubt. To be able to go back to the way things had once been between them, when she thought he could never hurt her. In the light of his side of the story and this new revelation, if it were true, he never really had. Gia wasn't sure what to believe.

Had he slept with Lorena? Had he not? The answers had swung back and forth so many times, even she couldn't keep them straight. How could he be sure he wasn't Bella's father?

"How did you find out?" She stared into his dark eyes, lit only by the moonlight, but trying to garner the truth from him.

"I had a paternity test done."

"When?"

"Earlier today. It was a rush job, a friend doing a favor."

"So, it *could* be wrong."

"I didn't sleep with her," he repeated, leaning in closer. "There were some weird things that didn't connect in my head about that night."

"And suddenly they do?" She took a step back, but not so far as to break away from him. "That's a bit too convenient."

"Until now, until I thought there might be an us, I just put that night out of my head and pretended like it never happened. I was drunk, Gia. Things weren't exactly clear. But since you came back, I've been trying to piece everything together. Then I found out from someone I trust that your sister wasn't even at Fool's Point with me. She left me there, passed out in her car. When she came back, she made it look like we'd slept together."

"Why would she do that?" Andrew's face clouded, and she knew he wasn't telling her everything. "Tell me why," she pressed.

He clenched his jaw and sighed. "I'd seen you the week before, Gia, with your dad, and it got to me, more than ever before. I just . . . I'd just screwed it all up. So, New Year's, I was just wallowing all day in regrets and memories. I didn't know you'd already headed back to San Diego, so I went to the restaurant to get shit-faced. I was hoping to run into you and that being drunk would give me the nerve to finally tell you the truth."

"Which is what?" Gia's voice was a tentative whisper, afraid to ask the questions she wasn't sure she wanted answers to but knew she needed.

"That I've never stopped loving you."

"Andrew." Gia closed her eyes, unable to face the raw emotion she could see in his face.

"So, I started talking out my ass. I remember that much. I kept saying I was going to leave town, get on with a bigger department some place like LA like I'd always said I would. Lorena had been bitching all night about how your parents pulled the plug on the second restaurant and how they screwed her. She must have thought she could convince me to take her along with me, especially if I thought she was having my kid."

He shook his head. "After that night, I heard a few rumors were going around about how Lorena tamed me. She kept calling, texting or running into me while I was on duty but I avoided her. When people didn't see us together, the rumors died down quickly. Then, come April, she took off and I thought that was the end of it. I didn't even know she was pregnant."

"But why?"

Andrew slid his hands up her arms and she braced

herself for the painful truth, even though she already knew it.

"Because it accomplished both things she wanted—to get out of Hidden Falls and to hurt you."

Gia's breath caught in her chest. The scenario was so like what Lorena had claimed happened after Lorena found out Gia and Andrew were engaged. She claimed Andrew had met with her at the restaurant after closing, that he'd made love to her, saying he wanted her to leave town with him. But Gia had never told anyone what Lorena had said.

She bowed her head. "Oh, Lorena," she whispered. She looked up at Andrew. "I'm sorry you've gotten caught in the cross fire of this war my sister has started with me. I don't know why, but—"

"Stop."

His hand plunged into her hair and he took a step toward her, closing the mere inches between them. Their gazes fused and their bodies connected. Gia felt the jolt of desire course through her at that simple touch, attraction running between them like an electric current, sparking and igniting.

"I don't care about that. I just need you. That's all I've ever wanted."

Her heart lurched in her chest, pounding against her rib cage heavily as it raced. She wanted to believe what he said.

"I love you, Gia. I've always loved you. There's never been anyone but you."

"Andrew, it's not just me now. I can't just worry about my feelings. I have to do what's best for Bella. If you're not her father . . ."

"I have custody. I assumed paternity and, according to Erik, unless someone else is willing to come forward contesting it, it will stand." He tipped her face up toward his. "Until I sign my rights over to you."

"You'd do that?" Tears filled her eyes and through them, she thought she saw the same in his.

"But I'd rather raise her *with* you."

The breath caught in her lungs, and she couldn't wrap her mind around what he'd just offered.

"If you really want to leave, Gia, I'll sign the damn papers, but consider staying here. With me."

She wanted to sound confident and sure, but this was all happening so quickly. What came out instead sounded low, husky and uncertain. "What are you saying, Andrew?"

"I'm saying we should finish what we started ten years ago. Marry me, Gia."

Chapter Twenty-Four

ANDREW HADN'T MEANT to blurt out a proposal that way. He'd meant to talk with her, to explain what had happened with Lorena that night, then somehow break the news that Bella wasn't his, but that he wanted them to stay. He knew Gia still didn't trust him. He hadn't given her enough reason to yet. Common sense should have made his next step clear—wait and take it slow. Maybe after a few months together, he could plan some elaborate proposal. That was what Gia deserved from him. Not this desperate-sounding attempt.

However, his mouth ran ahead of his brain. Again.

Gia stared up at him in disbelief, her mouth dropping open. At the horrified look on her face, self-preservation bubbled up, making him consider taking back his words. Shit, part of him wanted to, but the truth was, a bigger part of him didn't want to. He wanted to marry Gia.

He'd never stopped loving her, and now he couldn't bear the thought of her and Bella walking out of his life. He needed her, needed them both. Without them, his life would go back to being a hopeless meandering between work and meaninglessness.

"You're not serious."

It wasn't a question, and Andrew wasn't sure how to explain to her that he was completely serious. Her voice was steady, far more than he was sure his would be if he spoke, and she took a step away from him, breaking the physical connection between them. He could see her withdrawing, and that was enough to shake him from his stupor. He had to try.

"Gia, I am. I just . . ." He broke off, running a hand through his hair again.

"No, you're not." She pressed her palm against his chest, and Andrew could feel the heat that emanated from her, scalding him. But he also felt the tremble of her fingers. Her voice softened. "You can't be," she insisted, sounding less sure than she had a moment ago.

She was afraid.

Andrew moved toward her, wrapping one arm around her waist. "I am serious. Marry me."

Her gaze met his again, but this time, hers was hungry. She wound her arms around his neck and stood on her toes, her mouth pressing against his. This wasn't a sweet kiss. This was an explosion of yearning, violent and desperate. Her kisses devastated him, rendering him weak as her tongue tangled with his. As quickly as she'd started it, she backed away.

"I need to think." She held up her hand, warding him off. "I need some time."

Before he could even catch his breath, Gia disappeared, leaving him wondering if he'd just watched her walk away for the last time.

GIA THANKED HER guardian angel that the back door was open as she hurried into her room and closed the door behind her, pressing her hand to her racing heart. Andrew McQuaid had just proposed to her.

Again. Twice.

And she hadn't given him an answer. In spite of the chorus of screaming *yes*es in her head, she could focus only on the solitary, quiet *no*.

She had no doubt about the fact that she loved Andrew, had been in love with him since their very first date when he'd given a somewhat awkward bookworm a sweet goodnight kiss at her front door. But there were so many reasons they couldn't make their relationship work, including the fact that her sister seemed inclined to believe he was the father of her child, or lie about it.

And was it even possible that they hadn't had sex after all? Gia's mind swirled with the conflicting stories, clouding her judgment and making her want to bury her head under a pillow.

Bella sighed softly in her sleep, a quiet little *coo* that caught Gia's attention. She leaned over the side of the bassinet. This had to be her first consideration for any decision she made from now on. Whatever choice she made about Andrew, it had to be what was best for Bella. She ran a hand over the child's back, and the smile that opened the baby's mouth was sweetly heart-wrenching. This poor little girl had no idea she'd been caught in the middle of a sadistic, emotional game of tug-of-war. Whether it was some sort of revenge or just a cat-and-mouse thing her sister got off on, Gia wasn't certain—only that Bella was the one being used as a weapon, and she was the target.

Her chest ached as she realized that as much as she wanted to trust Andrew, there were still doubts that held space in her heart, and until they were vanquished, she couldn't give him an answer. Not yet. Once the concert was over, she could make decisions about what her future would bring, including his revelation that he was giving her custody of Bella.

It had been a roller-coaster ride the past few weeks, from her sister's appearance to Bella's birth to having, losing and, if Andrew kept his word, regaining custody. But the whirlwind had yet to settle.

She scooped Bella from the bassinet and tucked the baby against her chest, the powdery baby scent filling her senses as she lay on the bed with her. She felt her phone vibrate in her pocket but she chose to ignore it, letting the serenity of this moment overtake her, settling her worries and doubts. She had Bella and, somehow, everything else would fall into place.

GIA WOKE TO Bella nudging her face against Gia's neck, demanding her breakfast. The sky was still darkened and the sun was barely coming up over the horizon as she peeked through the curtains. She carried the baby into the kitchen, surprised to find Sarah still in the kitchen, cleaning up several dishes in the full sink. The woman laughed, no doubt at the utter confusion in her face.

"Do you really think I want to be out with those cows? I was just about to finish up here and come sneak Bella out so she didn't wake you. You got home late last night." Sarah cast her a sympathetic smile. "You're putting in some long hours at the restaurant."

"Better I do it than my dad try to." Gia cradled Bella carefully as she reached for a bottle in the cupboard and the formula on the other shelf.

"You sit," Sarah instructed. "I'll fix the bottle for you." She expertly prepared Bella's formula and tested it on the inside of her wrist before returning to the sink. "I hear Linc's performing for you this weekend. I can't wait to have him home again. It's been a long time."

"I really appreciate the way he's helping me out." Gia tried not to look too conspicuous as she glanced around the room for Andrew.

Sarah chuckled. "Everyone is already gone. Separating cattle this morning. They'll be out all day." She turned and gave Gia a conspiratorial wink as she walked over and wiggled one of Bella's bare toes. "It's just the two of us. Want to head into town and do some shopping for this princess?"

Gia couldn't help but wonder if Andrew had told her about the results of the paternity test yet. She certainly wasn't going to be the one to break the news, but she also didn't want to look like she was taking advantage of the woman's generosity.

"I have to get a few last-minute details finalized for the concert," she lied, praying Sarah wouldn't hold it against her if she found out. "And I need to work a double shift at the restaurant today." Thanks to her sister, that much was true.

"Oh." Sarah's face fell and she twisted her mouth to one side. "Who's staying with Bella?"

"I was going to take her to Rossetti's with me."

Sarah waved a hand. "Why don't I take her shopping with me?"

Gia could hear the hopefulness in the woman's voice and didn't have it in her to disappoint Sarah twice in as many minutes. "Sure."

Now what was she going to do until her shift this afternoon? As if reading her thoughts, Sarah cocked her head. "You sure you don't want to come with me? The craft store has some really cute new décor. Maybe you could find something for the restaurant." She slid the newspaper filled with store advertisements across the table, tugging out the one she was looking for and tapping it. "See?"

Gia didn't see the ad. Instead she focused on the headline of the newspaper:

Family Troubles Doom Rossetti's

"I don't think so, Sarah," she murmured, tugging the Local section from beneath the ad.

Gia scanned the article, the dread growing in her stomach with each and every line. Somehow the reporter was under the assumption that Gia was not only attempting to get custody of Bella against her sister's will but that she was trying to ruin Lorena's relationship with her parents and Andrew, the father of her child. It went on to insinuate that Gia had been working with Andrew on the concert, which was when she first made her move on him. It portrayed Gia as nothing more than a money-grabbing home wrecker with Andrew and Bella simply pawns in her master plan. She fought back the tears of fury, taking a deep breath as she folded the paper and finished feeding Bella, pretending to scan the rest of the ads when she was inwardly deciding how to best proceed with Lorena.

Her sister had gone too far this time. It was bad enough that she'd made Gia look like a heartless witch, but she was ruining Andrew's reputation and destroying any chance of the concert being a success, which meant her father would be forced to sell. What the hell was she thinking?

As Bella finished her bottle, letting out a loud burp, Sarah laughed. "That's my signal to get her ready to go." Gia let her scoop the little girl into her arms. "You go right ahead and relax until you need to go to work. You deserve some time off." Sarah surprised her by circling one arm around Gia's shoulders and giving her a motherly squeeze.

Forcing a smile of gratitude to her lips, Gia had a hard time thinking about anything but how she was going to find her sister and they were going to hash this out. One way or another, Gia was getting to the bottom of her sister's behavior and ending it for good.

ANDREW SAT WITH one leg looped over the saddle horn as his brothers drove the herd into the pen. Once inside, they would separate the cows from their young, but until then, Andrew was just sitting here, bored out of his mind, thinking about how he could be back in the nice warm bunkhouse, curled up on his couch with Gia and Bella. His dad rode up alongside him.

"Jackson and Jefferson are bringing in the last of the cows. Once we get them separated and vaccinated and check to see which cows are bred back, we'll push the pregnant ones to the south pasture, where they have the rich grass until after winter."

Andrew simply nodded and shot his dad a patronizing grin. "Not my first rodeo, Dad."

"Maybe not, smart-ass, but let's hope shooting your mouth off isn't your only skill." Andrew knew his dad was screwing with him. It was their way of connecting, so he didn't take the razzing personally.

"Well, at least I *have* more than one skill, old man," he teased back.

"I hope diffusing the situation between Gia and her sister is in your skill set." His father dropped his rope over the saddle horn and leaned down on his elbows, letting the reins dangle between his fingers. "Because according to the paper this morning, it's gotten ugly."

"What are you talking about?" Dread rose in Andrew's chest, bubbling at first, then roiling like lava.

"There was an article this morning that says Gia tricked you and Lorena into giving up custody of Bella. That the two of you are having an affair and Gia's trying to con her parents out of millions. It's pretty juicy stuff."

"They don't have millions," Andrew protested, sitting upright.

"According to the article, they would if they sold the restaurant, which they wanted to do until Gia convinced them otherwise."

Andrew dropped his leg back over the saddle. "That's not what happened."

His father gave him a half-hearted shrug. "I believe you, but that doesn't mean everyone else will. I have no clue how Gia's going to do damage control over this one." His father sat up, sucking a deep inhalation. "Or how Linc can still do the concert."

"You don't think he'd bail on her, do you?" His dad gave him another half-shrug. "Shit."

Andrew pulled his phone from his back pocket, but his dad placed a weathered hand on his arm. "Before you go calling your brother, you might want to make sure Gia's okay."

"Shit," he repeated.

"Instead of 'shit'-ing about it, why don't you head in and see what you can do to help her fix this?" His father tapped the edge of his rope against his knee. "You know, this reporter must have it out for our family, or they really like sensationalism, because he sure stirs up a lot of crap. Maybe that's where you should start."

"With the paper?"

"Find out who wrote the story, where they got their information. Chances are, it's a bunch of crap, just like it was when they reported on Grant last year."

Andrew twisted in the saddle, watching as the twins drove the cattle through the gate, and looked back at his father. He didn't like letting his dad down. This was one of those situations when the entire family pulled together, but he really needed to find out what was going on. To do that, he had to find Gia. "You sure you don't want me to stay? Gia and I can take care of this tomorrow."

His father laughed. "Sure you can. When? While you're on shift? Go. You won't be able to keep your mind on cattle anyway until you get this settled." Andrew tugged on his reins, his horse instantly alert. "But son, maybe this time around you could just marry that girl *before* you screw up." His father gave him a lopsided grin, letting him know he was joking.

"Don't worry, Dad. I'm trying."

The grin slid from his father's lips for a moment as realization dawned. His father's surprised smile beamed from ear to ear. "Well, all right then. Go get her."

GIA SLAMMED THE door to her parents' house shut. "Lorena!"

Silence greeted her and she hurried to her sister's room, shoving the door open with enough force for it to bang into the wall behind it. Her mouth dropped open as her gaze fell on the empty bed. The entire room had the air of being abandoned. Taking in the neatly made bed, Gia opened the closet. It was emptied except for a few of her father's flannel shirts hanging along one side. She hurried to the dresser, trying to ignore the snapshot in a gold frame, the one of her sister hugging her around the neck, her smile wide and bright while Gia had only an annoyed grimace for the camera. Lorena couldn't have been more than six, which would have made Gia almost eight. It had been so long ago. And facing what she was now, Gia could barely believe they'd ever been that close, that Lorena had ever seen Gia without anything other than malice.

She picked up the scrolled frame, surprised by how light it was. Plastic. What a perfect metaphor for her relationship with her sister. On the outside, it looked real, beautiful and sturdy. But if you looked at it closely, it was nothing more than a sham, a fake imitation, weak and brittle, ready to break if held wrong.

"Where's Bella?"

Gia spun at her mother's voice in the doorway, setting the frame back on the top of a pretty doily her mother had on the dresser. Just like everything in their family, it was nothing more than fancy dressing to cover the scarring beneath.

"With Andrew's mother. She wanted to take her shopping."

"Humph," her mother huffed, rolling her eyes. "*Sostituito*."

"You have not been replaced. I needed to come talk to Lorena, and Sarah offered. I didn't even know you'd be here."

"I see." Clearly, her mother didn't. "Well, she's gone again."

"Gone where?"

Her mother glanced around the room and sighed in defeat. "I don't know." Her dark gaze met Gia's, and she could see the blame in her eyes. "What did you do?"

"Me? Why would you automatically assume that I did anything?"

This was so typical of her family. Her mother automatically took Lorena's side, and her father would try to play the peacemaker between them. This was one of those situations where there weren't sides to take. Her sister had lied, blatantly, publicly and destructively. Her mother couldn't possibly blame her for Lorena's actions.

"You pushed her. You pushed her to come back and make a decision about Bella. She wasn't ready. She's fragile, Gia. She's not strong like you."

"Wait a minute." Gia held up a hand. "You're saying that by telling her she needed to come back here and be responsible for her daughter, to come back and help you and Daddy with the restaurant, I drove her to run away again?"

Her mother pinched her lips, and Gia could see the anger flare in her eyes. "Yes, exactly."

"But you don't have a problem with the fact that she left her newborn daughter in my arms, literally? Or with asking me to take time off from my job to come home and help save the restaurant? Or with asking me to help you guys solve your financial crises?"

"It's different for you." Her mother's words sparked Gia's rage at the injustice of the double standard.

"Why? Why is it different? Why do you have so many expectations of me and none of her?" She crossed the room, standing in front of her mother, ready to demand an answer for the first time in her life. Tears burned in her eyes and Gia fought them back. "Why do you care so much about how she feels and not at all about how I feel, or what I'm giving up?"

"She's not like you, Gia." Her mother's voice had

quieted and her gaze fell to the floor. "You're like your father—strong, intelligent, resilient. You're my *donna bella e forte*, but your sister . . ." Her mother shook her head sadly. "Lorena is like I was until your father. A leaf on the wind, a butterfly looking for a safe place to light. She needs our understanding. She needs to know she can always count on the people she loves."

"She's a spoiled brat who doesn't care about anyone or anything except what she wants. Do you even know what she's done? Have you seen this?" She shoved the newspaper at her mother.

Pain filled her mother's eyes as she let the paper fall to the ground, but it was quickly replaced by anger again. Her mother wasn't going to recognize the truth of her sister's selfishness. She didn't want to and would continue to ignore it in favor of the fantasy daughter she'd created in her mind.

"You realize she's ruined any chance of this concert succeeding, and if it doesn't, Daddy is going to be forced to sell."

"Good." The terse severity in her mother's voice shocked her. "I've been telling him for a year he needs to sell. He's not healthy enough to run that place. It will kill him."

She reached for her mother's arm, inhaling slowly at the realization of what she was about to say. "Mama, have you thought that he might not want to live without it? That he just might want to spend what time he has left doing what he loves most?"

Her mother's eyes snapped up to hers, as if she'd just slapped her across the face. "No, Gia." She made a quick sign of the cross like she was warding off evil spirits. *"Dio Mio! Non anche dire che."*

Don't even say that.

As stubborn as her mother was, she refused to acknowledge that her husband's desires for the rest of his life might not mirror her own. But at this point, Gia couldn't worry about the miscommunication in her parents' marriage. Her concern was clearing up her sister's lies and making this concert succeed so that her parents had options. As long as the medical bills were paid, they could make a decision about whether or not her father retired without that dark cloud hanging over them.

"I have to find Lorena." She tugged her phone from her back pocket, calling Lorena.

"She won't talk to you," her mother warned, shuffling behind her as they headed for the front door.

"Why?"

"She told me to tell you that now you know what it's like to lose everything too."

Chapter Twenty-Five

ANDREW STARED AT the screen of his phone in disbelief as he sat outside the newspaper office.

> Stay away from Gia or I'll ruin your career. I'll say you perjured yourself to gain custody.

Lorena was pulling out all the stops now, not only going to the media to destroy Gia's credibility, but now she was threatening his. She was grasping at straws, and he wondered if she even realized how desperate this last attempt was. Even if she tried to go after him, he had the truth on his side. He'd had every reason to believe Lorena when she said they slept together, plus there were plenty of people who'd vouch that she'd bragged about sleeping with him. His signature on the court documents would be chalked up to nothing worse than him naively trusting her.

However, Gia was a different story. This article would make it nearly impossible for her to save her parents' restaurant or to stay in Hidden Falls. Which, if he had his way, she would.

He got out of his car and slipped the phone into his pocket, ignoring the vibration as it notified him of another text, followed by three more in quick succession. Jerking open the office door, he was greeted by a college-age intern at the front counter.

"Can I help you?"

"I need to speak to your editor."

"Do you have an appointment?"

Appointment, damn it! "No."

"I'm sorry, but you'll need an appointment." She flipped open a scheduling book, scanning the dates. "He has an opening next week, Tuesday morning."

Andrew scanned the office, which was nothing more than several desks scattered around the open newsroom. Along one side, he could see two enclosed offices, both with doors shut, but through the glass windows, he could see Lorena, seated with her back toward him, in deep discussion with someone he couldn't see. It took every bit of self-control to keep him from bursting into the office to not only let her know he would beat her at her own game but to see who she was talking to. He turned back to the girl at the counter.

"I need you to pass along a message to him." Her brows lifted slightly in surprise, but she picked up a pen and poised it above a notepad, ready for his message. "Tell him that my name is Andrew McQuaid. The same Andrew McQuaid mentioned in the article you ran this morning," he clarified. "My lawyer, Erik Masters, will be contacting him on behalf of myself and Gia Mancuso for libel."

"Libel?" She glanced up at him. Then she glanced backward toward the office where Lorena was seated. "Um, maybe . . . Hold on." She picked up the phone and punched one of the lines.

Andrew listened as the girl explained the situation to the person on the other end of the phone. He watched, slightly amused, as Lorena spun in her chair to look back at him. A man rose from the desk in front of her and closed the blinds before opening the door of the office.

"Mr. McQuaid," the man said as he approached the reception area. "I'm Mr. Wales, the editor of the paper. I believe there's been some sort of misunderstanding. Won't you follow me and we can discuss it?"

Andrew leaned against the counter and arched a brow. "I'm not sure there's anything to talk about, sir. Unless, of course, you'd like to discuss the matter of a full retraction and public apology."

The editor frowned and cocked his head to one side. "Well, sir, you see, that's not going to be easy, because we technically haven't libeled anyone. We were brought this story with the assurance that—"

"You've published libelous statements regarding both Ms. Mancuso and myself." Andrew crossed his arms, knowing his size made him look even more imposing. "I'm not sure what else you might call it." He shrugged. "But if you'd like to debate semantics, I'm sure my lawyer would be happy to debate them with you."

"Sir," Wales started to argue.

Andrew jerked a chin toward the man's office, cutting him off. "Don't worry. We'll be naming Lorena Mancuso as well. For future reference, you should probably do a background check on your sources before you proceed with printing a story."

Wales glanced toward his office and back at Andrew, looking thoroughly confused about his best course of action. Andrew spun on his heel and started for the door.

"Wait a second." Andrew heard the slightly panicked note in the editor's voice and knew his threat had the impact he'd hoped for. "Is that all it will take? An apology and for me to retract the article?"

Andrew looked back at the man over his shoulder. "What else would you suggest? I mean, you did paint Ms. Mancuso in a very bad light, and she does have a concert this weekend that will probably only have minimal sales now." He left the statement hanging, waiting for Wales' proposal.

"I could run ads for the concert as well, promote the event. Free, of course." He glanced back at his office. "But you must understand that this story was time-sensitive, and my reporter promised me that the necessary research was done. Our source—"

"Was full of shit."

Mr. Wales brows knit between his eyes. "Obviously my reporter must not have done as much research as she claimed to have done. Sir, I do apologize and promise you that I will take care of this. There is no need to bring legal action. I will personally make sure this is taken care of to both your and Ms. Mancuso's satisfaction."

GIA LET HER forehead fall into her hands as she listened to the dinner noises down the hall. It was quieter tonight. More so than it had been since her return. The article that had run this morning was certainly to blame, and she had no clue how to spin it now. This was a publicist's nightmare, and she knew Linc didn't want this kind of attention. She hadn't heard from him yet but didn't doubt he'd be calling to cancel the concert soon.

"You know how to fix all of this, don't you?"

Gia jerked her head up to see her sister standing in the doorway, smug satisfaction written all over her face.

"Just go back to San Diego. Go back to your boring job with your nice car and your stupid empty condo. Let Mom sell the restaurant."

"Why do you even care?" Gia rose and moved around to the front of the desk, sitting on the edge. She didn't want to feel like she was hiding behind anything. She was ready to confront her sister head-on. "I'm surprised to see you here. Mom said you bailed again. You're getting good at it."

"Left town. Got out. Escaped," she clarified. "You, on the other hand, seem sadly stuck, weighed down by too much responsibility." Lorena pursed her lips before chuckling. "When are you going to learn?"

"One of us should have some sense of responsibility, don't you think?" Lorena was trying to bait her and she wasn't going to bite.

Lorena inhaled slowly, looking around their father's office, her gaze searching the photos on the wall as she wandered past the desk, letting her hand trail over the surface. The old desk had been purchased secondhand years ago, and now it was weathered and in desperate need of varnish. He'd never gotten around to it. Most of the place had the same problem. If it didn't affect the daily use or an area that customers frequented, her father let it slide for later. Gia didn't miss the reminiscent look in her sister's gaze and hoped it might trigger some sort of emotion for their parents' plight.

"It's going to be sad to see Dad without this place," Gia said. Lorena turned back and let her gaze slide over Gia as she purposefully chose her next words, wanting Lorena to feel the impact of her actions. "Keeping it would've made Dad happy."

"Aw, aren't you just such a good daughter." The bitterness in her sister's voice was sharp, stinging.

"What did I ever do to you, Lorena? Why do you hate me?"

"Me? Hate you?" Her sister gave her a look of mock surprise. "Who could ever hate *Santa Gia*?"

"We used to be close. What happened?"

"I woke up."

"What's that supposed to mean?" Gia wanted to retreat from the pure contempt she could see in her sister's expression.

"I think I was eight the first time Dad told me I should be more like you. No matter what I did, I could never live up to the perfection that you seemed to shine with. It was always 'Gia this' and 'Gia that' and 'maybe Gia can show you how.' I've been living in your shadow forever. Do you have any idea how that feels? Trying to measure up but knowing I never would?"

Lorena grew more animated as she walked into the room, her hands thrown into the air. "And it never got any better. You were just Miss Popularity. Teachers used to compare me to you and tell me how smart my sister was. There was nothing I could do that you couldn't do better. So, I quit trying."

Gia remembered her mother's explanation for Lorena's troubles. *A place to land . . . needs to know her family loves her.* Lorena's jealousy had blinded her for so many years that she'd allowed herself to be consumed by it.

"Lorena," she began, "you know that Mom—"

"Mom tried to understand," Lorena agreed, waving her sister off. "But she was only one person in a town of hundreds singing your praises. You think her voice didn't get drowned out? Even after you left, I had to hear people telling me how *lucky* I was to have a sister like you. I had to listen to everyone ooh and ahh over you and Andrew. No one cared about what I wanted, what I could do. It was always about Gia."

Gia had been oblivious to what her sister had gone through. She'd been so wrapped up in her own life that she hadn't noticed what had been going on in Lorena's. Whether she'd meant to or not, she'd played a part in Lorena feeling inadequate. If only she'd seen, she could have encouraged her sister.

"I'm sorry."

"Yeah, now." Lorena laughed, the sound brittle and painfully harsh. "After you know what it's like to have nothing. I had Mom convinced to let me open that second restaurant. Dad was on board. I was going to be the one to save the family, to prove how much they could count on me."

"That wasn't my fault, Lorena."

"No? You were the one who pointed out to Dad that it wasn't a good time. You ruined my future. So I ruined yours." The pure hatred Gia could see in her sister's eyes was staggering. "Do you have any idea how good it felt for me to watch your perfect life fall apart at your feet? To watch you cry for the first time? I'd never seen that before. You were always smiles and sunshine. But not that night."

Andrew. Gia didn't need to ask Lorena if he was what she meant. Gia knew. She shook her head, wondering at the bitterness that had to have accumulated in her sister for her to maliciously hurt her that way.

"That was a long time ago."

Gia turned her back on her sister. She could feel empathy for the jealous teenager Lorena had been, hurting, seeking approval, but it didn't excuse Lorena's vicious actions now.

"We both know that's not true." Her sister laughed again, her voice carrying through the room and stabbing Gia in the chest. Gia turned back around, eyeing her sister, waiting for her to explain. "Everyone in town knew that wasn't true. You never got over him, any more than he did you. It was just a matter of time—although you both lasted longer than I thought you would—but to watch your misery every time you came home was priceless. How bad did it hurt when you found out Andrew was Bella's father? To imagine us together? To know he wanted me?"

The barb was meant to wound, meant to tear Gia down, but it made Gia realize that Lorena didn't know Andrew had discovered he wasn't Bella's biological father. She pinched her lips together, refusing to answer. Lorena's smirk widened.

"That much, huh? Sucks when you aren't the first choice, doesn't it?" Lorena tipped her head to one side.

Gia felt the rage bubble up in her chest. Her sister had destroyed her relationship with Andrew once, had tainted the purest love she'd ever known, because she wanted Gia to feel the same jealousy she had.

"You weren't his *choice*, Lorena. The first time never happened and the second, he was drunk. You used that to your advantage."

"Oh, lookie who thinks she has everything figured out." Lorena narrowed her eyes.

"I'll give you points for being creative, because you almost got away with it." Gia shook her head, unable to believe the extent her sister would go to get her vengeance.

"What do you mean, 'almost?' That article this morning worked even better than I'd hoped. If you and Andrew try to get together now, you'll both be ostracized. People in Hidden Falls aren't that forgiving. He'll lose his job. I've already made sure of that with the interview I gave the newspaper today." She gave a short but cruel laugh. "Police departments tend to shy from officers accused of taking advantage of women in their patrol cars."

Lorena curled her lip up. "And your concert is going to be a bust so Mom and Dad will finally realize that you don't actually have the Midas touch. When they sell, I'll move back home to 'take care' of Dad," she said, wiggling her fingers in the air for quotation marks. "Mom and I can hire a nurse with all the money this sale will get them."

"You have to know I won't let any of that happen."

Lorena chuckled quietly. "You think you can stop me? Go ahead and try. I'll use the money I convince Mom and Dad to give me to take Bella away from Andrew too."

Dread pierced Gia's heart. Bella's future was the only thing Lorena had left to wield against her, and she knew it. She was Gia's one weak point, and Lorena didn't hesitate to drive that stake home.

"You can't," Gia reminded her. "You signed off your rights."

"Oh, you're right. I did, but she has two parents." Her sister arched a devious brow and gave her another of those smug grins. It made her heart stop as she realized what her sister had planned.

Lorena had signed off her paternal rights, but Bella's biological father hadn't.

Chapter Twenty-Six

ANDREW SAT ON the couch with Bella curled against his chest, sound asleep after finishing her bottle. Her soft breath brushed over his neck, smelling faintly like the formula, and he couldn't help himself from pressing a kiss to the top of her downy head. Bella sighed quietly, her mouth dropping open and the corners twitching into a smile that made his heart pound with adoration. This little girl had easily become such an important part of his life, enough that he'd lay his life down for her without thinking twice, even if she wasn't really his blood.

He'd had a few friends who'd married women with children from previous relationships—his brother Grant had done it—and he'd wondered how they could so easily love a child that wasn't their own. He no longer questioned it.

When Bella looked up at him with wonder, with eyes

that would likely turn brown, so filled with curiosity, her DNA didn't matter. He didn't care whose genes she had. He was the only father she'd know. He was more than willing to take care of her when she had a fever, to be the one teaching her to ride a bike as well as the man who would hold her hand and walk her to school. He would be the first man to love her to distraction.

More than ever before, Bella had made him realize that blood didn't make a family. Love did. And he loved this little girl.

But he wouldn't get to do any of those things if Gia left Hidden Falls.

Andrew couldn't entertain the thought of Gia returning to San Diego. Losing her again would devastate him, but losing them both would destroy him.

As if the thought of her conjured her from thin air, Gia appeared in the doorway, leaning against the door frame. "You two look comfortable."

Her voice was husky, and he wondered if it was from emotion or exhaustion. "You okay?"

Gia took a deep breath and pushed herself from the doorway, nodding. "I went to my parents' house today. My mother is upset Lorena is leaving town again."

"That's good, right? I mean, about Lorena." He was confused by the despondency he could see in her eyes when she should feel like celebrating. "I mean, she won't be here to lend a hand with the concert, but her drama wasn't really helping matters anyway."

Gia shrugged. "She blames me. She refuses to see that Lorena has caused all of her own troubles." She bit the corner of her lip and he felt the trepidation creep into his gut, twisting it in knots. "Are you sure Linc still wants to do the concert?"

"I called him earlier and explained the situation. He said he's more on board than ever. I also went down to the newspaper office. They are printing a retraction in tomorrow's paper and running several advertisements for the concert." He shrugged, slightly disturbing Bella who protested with a grunt. "I won't pretend that the article this morning helped matters, but hopefully this will help mitigate any damage Lorena caused."

"I doubt it. Lorena said she'd given a second interview today."

He heard the defeat in her voice and it confused him. Gia was never one to give up in the face of adversity. Never. If anything, it spurred her to try harder. She always proved she could beat the odds.

"I suspected that's why she was there."

"You saw her?"

"When I went in." He carefully stood, readjusting Bella in his arms as he moved to Gia. "But you'd be surprised what a threat of libel can do."

She shook her head in denial. "She's wants to get you fired, Andrew. She won't stop until she does. Until she makes us both miserable."

"I'm not getting fired. I've got everything under control, Gia. Trust me." He slid his hand to cup her cheek. "I won't let her hurt you, or Bella, again."

"I don't think you realize the extent Lorena is willing to go to in order to hurt me, or anyone who tries to help me. She blames me for so much. I never knew how much."

"Lorena is a spoiled, jealous child bent on destroying anything she can't have for herself. And I don't think you realize the extent I will go to in order to make sure you and Bella are both safe and happy."

Gia's gaze locked with his. He could see her doubts, the fear eating at her, the fierce independence born of being let down by so many people she thought would be there for her, him included.

"Yes, I think I do," she whispered sadly. "What I don't understand is, why? We aren't your responsibility."

Andrew gave her a lopsided smile. "On the contrary, my daughter *is* my responsibility, and I took that on willingly when I signed those papers."

"But you didn't know she wasn't yours then," Gia contradicted him.

"I suspected as much," he admitted honestly.

"Then why? Why didn't you do the paternity test first?"

"I did it for you, Gia. Well, and Bella. She deserves someone who loves her the way you do." She looked down at the infant in his arms, but he tipped her chin up to meet his gaze. "And I love *you*. If there was any way in my power to give you what you wanted, I would do whatever I had to. Even signing a paternity acknowledgment for a child that might not be mine."

Tears filled her eyes and she tried to blink them back. "After the concert, I need to go back to San Diego," she blurted, taking a step backward.

"Gia—"

"No, don't." She held up her hand to keep him at a distance. "I can't explain why, but I have to do this." She swiped at the tears that managed to escape. Her gaze, filled with longing, dropped to the baby in his arms before meeting his again. "You have to take care of Bella. Promise me you'll do that."

"Of course, I will, Gia, but—"

"I'm going back to my parents' house tonight." She ran from the room and, luckily, his legs were long enough to keep up without jarring Bella.

"Will you stop and talk to me? At least explain why." He tried to keep his voice down. The last thing they needed was for someone to hear and come running into the room, assuming he was causing trouble for Gia again. "Gia."

She dragged her suitcase from under the bed and threw it on the covers before moving to the dresser, pulling her clothes out and shoving them inside. Andrew could tell she was struggling to ignore him and wasn't going to let her off that easily. He hadn't fought this hard for her to watch her just walk away again without any explanation. If she didn't love him, he would learn to accept that. But he had the feeling this was something different.

This was Gia running away. This was fear.

He closed the door behind him. "Gia, you don't want to do this."

She glanced in his direction, tossed the last of her clothing into the bag and zipped it up. Lifting the bag from the bed, she carried it to where he stood, blocking her exit.

Taking a deep breath, she looked up at him. Gia pressed her lips together, but he didn't miss the lower one trembling. "You're right, I don't. But that doesn't change the fact that I have to."

"What is *that* supposed to mean?"

"It means, you signed those papers because you loved me and Bella."

"Love," he corrected. "I *love* you and Bella."

She closed her eyes, and he saw another tear slip from one corner. "Love," she acknowledged with a sharp nod. "And I'm doing this because I love the two of you."

Gia pressed a quick kiss to Bella's forehead, her cheek against where his heart lay broken in his chest. He heard her bite back a sob as she rushed past him through the door. Reaching out, he grasped her wrist. "Gia, wait."

She turned back to him, pulling her hand from his grasp and laying it against his cheek. Standing on her toes, she kissed his mouth, and he could taste her tears on his lips as she whispered against them.

"I love you. Trust *me* this time."

Her words rooted his feet to the floor, unable to comprehend what had just happened. She loved him. She was leaving. None of it made sense.

Apparently it didn't have to.

It HAD BEEN four days since Gia walked out of the McQuaid house. Ninety-six hours since she'd kissed Bella and inhaled her sweet baby scent or cuddled her warm body close. Five thousand, seven hundred and sixty minutes—Gia glanced at the clock—sixty-seven minutes since she'd heard Andrew's confused voice as he tried to convince her to stay, to discuss with him why she felt she had to say goodbye.

That wasn't exactly true. He'd called several times over the past four days, trying to talk to her, using the concert as an excuse, but she'd simply texted him back with the answers he needed or contacted Linc directly. She was avoiding him. She had to. There was no other way for her to maintain any sort of sanity otherwise. As it was, she wasn't sure she was going to be able to make it through the concert tomorrow without breaking down.

She wanted to stay. Gia made the decision to stay, had even typed up her resignation, before her sister changed her mind by threatening to take Bella away from Andrew. As long as Gia and Andrew weren't together, Lorena would leave Andrew and Bella alone, and Bella was safe with him.

However, if he went through on his offer to give her custody, or Lorena realized they were together, she'd go after Bella for the sole purpose of hurting Gia. It didn't matter who was caught in Lorena's wake. Gia loved both too much to see that happen.

She'd seen the look on Andrew's face when he held Bella, when he pressed a kiss to the top of her head. He loved that little girl as much as if she were his own flesh and blood, regardless of what the paternity test revealed. It was also in that same moment she realized she could fully trust him.

It was ironic, really. The moment she realized she could trust Andrew completely was the very same one she vowed to walk away in order to protect them both. At least for the time being, or until her sister gave up on this vendetta she had. Gia couldn't risk Bella's well-being for her own selfish desires.

Now, with Lorena gone, things were quiet, and it looked like the concert wouldn't be a total bust after all. The ticket sales weren't what she'd hoped for, but it would be enough to take some of the pressure off her parents by paying most of her father's medical bills.

However, Gia still felt like she was failing them. All she'd managed to accomplish by returning was to lose custody of their granddaughter and put them at odds with one another. Her mother still insisted they sell; her father still insisted they keep Rossetti's. Gia had no doubt her mother would win the argument because, once she returned to San Diego, there would be no one left to help her parents run the restaurant. It would once again become too overwhelming, and they would be forced to sell.

Despite Gia's best efforts, Lorena was going to get her way. Her parents would sell, she'd lost Bella and her heart was broken again.

"Well, my day is just getting better."

Gia looked up to see Lorena standing in the doorway of the office.

"Why so sad, sis? You have a concert to put on? People you need to be *perfect* for, remember?"

She fought the urge to jump out of the chair and rip her sister's hair out. She wanted to slap the smug look from her face. Lorena needed to grow up and move past this petty jealousy. This wasn't a game; she was playing with lives. But Gia was too weary to argue with her. Not that it would do any good.

"I thought you left."

"Yeah, well, I did, but then I came back." Lorena flounced into the room and flopped into one of the chairs.

Like a bad habit.

"I need a favor."

Gia arched a dark brow. Surely her sister was joking. Why would she willingly do anything for her after everything she'd done? Lorena must have noticed Gia's outrage in her expression.

"Don't give me that look. It's not a big favor. I just want you to have Bobby open for Linc."

Gia silently stared at Lorena, astounded at her sister's audacity. "You tried to sabotage this concert," Gia pointed out.

"Since you're insisting on going through with this concert, I assumed that you'd want to help him."

"Him? Or you?"

"Both of us. And you." Lorena gave her a bright smile, and Gia was amazed at how much she looked like a lioness ready to attack. "Linc's name tied to his would go a long way in his career. Then the two of us will be off on tour."

"You've got to be kidding me?" Gia rose from behind the desk. "Get out."

Lorena rolled her eyes and stood slowly. "Gia, we can either do this the easy way or the hard way. Either you convince Linc to let Bobby open for him or we'll take a trip down to the courthouse tomorrow."

"Did you lie to him about being Bella's father too?"

Gia hadn't meant for the thought to sneak past her lips. Lorena narrowed her eyes. Provoking her sister wasn't going to get her anywhere.

"Judge me all you want, Gia, but I'm going to get out of this shithole. Since Andrew turned out to be a loser, Bobby may just be my ticket. So, you're going to help me."

Gia shook her head. "If you want to leave so badly, just leave."

Lorena rose quickly, sending the chair skittering backward. "It's easy for you, Gia. I wasn't engaged to one of the most eligible men in town. I didn't get a full-ride scholarship. I didn't land a fancy job. I had nothing. Nothing but this stupid restaurant and a promise of someday."

"Wait a second." Gia was suddenly seeing her sister clearly, recalling how Bella's father had never wanted a child, how she'd lied to convince him to take her back. "You got pregnant on purpose, hoping Bobby would propose? When that didn't pan out, you tried to blackmail Andrew, didn't you?"

Lorena refused to answer and stormed toward the door. "Just set it up, Gia. Make sure he goes on before Linc."

The door slammed behind her, hard enough that Heather came running. "Are you okay?"

Gia nodded, but an idea began to form. She ran after her sister. "Okay," she yelled down the hallway. Lorena stopped and turned around. "I'll set it up. Tell him to be here tomorrow at nine for a sound check."

Lorena gave her a quick nod and disappeared into the front of the restaurant, leaving Gia with only a few hours to make sure she could pull this off. It was going to take some planning and a lot of luck, but she was going to make sure her sister couldn't threaten her, or Bella, again.

"WHAT THE HELL are you waiting on, you pussy? Nut up and go talk to her."

"Shut up, Linc. You don't realize what's gone on before you showed up."

Linc rolled his eyes and picked absently on the strings of his guitar. "Gia thought you boned her sister so she dumped your ass. Then you *did* bone her sister, but not really, and she shows up with a kid that she dumped in Gia's lap, claims it's yours, but it's not. And now you have a kid and no Gia. Does that about sum it up?"

"Something is going on and Gia's refusing to talk to me about it. She's afraid, Linc. Really afraid, and losing Bella would be the only thing that would scare her like this."

Linc sighed. "Again, then why are you sitting here, talking to me about this, instead of down at Rossetti's talking to *her*?" He reached for his phone on the table and tapped a few buttons. Within a few seconds, his phone buzzed with a reply message. "There. She says I can come down right now and make sure the guys put everything where I want before the sound check. If I take you down there with me, will you quit whining like a bitch?"

"Fuck off."

Linc shot him the lopsided grin thousands of women had been drooling over for the last seven years as he slid the guitar into its case and threw his arm around Andrew's shoulders. "Exactly what a bitch would say. Come on."

Andrew knew his younger brother was trying to make him feel better, but it wasn't working. He'd been on edge since Gia walked out without any explanation. He wanted to trust her, the way she'd asked him to, but he also knew she was stubborn enough to get in way over her head.

"Mom—" he paused, pressing a kiss to his mother's cheek "—can you watch Bella for a few minutes?"

She arched a brow. "I guess that depends on where you think you're going? You," she said, pointing a scolding finger at Linc, "just got home last night."

"I need to talk to Gia," Andrew said.

"To get a few things settled before the concert tonight," Linc added slyly. Their mother eyed them, looking from one back to the other.

"Lincoln McQuaid," she warned, "just because you can lie to other women on tours of yours doesn't mean you can lie to your mother and get away with it." She turned to Andrew, her gaze softening with motherly adoration. "Fix this with her, Andrew, and bring her home."

"I'm going to try, Mom."

Chapter Twenty-Seven

GIA STARED DOWN at the paperwork Erik Masters had e-mailed her this morning. If her hunch was correct, Bobby would be happy to sign the documentation and her sister's threat would become a moot point. She'd be free of that black cloud hanging over her and she wouldn't have to leave Hidden Falls after all. But only if she was right about Bobby being Bella's father.

None of her plan even took into account the fact that she had to somehow get Bobby away from Lorena to sign the papers. Or that she might have to sell her soul, jeopardize her own reputation and convince Linc to let him perform a set. Gia moved her hands over her body in the sign of the cross. She might not go to church like her mother, but she prayed there was someone up there listening to her pleas.

She reached up, twisted her long waves into a messy bun on the top of her head and scrubbed her hands over her eyes. Linc was on his way in, Bobby should be arriving any moment and, hopefully, Lorena was too busy tormenting someone else to come until tonight.

"Come on, Bobby." Gia heard her sister making her way down the hall toward the office, presumably with the infamous Bobby following.

Wishful thinking.

She slid the papers from the lawyer into a file folder so they wouldn't be seen.

"There you are," Lorena said, pushing the door open enough for the man behind her to come inside. "This is Bobby McGee."

Gia arched a brow in disbelief. "Really?"

"What?"

Lorena looked nonplussed, glancing back at her country-singing boyfriend, and Gia bit back a laugh. "Some sort of unfortunate prophecy?"

The man stepped toward Gia. Tall and lean, with hair that looked in desperate need of a haircut, and a wash, he looked like a hippie-surfer in his torn jeans and red flannel shirt. The T-shirt beneath it was slightly dingy, like it hadn't been washed anytime recently, but Gia forced herself not to make any judgments as her gaze slid up to meet his. Deep blue eyes locked with hers and his full lips slid into a gallant smile, showing perfectly straight teeth, as well as a single dimple in his left cheek, nearly buried in scruff. It wasn't hard to see what had attracted Lorena to him. He had a sexy grunginess about him. Like a movie-star lumberjack.

"Yeah," he chuckled, his voice more gravelly than Gia had expected. "My mom was a big Janis Joplin fan. Guess that's where she got it from." He held out his hand. "You're Lorena's sister?"

His gaze slid over her, not-so-subtly taking in her every curve. His tongue slid out, licking his lower lip, and Gia withdrew her hand, rubbing it on her jeans, feeling the urge to cover herself.

She bit back a nasty retort, not willing to shoot herself in the foot for the sake of her pride, and simply answered, "Yes."

"You two look a lot alike." He glanced pointedly at her ample breasts, thankfully well covered by her T-shirt bearing the restaurant's logo.

"How did the two of you meet?" She glanced at her sister, who moved closer to Bobby and wound her arm possessively around his waist.

"She's my manager," he explained, pulling her in for a squeeze.

"And your fiancée," Lorena added with a squeal as he ducked his head into her neck and nibbled. Gia thought she might gag.

He lifted his head, flipping his hair back from his face with a laugh. "She says you're going to let me open for Linc McQuaid tonight."

"The final decision will be Linc's, of course, but I'll put in a good word for you."

"I'm sure she can persuade him, baby," Lorena added quickly, glaring at her sister in warning.

"I'll certainly do my best," Gia agreed. "As a matter of fact, he should be here in just a few minutes for the sound check. Why don't you two figure out a set list, work on a couple songs, and then you can audition for him. That way he'll know you're the real deal."

Bobby shook a finger at her and narrowed his eyes. "That's a good idea." He looked around Gia's office. "You, uh, got another room I could practice in? Something with better acoustics?"

"Lorena, why don't you find somewhere that will work for Bobby? I'll text you when Linc is ready for him."

Lorena opened the door and ushered Bobby down the hall, toward the storage room. She had barely walked away when Gia felt her phone vibrate. Glancing at the screen, she saw the text message from her sister.

Don't fuck this up.

Without responding, she slid her phone into her back pocket. No, she knew exactly how important it was for her not to fuck this up.

GIA WAS OVERSEEING the setup in the ballroom when she heard several of the newly hired waitresses whispering. She followed the direction of their mooning gazes and smiled when she saw the heart-stoppingly handsome Linc McQuaid step inside the room with his guitar slung over his shoulder. Her smile slipped a notch, however, when she caught sight of the broad-shouldered man behind him looking more like his bodyguard than his brother. Even with his features shadowed, she'd have known Andrew anywhere.

Correction—her body knew him and instantly responded. Gia's pulse kicked into high gear, racing, making her blood pound hot and heavy. Her breathing grew shallow, and she felt the familiar flutter in her stomach, not to mention the regions below.

"Gia." Linc hurried across the ballroom and wrapped her in a bear hug. They'd been friends throughout high school since he was only a year older, but they'd lost contact after graduation and her breakup with Andrew. "How's life treating you, kiddo?"

She grinned at his nickname for her, even though she was two months older. "Not as well as it's treated you, apparently." He shrugged and gave her a guilty smile. "Who'd have guessed that all those theater musicals would pay off?"

"Shh!" he said, draping an arm over her shoulder. "Please, do not let that secret get out."

Faint guitar music carried through the ballroom as another waiter slipped through the double doors. Gia needed to get Linc to her office and talk to him before Lorena saw him. "I have a favor to ask you, but let's head to my office.

"Heather, can you make sure the dessert table is set up over there?" She pointed to one corner, trying not to be conspicuous as she glanced back at Andrew.

"You got it, Boss."

Linc leaned down to her ear. "Gonna just pretend he isn't here?"

"It's better if I do."

Linc gave her a knowing look and shook his head. "For now." He turned toward his brother. "I'll be right back."

Andrew's mouth dropped open, like he was about to speak, and then he thought better of it. He gave a sharp nod and headed toward the bar, walking behind it to grab himself something to drink, wearing a scowl on his face that dared anyone to question his presence there.

She steered Linc toward her office. He made himself comfortable on the edge of her desk, toying with the picture of her family in a frame. It had been on the desk as long as she could remember, something her father must have set there, but until he turned it toward her, she couldn't even remember what it was a picture of.

"I hear your sister's still causing you trouble."

Gia looked at the picture in his hands. She and her sister were in front of her parents, but while everyone faced the camera, their faces plastered with cheesy smiles, Lorena's eyes held a contempt she'd never recognized.

Not until now. She'd see the same look in her sister's eyes so many times in the past few weeks.

"I guess some people never change," he said.

"That's sort of the favor I need," she said, slipping the picture from his fingers and placing it facedown on the desk. "She's insisting her boyfriend open for you tonight."

"Um, no." He rolled his eyes, pushing himself off the desk.

"Before you refuse, hear me out." She needed Linc to listen to reason. She'd plead if she had to. Because if one stupid set was what it would take to get Bobby to sign off his parental rights, then she'd make sure he got it. "I'm asking, too, and you know I wouldn't put you in that kind of position unless I really needed this."

Linc looked thoughtfully pensive. "Why do you need this?" When Gia shrugged, he laughed, surprising her. "Bullshit, you don't know. You have something up your sleeve."

She arched a brow at him, wishing she could tell him. "Just shut up and agree. Please."

"Okay," he conceded.

Inwardly Gia wanted to jump for joy. Now she only had to get Bobby away from Lorena for a few minutes.

"On one condition."

Crap! She should have known he'd made it too easy, especially for one of the McQuaid men.

"Talk to Andrew. Work this out between you guys.

You know that the two of you belong together, Gia, you always did."

She wasn't about to argue with him, especially when he was saying something she agreed was one hundred percent true. "Okay."

"Well, crap," he muttered, echoing her earlier thought.

"What?"

"If I'd known you were going to agree so easily, I would have added a few more conditions."

She smiled at him smartly. "Too late. Go wait in the ballroom and I'll bring him out for an audition in a few minutes, but make it look like the real thing, okay?"

"You got it, kiddo."

Gia's stomach did a nervous flip before winding into a massive knot. She pressed a hand against it, wondering if one of her plans was finally going to work out the way it was supposed to.

GIA HEADED TO the supply room and found Bobby in the back corner, wedged into a small area of the concrete room with boxes of toilet paper and Styrofoam to-go boxes towering above him. The soft notes of a ballad greeted her, and she realized he wasn't half-bad. In fact, his voice with its deep gravel held a mournful plaintiveness that gave his music a bluesy feel. Lorena wasn't in the room, so Gia knew not to waste this opportunity.

"Bobby, why don't you come back to my office? Linc is getting a few things set up for tonight and then he'll be ready for you. In the meantime, I have some papers for you to sign."

The man jumped up from his seated position on an old metal chair, bumping his guitar against it and causing it to clang loudly. Gia instantly looked back, waiting for Lorena to come running in, but no one else entered.

"Papers? Like a contract?"

"Sort of," she hedged, not wanting to commit to anything.

Gia opened the door of the office for him, closed it behind them and walked to her desk. Lifting the file folder, she felt her heart stop in her chest. It was now or never.

"How serious are you and my sister?"

Bobby's brows knitted together in a frown before lifting in pleasant surprise. A sly grin slipped across his face. "Aw, baby, I've never had sisters before, but—"

"Ew, no. I mean, if you're really her fiancé, you have to know she just had a baby, right?"

His face clouded. "Lost a baby, you mean."

"No, *had* a baby. A little girl."

"Yeah, she died, was . . ." He paused, searching for the term. ". . . still . . . stillborn."

Gia shook her head. Bobby's blue eyes turned stormy as he ground out, "She lied." Gia nodded even though he wasn't really asking a question.

"Motherfucker," he cursed beneath his breath. Bobby took a deep breath. "So? What do you want from me? I told her I didn't want kids."

Relief coursed through her, flooding every fiber of her being. Bobby set the guitar to one side of the chair and slid into it, as if his legs wouldn't quite hold him, in spite of his bravado. His hand tangled in his messy hair.

"I didn't even agree to this fiancé crap. That was all her."

"You don't love her?"

"She's using me to get out of this town. I'm using her." He shrugged. "Don't get me wrong. I like her, so it works for us, but love?" He rolled his eyes and shook his head. "I'm not going to be tied down, especially with a kid I'm not even sure is mine."

Gia felt her stomach knot up at the thought of yet another man being Bella's father. How many men had her sister slept with?

"What do you mean?"

"There was this other guy. Some cop or something. She said she roofied his drinks. It was just a joke and she said she didn't sleep with him, but come on, Lorena's not exactly a girl to say no, if you know what I mean. And I covered my shit." He flung his hand toward his crotch.

This guy is all class.

"A cop?"

"Yeah. Said something about it being payback and

a long time coming, but I don't know what she meant. Most of the time, she talks but I can't figure out half of what she's saying."

Andrew.

Gia slid the folder across the desk toward him. Bobby opened it and glanced down at the documents, shoving it back at her.

"I told you, I'm not signing anything saying I'm the father of this kid. Not until there's a paternity test done proving it's mine."

"Read these again." She slid it back. "These documents simply say that if, at any time, you are proved to be the father of Bella, you're signing off any and all parental rights to the child."

"Really?" He grabbed them and scanned them again. "So, like, this means I don't have to pay any kind of support?"

Was this really about money for him? *That* was his only concern?

"By signing these, you're saying that you'll never make any claims that this baby is yours, nor are you responsible for her in any way. It also means she can be put up for adoption."

"Shit, show me where to sign." He tugged the documents toward him as Gia handed him a pen.

"Be sure, because this isn't something that can be easily reversed," she warned, hating the part of her that demanded she be completely forthright.

He cocked his head at her. "I'm a broke musician,

on the road, and can barely feed myself. How would I take care of a kid, even if I did want one? Which, for the record, I don't."

Gia stared at the man across from her, realizing that sadly, he was making a more mature and responsible decision for Bella than her sister by focusing on Bella's needs and his inability to provide for them. She could almost feel sympathetic toward him and was glad she'd talked to Linc about letting him open. Maybe it would be the break this guy needed.

He glanced up from his signature, passing the papers back to Gia. "So, is that a no on the sisters thing?" He wiggled his brows suggestively.

And there went any sympathy she felt toward him.

"It's a no," she assured him.

Bobby shrugged his shoulders and rose with a chuckle. "Can't blame a guy for trying."

Gia made sure that the papers were signed correctly before closing the folder and rising. "Yeah, I can. If you want to go out and get ready in the ballroom, I'll be right there."

Bobby reached for his guitar, heading for the door. He stopped with his hand on the knob. "Gia?"

"Yeah?"

"I appreciate this. I really do."

She might not like the guy. She might think he was a total douchebag, but she could empathize with someone chasing his dream. Especially when he'd just handed her hers so easily. "You still need to impress Linc."

"No," he said, shaking his head. "I mean, that too, but for telling me the truth about the baby. I might not want to be a father, might never want to, but someone should take care of that kid. Your sister . . ." He shook his head again, unable to meet Gia's gaze, and she could see the faraway look in his eyes, as if he was lost in his own thoughts. "Well, someone should have that kid's interests at heart. You seem like a good person. Not what I expected."

Gia felt a brief moment of guilt before she realized that, in this scenario, she was the only one who loved Bella and wanted to see her happy. Well, her and Andrew. They might not be her biological parents, but they loved her, and that more than made up for DNA.

"Break a leg, Bobby."

Chapter Twenty-Eight

ANDREW HAD BEEN waiting all day. He couldn't claim that he'd been patient about it. Once Linc put him to work, the time had passed more quickly than it had before as people began arriving for the private VIP concert. It was no surprise that three quarters of those who'd purchased tickets had been women and, for a concert that had been boycotted thanks to a bullshit article by the local paper, the ballroom was packed.

Some hippie-grunge dude was up front strumming on his guitar, and the women who'd come to swoon over his brother seemed to be eating this guy up as well. He didn't get it. The guy looked like someone Andrew would have run in for loitering and ended up busting on possession charges, but whatever. If the women around Hidden Falls were into some Kurt Cobain–looking wannabe, more power to the guy.

Andrew had eyes for one woman and cared only what she was thinking. Unfortunately, Gia had completely avoided him at every turn tonight. He'd tried to catch her alone, but whenever he came close, she would slip away, only to be seen serving tables or mingling with the diners. When he'd first walked in with Linc, she'd been in jeans and a T-shirt, but at some point she'd managed to sneak off and change into a cute little sundress. The long, flowing skirt twisted around her cowboy boots as she danced around the room, smiling at everyone. Everyone but him.

"Chill out! Shit. She promised me she'd talk to you." Linc slapped him on the shoulder. "Geez, I thought *I* was the one who was supposed to get nervous."

"I'm not nervous." Andrew shrugged off his brother's hand. "I'm concerned. There's a difference."

"Yeah, you're right. They just both look like nerves." Linc rolled his eyes before jerking his chin toward the stage. "This guy is actually pretty good."

"I guess." Andrew wasn't exactly in the mood for small talk, at least not with his brother. He wanted to talk to Gia and wasn't going to be able to settle down until he did.

He watched her move toward the other end of the stage as the guy finished his set, clapping as she walked toward the microphone. The hippie rose from his seat, bowing slightly amid the applause and adoration.

"Thank you. Ladies and gentlemen, another huge round of applause for Bobby McGee." Gia's voice was engaging, with just enough low huskiness to make his body begin to ache.

Linc snorted beside him. "He's *got* to change his name if he wants to be taken seriously." He stepped up on the back of the stage. "You ready?"

"I'm not the one going onstage."

"No, but now's your chance to kidnap that woman, while I work the room, so you can figure out what's going on between the two of you. Convince her that you're worth sticking around for, dumbass."

Before Andrew could respond to his brother, Gia introduced him and the crowd went wild. Gia had to be thrilled with the turnout. She might not have been happy with the article her sister instigated, but if the sold-out crowd here tonight was an indication, the retraction and subsequent advertising more than made up for it. Just as Gia settled the microphone in the stand for Linc, he reached out, grasping her hand in his.

If it had been anyone but his brother, Andrew would've come unglued.

"Hold up." His brother covered his wireless mic and leaned down to whisper something in her ear. Gia's cheeks colored and her eyes widened, her gaze shooting toward where Andrew waited at the back of the stage. Linc gave her a little nod and she returned it with one of her own.

"Ladies," Linc began, his voice low and husky, "and gentlemen. I just want to take a moment to thank this woman right here. She's pulled this concert together in a very short time, and I think she's done a phenomenal job, don't you?"

Applause sounded from the crowd, but Linc wasn't letting it go. "And what about this food?"

More applause, followed by several whistles. "This is the one place I always look forward to coming when I'm home, and now that the cat's out of the bag and the rest of the world knows how great Rossetti's is, I just hope you'll save me a table, Gia."

"Always," Gia replied with a dazzling smile.

Linc slid into the chair one of his crew set up in the middle of the stage for his rare acoustic performance. "In fact, most of you probably don't know it, but Gia here was part of the inspiration for one of my songs. About a pigheaded man, too stubborn to go after the woman he loved when she left town. Gia, this one's for you and my brother."

Linc began to pluck at the strings of his guitar, and Andrew immediately recognized one of Linc's most popular hits, the one that had first gotten him on the charts nearly eight years ago. As many times as he'd heard it on the radio, he'd had no idea his brother had written it about them.

The crowd began to sing along as dessert was served to each table, and Andrew saw Gia practically run off the stage, hurrying through the double doors. He followed her, determined that he wasn't letting her get out of his sight again.

"Gia, stop," he called as she walked swiftly down the

hallway toward her office. She paused but didn't turn around.

Andrew could hear the haunting notes of the song, could feel them as they squeezed at his lungs, making it hard for him to breathe.

> *I watched you walk away.*
> *Let us slip through my hands.*
> *My heart's in too many pieces for me to*
> *   ever love again.*

He'd been so stupid all those years not to fight for Gia, not to go after her. He'd lost out on ten years they could have been together, and now that she was back in his life, he wasn't going to let her walk out with fighting again. Somehow he had to convince her to stay.

She turned around slowly. "I have something for you."

Andrew felt every part of his body clench as he speculated what she might have in comparison to what he wanted. The last time she'd uttered those words to him, she'd given him back his ring. "For me?"

"Come here."

She opened her office door and he followed her inside. Shutting the door behind them, she leaned backward against it, a sly smile slipping over her lips and her eyes alight with heated excitement. It confused him after the way she'd acted all night. She jerked her chin slightly toward her desk.

"Go, look."

Andrew moved toward the empty desk where nothing but a manila envelope lay on the surface. He lifted it, holding it toward her, trying not to acknowledge the disappointment he felt. "This? What is it?"

Her smile widened. "Open it."

Taking a deep breath, Andrew unfolded the clasp and reached for a stack of papers inside. Before he could even look at them, she moved toward him, her smile as big and bright as the morning sun. "I mailed the originals of all of these to Erik Masters today."

Andrew shook his head, unable to look away from her dazzling smile to even read the papers in his hand. "What are they?"

"Well, this one," she said, tapping a finger on the top page, "is my resignation from my job. He didn't actually get that one. My boss did."

Andrew's gaze dropped to the page in his hand in shock. "You quit your job?"

Gia nodded. "I probably should have gone back and done it in person, but I informed them that I'm moving back to Hidden Falls due to my father's health concerns. I'm going to run Rossetti's with him. I'm not letting him give up his dream and sell."

"You're moving back?" he repeated dumbly, unable to believe he was hearing her correctly. Just a few days ago, she'd left his place in tears. "Wait a second, slow down."

Gia moved closer to him, laying her hands against his chest, her fingers inching toward his shoulders. "I am staying, Andrew," she repeated, saying each word slowly.

He dropped the papers onto the desk, unable to resist the temptation of this soft, willing woman. He wound his arms around her, almost afraid to ask his next question. "What made you change your mind?"

"This."

She leaned over to the papers and slid her resignation from the top. He immediately saw the words *terminate* and *parental rights*. Andrew shook his head at the signature along the bottom. "What is this?"

"This is my insurance policy. My sister can't threaten me now."

"Wait, what?" Andrew drew back. "What do you mean 'threaten'?"

Gia's smile didn't even falter. "I had to leave because Lorena was threatening to have Bobby challenge your custody. She was going to use him to take Bella from you if we were together."

"He's the other guy Lorena was with?"

Gia nodded. "But he never wanted to be a father and signed off any rights to Bella. I talked to Erik and, since he was never on the birth certificate, as long as he signed this . . ." She shrugged. "Bella can't be taken away from you now. No matter what Lorena tries to do. They've both terminated any rights and custody. Bella is safe, and if you're telling the truth about Lorena not being able to come after you and your job . . ."

Andrew closed his eyes and dropped his forehead against hers. She'd been so busy trying to take care of this situation alone that she didn't know he'd been trying to do the same. This woman had been ready to walk away again to protect him and Bella.

"I love you, Gia. Do you even realize how much?" He could see he'd confused her and chuckled. "I already took care of any issues Lorena might try to cause with my job, while I was making sure she couldn't touch you and Bella. Even if I hadn't, it wouldn't have mattered. I'd rather have you and Bella in my life than some job."

"Boloney," she whispered, her lips brushing against his. "You love your job."

Andrew's fingers clenched the material of her dress as he pulled her closer. "You are everything to me. I love *you*."

"Good." She ran her tongue over his lower lip and he groaned in desperate need. "Because I love you, Andrew McQuaid. I've never stopped and . . ." She pulled back and looked him in the eyes. "I plan on holding you to that offer."

"About giving you custody of Bella? Absolutely. Just don't try to run off again." He bent down to nuzzle her neck, but she placed a hand on his chest. Andrew tipped his head to one side.

"Um, no. The one where you proposed," she corrected him, her eyes glinting mischievously. "You didn't think I'd let you get out of that twice, did you?"

"Oh, honey, I have no intention of trying to get out of it."

The door slammed open and they turned to see who'd come in. Lorena stood in the doorway, her dark eyes glittering at the two of them.

"Normally I'd be pissed, but I'll let this—" she said with a wave of her hand "—slide this time."

Andrew rolled his eyes, holding Gia tighter and refusing to let her wiggle out of his grasp to appease her sister. "Gee, how generous of you."

"I told you it would work, Gia. Linc's manager already contacted Bobby and wants him to come to Nashville. We're leaving tomorrow."

"What about the next two nights? He was supposed to open for Linc then too."

"Who cares? Find someone else." Andrew looked down at Gia as if to say she should have expected this sort of irresponsibility from Lorena. "I told you, I'm getting out of this shithole and I am never coming back."

"What about Mom and Dad?"

Lorena rolled her eyes. "We both know that you'll come rushing back to take care of them, Gia. I'm grabbing my brass ring and no one is going to force me to let go. Not you, not Mom and Dad—"

"Not your daughter," Andrew added.

Lorena glared at him. Gia slipped from his arms and went to her sister, wrapping her arms around Lorena's stiff, unexpectant frame.

"You're my sister and I want to see you happy. I hope this works out the way you want it to."

Lorena eyed her, as if trying to judge the truth of Gia's words. Lorena might not believe it and Andrew couldn't understand how, but he could hear the genuine affection in Gia's voice.

"I guess this is it, huh, Lorena? Should we say good-bye now?" Andrew knew he shouldn't sound so pleased with the way this situation was turning out, but Lorena leaving was best for everyone.

"You're staying here, aren't you?" Lorena glared at her sister suspiciously before shooting Andrew a dirty look.

"Yes." Gia's voice was steady, strong . . . fearless. Damn, he loved her lionhearted boldness.

"With him." Lorena arched a brow, daring Gia to contradict her. "You know what I can do."

Gia didn't even blink. They knew Lorena couldn't do anything, but she didn't know that yet.

"Yes," Gia agreed. "I know exactly what you can do. But why would you? You have what you wanted. A new life away from here with a man you love. You've won, right?"

Neither looked away, both just as stubborn as the other. Finally Lorena let the corner of her mouth tug up to one side. "Whatever. I'm heading to Nashville and Bobby is going to be famous with my help. Peace out, bitches."

Turning on her heel, Lorena disappeared from the

office. Andrew immediately saw Gia's shoulders relax as she stared at the empty doorway, as if Lorena's departure had lifted a fifty-pound weight from around her neck.

"She'll be back." Gia turned back toward him. "It's not going to work out between them. They don't love each other."

Andrew walked toward her and wrapped his arms around her shoulders, pressing a kiss to the top of her head. "You can't make her choices for her." He turned her toward him. "It's time for us now. Us, and our daughter."

Her eyes brightened and he saw the sheen of tears fill them. "I like the sound of that," she whispered.

"Good, because I am never letting either of you go, Gia. Come home with me."

She arched a saucy brow. "To the bunkhouse?"

"For now. Until I can build you a proper house." He looked down at her. "Besides, everyone is here at the concert, which means the bunkhouse is empty and we can toast our engagement."

"To us?" Her smile made his heart skip a beat.

"To our family. But it's going to have to wait until after the concert, Romeo."

GIA HAD CHANGED back into her jeans and T-shirt to clean up after the concert. The temporary wait staff had left, but Rusty and Heather had both refused to go without helping clean up. They'd tried to convince Gia to leave, offering to close up, but she didn't think anyone really expected her to go.

"*Piccola*, you should go home. It's been a long, eventful night." Her father draped his thin arm around her shoulder. "I can't thank you enough for everything you've done. If the next two days are half as successful, we'll be back on track."

She wound her arms around his waist, still shocked by how thin he'd become but feeling a spark of hope. After the concert tonight, they'd raised almost enough to get his medical bills out of collections, enough that they would begin treating him again. The rest of the income from the next two nights would go a long way toward paying off the rest and getting her father the treatment he needed.

"Daddy, go ahead. I'll finish taking care of things here, but then I'm going to head back to the ranch with Andrew and Bella."

Her father smiled. "I thought that you might." He pressed a kiss to her temple. "He's a good man, *piccola*. He will take good care of you both when I can't."

"Stop," she ordered, trying to keep the fear from choking her. "You're going for the treatment. I'm not moving back here unless you promise to get well." She felt him take a deep breath, relaxing even as she hugged him. "We're going to run this place together, Daddy, as a family, the way it should have been all along."

"Humph," her mother scoffed as she came into the room, setting the broom off to one side. "As a family?

You chased your sister away and now you want to talk about family."

Gia was tired of being blamed for her sister's choices, tired of trying to fix what her sister destroyed. She stepped out of her father's comforting embrace to face her mother's accusatory stare. "Mama, I didn't chase Lorena away. She chose to leave, has been wanting to for years."

"I trusted you to convince her to stay."

"Isabella, stop." Her father's voice was stronger than it had been since Gia's return. "Gia has done nothing but sacrifice for us, and her sister. Lorena has caused enough hurt in this family, enough divisiveness. She continues to make poor decisions and you continue to enable her. I won't tolerate any more."

"You . . . won't . . ." Her mother sputtered, blinking in shock.

"No," he interrupted. "You have allowed our daughter to run wild, like a hurricane, over this entire family. It's time she learns that actions—her choices—have consequences."

"She *knows* that, Giovanni. But she's searching—"

"No, Mama. She's doing whatever she wants because she knows no one will stop her. This time, I did. I refused to give in to her bullying and demands."

"You," her mother reproved, jabbing a finger Gia's direction, "are the reason she is seeking to be more, to prove herself."

"Me?" Gia glanced up in time to see Andrew and Linc come back in the room.

For years, she'd felt like she wasn't enough. That if she'd been more, she could have held on to the one man she'd loved. Lorena had made her feel that way with her lies and deception. As much as Gia was willing to accept that her sister had been jealous of her, she also accepted that she hadn't done anything to cause it. She'd chosen to make a life for herself, both with Andrew and after her sister had tried to destroy that relationship. She'd pursued her own life, but Lorena had remained so blinded by her envy that she let herself be held prisoner by her resentment.

Gia took a deep breath, grateful that her sister's mistakes had led her full circle, returning her to the man she loved, helping her find her passion working with their father and gifting her with the child she'd been told she would never have. Lorena had given her far more than she'd taken away.

She was finished shouldering Lorena's mistakes. "I'm sorry, Mama."

"You should be."

Gia stepped closer. "I'm sorry I'm such a disappointment to you. That I grew up to be responsible, to take care of you and Daddy. I'm sorry that you can count on me and rely on me to be there when you need me."

She could see the rage building in her mother, but it was time someone made her realize how asinine it was for her to continue defending Lorena's actions. She'd lied, slandered both Gia and Andrew, could have cost him his career and had one or both of them arrested.

This wasn't about being loyal to family. This was about facing her daughter's criminal actions.

"How dare you . . ." Her mother's eyes widened as she sucked in a ragged breath.

"Isabella," Gia's father warned as he approached, stepping between Gia and her mother. The crack of her palm against his shoulder was loud in the shocked silence of the ballroom.

Surprised, Gia took a step backward. Her mother had been about to slap her. She'd never raised a hand to either of her daughters before. If it hadn't been for her father . . .

Her mother clutched her hands to her mouth, realizing what she'd just done. "Giovanni, oh!"

Gia's father grasped his wife's hands, pressing them together and bringing them to his lips with a sigh. "Isabella, I love you. You're the mother of my children, the love of my life, but you're blinded to what she's doing to you, to this family."

She tried to pull her hands away. "I'm not—"

"You are. Go to her. Go *with* her. See for yourself. Watch how she treats you, how she treats those who love her most. She will take from you until you have nothing and return." He let go of her hands and cupped her cheek. "Go, see for yourself. Gia and I will take care of the restaurant. We'll be here when you return."

Her father glanced back at Gia, waiting for her to confirm what he'd said. Her father needed his wife here while he faced this battle for his health, and Lorena was conniving. It was a risk to send her, but Gia could see it was the only way she would ever understand.

"I'll take care of Daddy, Mama."

Her mother glared at Gia. "Lorena will prove you both wrong. You'll see."

Gia watched her father let go of her mother's hands, watched her mother walk out of the restaurant and leave them behind. Steady hands fell on her shoulder and she felt Andrew silently offer his strength. Reaching down, she grasped her father's hand, offering him whatever support she could for as long as he needed it.

Epilogue

GIA STRETCHED IN the bed, reaching for the warm man who should have been curled beside her. Instead her hands grasped nothing but cold sheets. Frowning, she opened one eye, scowling at the sunshine blazing through the window. "Andrew?"

"We're in here," she heard him answer from the kitchen in a singsong voice that made her smile. It meant he was with Bella.

Gia shuffled into the kitchen in bare feet, wrapping her arms around Andrew's shoulders from behind and pressing a kiss to his raspy cheek as he tried to convince eight-month-old Bella to take a bite of baby cereal. Her giant baby smile brightened at Gia, who laughed at her daughter's antics. Just as the spoon neared her laughing mouth, she slapped her hands against the high chair and knocked it from Andrew's hands, spraying cereal, with Andrew taking the brunt of it.

"Okay, apparently we're done."

She could hear the smile in his voice and felt the soft rumble of laughter where her chest was pressed against his shoulders.

"Want me to finish?" she offered.

"Sure."

Andrew rose from the chair and turned toward her. She burst out laughing when she saw the glob of cereal dripping from his forehead, down the bridge of his nose. She passed him a towel from the table and slid into the chair he'd vacated.

"The contractor called while you were at work yesterday. He said the house should be ready for final inspection next week." She glanced over at him to judge his reaction.

"It's about time," he grumbled. "It's been two months longer than he planned. The bunkhouse is too crowded."

"Cut him some slack. He built us a house from scratch in less than seven months. And if you're in that much of a hurry to move out, we could move in with my parents," she offered.

Andrew rolled his eyes. "No, thanks. Your mother still thinks I'm a *stronzo*."

Gia's eyes widened. "She does not!" He arched a doubtful brow. "Okay, maybe a little, but that's still a holdover thanks to Lorena."

"Speaking of which . . ."

"She's only coming home for a week, and Mom has informed her that she needs to find a hotel room. She still doesn't trust Lorena after she stole Mom's credit card from her purse. I guess she just wouldn't believe what Lorena was capable of until she saw it for herself."

"It was a good thing you suggested your dad put the alert on the card so it was caught right away."

Gia shrugged and let out a sigh. "At least he and Mom have gotten on the same page again, and with the restaurant doing well and Dad's treatments working so far . . ." She pursed her lips before easily spooning cereal into Bella's mouth.

"Don't go looking for trouble. Life is good," he reassured her, pressing a quick kiss to her lips. "How is it that you can get her to eat that so easily and I can't?" He stuck out his tongue at Bella and she giggled, spitting out the food. Andrew handed Gia the towel. "Sorry."

He didn't sound sorry at all, but she didn't mind. Bella loved her father and he was wonderful with her, better than Gia could have ever hoped he would be.

"At least the house will be finished just in time," he pointed out.

Gia knew he meant because they'd wanted to have the wedding at their own house next month. "Yep," she agreed, trying to contain herself.

"You'll have to decide where you want the ceremony, but I think that spot overlooking the creek would be nice."

He took the bowl and towel from her, set them on

the table and tugged her to stand. Wrapping one arm around her waist and sliding his other hand up her rib cage, he made her squirm with anticipation.

"We'll also have to move your man-cave to the garage."

His hand paused at the curve of her breast, and she couldn't help herself from arching into it. He clenched his jaw, smiling slightly at her obvious arousal for him, and brushed a thumb over her sensitive nipple. A sigh of pleasure slipped between her lips at his touch.

"I don't think so. We agreed that I could have the spare room to use as a game room—"

"—until we needed it," she interrupted. "We're going to need it."

"For?" he prompted, not really listening as he dipped his head to press kisses along her collarbone, tugging her T-shirt aside to give him better access.

"For the baby."

"Bella has her own room already."

Gia shook her head. "Not Bella."

Andrew's head snapped up. "Wait, what?"

"You're going to be a father. Again."

"But I thought you couldn't . . . that the doctors said—"

She shrugged. "They said it would be very *difficult*. I guess they were wrong. I've already been in," she reassured him. "They told me everything is right on track and I'm almost ten weeks."

"Ten weeks," he repeated. "We're going to have another baby?" Gia nodded, trying to discern whether his

reaction was shock or disappointment. "Another baby."
His mouth curved into a lopsided grin and the dimple
deepened in his cheek, flooding her with relieved joy.
"You realize what this means?"

Gia nodded and tipped her head to one side. "Yeah,
I'm going to be fat at our wedding."

His hand slid down to splay over her stomach, his
smile beaming. "Pregnant, and beautiful." He covered
her mouth with his, his kiss filled with promise. He
broke it off with a laugh and turned toward Bella in
the high chair. "You hear that, Princess? You're going
to be a big sister." Bella pounded her hands on the high
chair excitedly. "See, she's happy about it too."

"Are you?" Gia asked. The smile slid from his face. "I
mean, we're going to be moving and have two in diapers
and we just got Bella to sleep through the night and—"

"Shh." Andrew kissed her quiet, his lips plucking
at hers. "Gia, we are going to be together forever. What
could make me any happier? You are everything I've
ever wanted. Anything more," he said, jerking his chin
toward Bella and sliding his hand over her stomach
again, "is just icing on the cake."

"Promise?" she whispered, her lips meeting up with his.

"You can always trust me."

Acknowledgments

WITH EACH AND every book, I wonder where to begin thanking people. When you have an entire village, it's tough to pick one to kick it off.

First, I'd like to thank my readers. Without you, I'd still be writing at my kitchen table, dreaming of the day I could one day tell my stories for a living. You are the reason these characters have become real people and you continue to inspire me each and every day with your messages. I love you all!

Next, thank you to Suzie Townsend, who continues to be the best cheerleader I could ever ask for, all while always keeping me on my toes and busy. Thank you for never letting me rest!

Thank you, Tessa Woodward, for giving me my first opportunity and returning for more. You've been an amazing sounding board and I love working with you and the rest of the Avon Books team!

For my writer besties, thank you for listening to me go on and on about these characters and for forcing me to gather all of my thoughts into a coherent outline so that my stories can be more than gibberish. I don't know where I'd be without our phone calls, coffee dates and wine sprints!

A big thank you goes out to the Country Crew! For always being the first to read, review and cheer me on. Without you ladies, I'd still be spinning my wheels dizzily!

I want to thank my family. You've believed in me even when I didn't believe in myself. You've always been right there to celebrate every success and pick me up with every frustration. I know I don't tell you enough (is it ever enough?) but I love you all to the moon and back again!

And, finally, I want to thank the man who has given me the freedom to be myself, to live the life I choose and to support me the entire way. Bryun, know that you are the inspiration for every romantic moment of every story. My heroes can only hope to grow up to be like you. I love you!

**Keep reading for an excerpt
from the latest romantic novel
in T.J. Kline's Hidden Falls series**

Daring to Fall

Emma Jordan has returned home after her father's death to run the animal sanctuary that had been his legacy. But strange things start happening, and it seems that someone is out to shut her down, someone who doesn't mind putting lives in jeopardy to see it through. When Hidden Falls' sexiest fireman starts to ask questions, Emma needs to make sure his charm doesn't distract her from keeping her dreams alive.

Ben McQuaid has an obligation as a local fireman to protect the community, even from a well-meaning wildlife veterinarian who's in way over her head. But, it's becoming hard to keep his loyalty to the town and his desire for the pretty vet separate. As Ben and Emma become caught in a dangerous game of cat and mouse, their feelings for each other are growing.

Will they let duty drive them apart
or will they dare to fall?

"HEY, BEN, I have a favor to ask."

Ben McQuaid rolled his eyes skyward. Of course, his brother Andrew needed another favor. Lately, Ben seemed to be the one *doing* the favors more often than receiving any. But, that's what brothers did for one another, right? And with six siblings, most of them younger, that added up to be a lot of favors.

"Make it quick, I'm on my way into the fire station for my shift."

"Good, because this is more of an official call than a favor anyway. I need you to head down to the Quinn place on Mosquito Road. Apparently, there's a cat stuck in a tree. It seems stupid to call it in to the firehouse and drag the engine out for a cat. See? I'm actually doing *you* a favor and saving you all that cleaning and polishing you have to do just for driving a truck out of the garage."

They'd be cleaning the engine anyway. Plus, without an engine, Ben had no ladder to get up the tree. "So, what you're suggesting is that I shimmy up the tree the way I did when we were ten to get the football you and Grant would get stuck."

Andrew's chuckle sounded through the receiver. "Pretty much. Look, the call just came in from dispatch and you've got to drive by there on your way into town anyway. No sense in making it an official call."

There was nothing about this that was a *favor* for Ben. "What's wrong, is there an apple fritter with your name on it? This way you save yourself the effort of having to fill out another police report, right?" Andrew wasn't fooling him.

"There's that too." Ben heard Andrew address someone else in the background. "Hey, I have to run. There's a domestic dispute at the winery. You got this, right?"

"Yeah, I'll take care of it," Ben said with a sigh.

"Thanks. I owe you one."

"One?" Ben muttered to himself as the receiver disconnected in his ear and he took the turnoff onto Mosquito Road. "You owe me more than that."

He wasn't looking forward to this. Hollister Quinn was one of those old guys who spoke his mind, loudly and often. He'd been the first in line to protest the latest upgrades being done to spruce up their small foothill town. Said he liked it rustic, the way it'd been for years and that it should stay that way. However, now that there was talk about Hidden Falls trying to become more of a tourist attraction along the way to Tahoe, an idea that would bring higher profits for local businesses which, in turn, kept the town thriving, Quinn was complaining even more. A visit with Quinn, even to retrieve a kitten, was sure to bring a lengthy lecture about how the people of Hidden Falls were selling out. Ben rubbed the knots of tension already building at the back of his neck.

Pulling into the circular driveway in front of the Quinn house, he maneuvered his pickup between several other vehicles, none of which were Hollister's. A crowd was already gathered under one of the tall pines in the front yard.

"Great," the old man complained as Ben edged closer to the chaos. "Please, tell me you're here to do something productive, not just here to gawk like everyone else. I need someone to get that damn thing outta my tree." He pointed to where a tabby kitten yowled loudly from a high branch on the tree.

Ben squinted, following the old man's gaze. "Are you sure that's a cat? It doesn't look—"

"What else would it be?" Quinn rolled his eyes before glaring at Ben and shoving him toward the god-awful howling the cat in the tree was making. "Do your job, fireman, and get that thing down." He turned away, muttering something about the woman running the animal sanctuary down the road but Ben didn't quite catch it and he wasn't about to risk having the old man rip him a new one again.

"Sure thing, Mr. Quinn," Ben agreed, wondering again why he'd wanted to be a firefighter. Sweating it out with the cattle on his parents' ranch sounded a hell of a lot better right now than climbing a tree to get the shit clawed out of him by a frightened kitten.

He glanced around at the large group of neighbors that had come to watch, curious at the interest for a simple kitten stuck in a tree. It wasn't a big enough deal to warrant this sort of hullabaloo. The kitten yowled louder and Ben had just lifted his foot onto the ladder Quinn had left braced against the side of the tree when Ellie Quinn, the old man's daughter, hurried to his side.

"Ben, I'm sorry. I tried to get my dad to just leave the poor thing alone, but you know how he is." She shot him a coy smile and her eyelashes fluttered.

Ellie was a nice woman. The same age as his younger sister and obviously interested in him. She was sweet, kind to everyone she met, a member of the local women's shelter planning committee and generous to a fault. In fact, she was exactly what he wanted in a woman, plus she had a "girl next door" quality that made her adorable. His mother had been trying to set them up for months, reminding him that he should be giving her grandchildren before she was too old to enjoy them. The problem was, Ben wasn't attracted to Ellie at all. He wanted to be, but every time he was around her, there was no stirring in him, no warm fuzzies like he'd had with other women. Nothing to get a rise out of him, so to speak, at all. It was almost like he *wanted* to continually find himself getting screwed over by crazy women. "Don't worry about it, Ellie," he said, waving a hand in her direction and looking up the tree. "I'll just get this guy down and he'll take off back home." Ben wasn't nearly as confident about his ability to get the cat down as he sounded but Ellie was sweet. He couldn't blame her for her cantankerous father.

She cocked her head and gave him a confused look. "Oh. Um, okay."

Putting one foot over the other as he climbed the ladder, trying to ignore the jeers and shouts from below, Ben pulled himself into a fork in the tree, hanging his legs over the branch as he straddled it. He could barely see the spotted fluffy coat of the kitten but, from what he could see, it was definitely young. He'd never understand how a stupid animal could get itself into a tree but couldn't get back out. Then again, it wasn't like people didn't get themselves into some pretty precarious positions they couldn't figure their way out of.

Tucking his feet under him so he was squatting on the limb, grateful for the heavy tread of his work boots, Ben reach for a thick branch to his right, using it to swing him to the V beside where the cat was hiding. The gasp from the onlookers below nearly made him laugh. Sure, falling would be painful but the fifteen-foot landing into mulch couldn't hurt any more than the second story floor of an old farmhouse collapsing from under him during a call and dropping him into the concrete basement below. Those two fractured ribs had hurt like hell.

Straddling the second branch, he watched the kitten for a moment. The poor animal was scared out of its mind. Its big blue eyes were round with fear and, from this vantage point, he could see that it was a matted mess. Tiny claws clung to the rippled bark of the tree and he wondered how he was possibly going to convince the frightened animal to let go without his very vulnerable bare arm replacing the tree trunk under its claws.

"Here, kitty," he called quietly. The cat turned toward him and he saw the unmistakable black tufts over the kitten's ears. It turned away again, edging out onto the branch and he saw the stubby tail.

Holy crap, that is not a cat. It's a freakin' bobcat kitten.

"Shit," he muttered. "That damn brother of mine owes me *big* time."

**And make sure you check out the
first in the Hidden Falls series**

Making the Play

Grant McQuaid has dedicated his entire life to his
football career. Now an injury threatens his place on
the team and he's forced to return home to rehabilitate.
But when he meets his "biggest fan," a precocious,
blue-eyed, hearing impaired boy named James—and
his beautiful mother, Bethany—Grant begins to
question whether football is the future he still wants.

Bethany Mills has been doing just fine since her
husband walked out on them . . . and she definitely
doesn't need another man to disappoint her—or her
son. But when James runs into his hero at the park,
Bethany admits there is a void in her son's life that
she just can't fill. Her attraction to the handsome
football star is undeniable, but a man in the limelight
is the last thing she wants for herself, or James.

Grant doesn't want to subject Bethany to the chaos
of dating a professional athlete. But the more
time he spends with her and James, the harder
it is to resist making a play for her heart . . .

About the Author

T. J. KLINE was raised since the age of fourteen to compete in rodeos and Rodeo Queen competitions, and she has a thorough knowledge of the sport as well as the culture involved. She writes contemporary Western romance for Avon Romance, including the Rodeo series and the Healing Harts series. She has published a nonfiction health book and two inspirational fiction titles under the name Tina Klinesmith. In her very limited spare time, T. J. can be found laughing hysterically with her husband, her children and their menagerie of pets in Northern California.

www.tinaklinesmith.com

Discover great authors, exclusive offers and more at hc.com.